DR. MASON ONLY DIES AT NIGHT

VAMPIRE ACCORDS
BOOK ONE

M.L. EADEN

Print ISBN: 978-1-962655-11-8
eBook ISBN: 978-1-962655-09-5

Edited By Victoria Flickinger: flickeringwords.com

Cover Art By Vanda Pinto: missviebookdesigns.com

Sensitivity Consulting: Dr. Joe Stahlman

2nd edition 2023
Previously titled: Death Warmed Over
For information, and CW's visit the author's website @mleaden.com

Reader's Note

The Universe you are entering is a contemporary one with magic, myths, and legends living and working alongside each other. There are many sentient and varied species. Some of them are out in the open while others are not. However, everyone knows they existed, knows there's magic in the world, and knows that whether something walks in the light or goes bump in the night, it's as real as the sunrise and sunset.

It's a world where science and magic work hand-in-hand, creating advanced technology and building a day-to-day life where you could easily meet a dragon astronaut, an orc mage specializing in medicine, or a fae working as a tailor. Moonbases exist, sustainable living is a reality, and promises which seem to be mere figments of imagination are woven into the fabric.

Enjoy!

TO DISCOVER MORE:
MLEADEN.COM/BOOKS

Dedicated to the memories and stories
of my fellow LARPers.
Love,
The Mel, your storyteller

CONTENTS

MONUMENTAL SHIFT

Summer 1878 — Somewhere in Europe, Necromantic War front

The night was hot. I was sweating through my uniform, and my fingers slipped as I tried to place the healing salve as salvos of magic flew overhead.

"Listen, you're going to be fine." Vampires could, in fact, die. The vampire under my hands was losing what little blood he had left as I tried to magically knit the hole in his neck using the salve as a medium. It was an old myth that vampires frenzy when they lose this much blood. The one I was working on kept blinking, eyes wide from the pain he was likely experiencing.

"What's your name?" I glanced at his uniform. He wore the blue wool of the United States military and was like me in a way. Our home country didn't send people, formally, to fight Europe's war, but that didn't stop us from volunteering.

"Gerald." The projectile hadn't hit his windpipe, which was good. At least his lungs weren't filled with blood. Though that might have been preferable in this case, since it would have kept Gerald's blood inside.

"How old are you, Gerald?" His charm bracelets warding against compulsion were still intact. The Dictator's necromancers wouldn't subvert him while I patched him up.

"Seventy-five," he gasped.

"Well, you'll live to see seventy-six." The guy didn't look over twenty-eight, maybe thirty, but you could never tell with vamps. "We'll get you into a foxhole for the day, and by tomorrow night, you'll be right as rain." The healing spell was working, even though it had proven difficult with the gloves I had magicked up to prevent being infected. We never would have found out about the vampire virus if some academic named Beijerinck hadn't been redirected by the war effort from studying sick tobacco plants. Thanks to him, we now had a word for what infected individuals and transitioned them into vampires. I just needed a few more seconds with the healing spell, and Gerald would be stabilized enough to move.

Our field training had been rushed at best. Anyone with healing magic, medical skills, or both, who had either volunteered, like me, or were drafted into the war were given the basics—keep your head down, stay behind the front lines, and always wear your helmet. Before the war, I mostly took care of farm animals with healing spells to clear up ailments or mend wounds from predators. That was several thousand kilometers away, back home in Boulder, in the newly formed state of Colorado.

"That's patched," I said as wrapped a bandage around his neck to protect the spell, and the newly healed flesh. "Let's get you moved." I stayed low, with a knee pressed to the ground, helping my patient roll to his knees. His eyes went wide, and I thought the spell had faltered. "You okay?" I reached for his neck to check my work, then realized, in that odd way where your brain doesn't process what's happening until it's too late, that someone else was reaching for mine.

"Shit!" Gerald yelled as he scrambled away on hands and knees, holding his neck wound.

I choked as I was snapped off the ground from behind. Fangs pierced my shoulder as a strong arm wrapped around my midsection.

Vampire bites were not the whimsical, romantic notion that seems to have spread through all the reading parlors. It was more akin to a snakebite than anything else. Once bitten, you had two choices: die or fight. You landed in category A without much trouble if the vamp broke your neck. But for whatever reason, this vamp hadn't done that. It gave me an opening for the second option. While my healing spells were useful for repairing skin damage, and closing wounds, they also came in handy when you needed to open a wound or a calving animal.

I placed my hands behind my back against the vamp's torso and pushed with my arms and magic. The resounding pop barely registered over the explosions from the fighting around us as we both dropped to the ground.

My gaze met hers as I turned my head. While her guts spilled out on the ground, the expression on her face went soft as her jaw slackened and the animated life went out of her eyes. Once her skin started to wilt, I knew she was finally dead.

My throbbing neck told me I hadn't come away with a simple bite. I slapped my hand over the gushing wound. The barrier spell I used to make gloves worked great when you didn't have a lot of supplies, but they didn't save you from being careless. I hadn't thought to shed the spells from my blood-covered hands as my own red vitae escaped with each beat of my heart.

The world suddenly lit up with a rainbow of lights and sounds as dragons streaked overhead. They breathed ice and then fire, stopping the zombies and vampires in the Dictator's army from advancing. I laughed at the colors and had a sad thought about missing ladies' night at the field hospital canteen. Agnes had promised to buy me a drink. It also meant that Gerald and I had likely been caught up in a retreat so the winged division could advance. So I was likely in a middle ground between both front lines. Which meant the possibility of being rescued or finished off was fifty-fifty, and that was only if I didn't bleed out first. I closed my eyes as my vision grew dark.

The first thing I noticed, after who knows how long, were voices.

"She's infected. It's the only way she survived."

"Maybe. She's a trained healer; she could have fixed some of the damage before she passed out."

"We'll know more once the mage unit finishes testing her blood."

Were they talking about me? I felt like the rough side of sandpaper. The friction of everything was too much. Cloth against my skin, sounds in my ears, the scrape of my tongue against the roof of my mouth. "Water."

I don't know how long I repeated myself until someone held a glass to my lips and poured a tepid liquid down my throat. I took a few big gulps before I asked, "Where?"

"Field hospital. About twenty kilometers from the front," a kind voice said.

"How long?" I drank more water and then grabbed for the cup.

"Easy, easy. You've been out for a bit, maybe four days."

I opened my eyes and saw a kind face. His skin was pale pink. Enough that it would trick someone into thinking he was alive at a distance, but up close, you could tell the pink shade was only because he'd fed recently. As my gaze raked him over for clues, I noted his short dark brown hair, brown eyes, and medic uniform, not unlike the one I'd worn, which was reassuring. He also had magical abilities, but what and how much, I wasn't sure. When I reached for his hand, I confirmed what I already knew.

"Don't panic."

Was I panicking? It wasn't like me to panic. I didn't mind vampires unless they were trying to chew on my neck. I let go of his hand and reached for the wound and the bandage that should be there. Instead, all I felt was smooth skin. That wasn't right. Even a knitting spell would leave a scar. I looked around the room, blinking twice to focus on auras. Most of the other people lying on cots were near death, dead, or had a dual aura, which was indicative of individuals who were vampires.

I probed the inside of my mouth with my tongue. Sure enough, my upper canines had elongated and developed sharper points. The match pair along my lower jaw were sharper too, but hadn't changed in length. My gaze dropped to my own hands, checking my aura. It was pinkish-red, typical for what I'd been through and how long I was out, but the soft gray haze layered on top was a giveaway. "This is the infected wing."

The vampire nodded. "We've never seen anyone infected from a bite. Most of these blokes had blood on them, or were injured somehow, and the wound became infected."

"And voilà. Yeah, I'm familiar with how it happens." I had to think about it for a minute. "Fuck, Gerald."

"Huh?"

"I was treating a wounded vampire named Gerald. His blood was all over my hands when the other vampire bit me."

"Ah, that explains it." He sighed. "You know your choices, yes?" He sounded British, though I wasn't sure from where exactly. Being from the United States, I'm sure my own accent sounded quaint.

"Yes." My throat was dry again. "How long do I have?"

"A day maybe. At the very least, spend today outside. It's supposed to be warm and clear, with lots of sunshine."

He'd done this before. I wondered how many times he'd helped people through their transition. "What's your name?"

"Ian." He blinked, then smiled, with a hint of his sharp canines showing. "If you decide to stay after today, we'll move you to the basement. It's muddy, but it's light-free, and no one snores."

I laughed despite myself. "Thank you." Ian clasped my hand, let go, then moved on to the next patient.

Some folks, the virus outright killed. Blood was a scarce commodity. The war effort couldn't afford to keep enough on hand for the vampires in their ranks. It meant that nothing went to waste, not even blood from those who died from the infection. It was collected, bottled, and put in a stasis cabinet for safekeeping, then rationed out each night to vampires on a schedule. Vampires could usually go a day or so without feeding. Those who preferred to feed each night often found willing donors.

It was considered an infraction if you were caught giving or receiving unless it was from another vampire. Mostly, the rule was meant to reduce accidental infections. Still, there were those that liked the thrill of a dalliance with a vamp—at least that's what I'd been told. I had been too busy in the six months I'd been assigned as a field medic to even consider any kind of dallying. If I managed to garner a hot meal and a few hours of sleep, I called that a victory.

For those of us who regained consciousness after being infected, we were given a choice. You could finish becoming a vampire, letting the virus mutate you, or you could find a delightful spot in the sunlight to kill off the virus, which also killed the host. Drugs made it a pleasant enough way to go if they were available. This ritual of greeting the sun was dubiously called a sun vigil, as if the name somehow made it more palatable. After a sun vigil, the head was always separated from the body so the corpse couldn't be raised.

That was learned the hard way during the first year of fighting. In a weird twist of magic and biology, the necromancers couldn't raise a vampire if they were killed, but they could certainly raise someone that hadn't fully turned. Anyone who died had their head removed now, no exceptions. The last thing you wanted to do was give the enemy an army in the midst of your own hospital camp.

SUN VIGIL

As a medic, you tend to sit with your patients after bringing them in. I've worked on many different kinds of folks during the war, and I'd seen my share of infected that chose the life they had over what happened next.

A few cots over from where I was convalescing, a fae was giving the staff hell in our little ward. Fae wear their emotions, literally. Only a glamour can hide them. This fae was not wearing one, possibly due to his wounds.

The fae cycled through anger and misery as his dulled light pink skin showed his shifting emotions in bluish-gray tones that burst across his body like polka dots. Neither his emotional state nor his thrashing about helped his gut wound any. It began seeping blood as I watched him berate the medics and guards, who were all likely from species immune to the infection since they weren't vampires, trying their level best to calm him. He was having none of it. I couldn't lie around and let him or the staff continue to suffer.

"What in all the realms do you want?" he yelled as I walked over to him. Medics glanced my way. They might have told me to go back to bed if they hadn't been at their wits' end already. "Are you here to convince me to become a creature of the night as well?" The fae was beautiful. They all were in some way. His light brown eyes were lit with untapped magic. His brown hair was twisted in elaborate braids that went the length of his back, highlighting his pointed ears instead of hiding them.

I shook my head and lowered my eyes. "No, I thought maybe you'd rather take a walk. Get a drink and enjoy the day. How does that sound?" He squinted while those around us looked at me as if I'd taken leave of my senses. I probably had, but it didn't matter.

"Will they let us?" he asked.

"How about this? We'll get some bracelets, so they don't worry, and go find the mess and see what hooch is there." The bracelets would inhibit our magic, which would keep a wounded person from misfiring around the hospital. The fae nodded, and I looked at one of the medics who seemed to be in charge. They nodded in agreement and quickly produced a few inhibitor bracelets, then helped us put them on.

A glance around the ward told me Ian wasn't present, so it was likely close to daybreak. "After you," I said as I pointed toward the ward exit. The fae nodded, and I followed.

"What's your name, healer?"

I smiled up at him. He had to be about half a meter taller than me, but that wasn't any surprise. Most people were fifteen centimeters or more over my head. I'd felt more comfortable with gnomes than I did humans at times. "Mason. What's yours?"

"Keegan." Others in the camp looked at us as we walked by, but didn't stop us.

"It would have been better to meet under other circumstances, but I'm happy to share a drink with you." I could be dead right now, so I felt like celebrating.

He nodded again as we went into the mess. The good stuff hadn't been around for a few years. All the mess could offer was piss poor whiskey they distilled nearby, but the alcohol content was high enough to make you forget it was shit after a few shots.

Keegan hated it. "I can't even lament my end properly. Who knows where the nearest bottle of spice whiskey might be." He sighed. "Damn war." He polished off his second bottle while I sipped the second glass I had poured from mine.

Early sunlight filtered into the mess hall. It wasn't even full light yet, but it was so bright that I covered my eyes. I saw Keegan do the same. "At least we still get to see sunlight. They say after you've been a vamp for a few years, even that goes away." Most new vampires, or yearlings, could tolerate dusk and dawn. The longer you lived as a vampire, the more sensitive you became, where even scant illumination from the sun could do bodily damage.

"You're staying then?" Keegan set down his bottle and looked at me, his gaze clearly assessing me.

"Since the virus didn't kill me," I shrugged, "I figured I would. I'm not exactly at peace with it, but I'm not ready to give up either. At least now I don't have to worry so much about injuries while I'm healing people."

"That's if you keep your magic. I've seen witches change and lose all connection to their abilities upon their transition."

"Keegan. You're kind of a killjoy."

"I am telling the truth."

"I know, I know." I watched him for a moment. "What about you? Planning to stick around?" I asked even though I knew his answer given his earlier altercation with the ward medics.

"No." He sounded absolute in his decision. "I shouldn't have survived. I don't know why I did, but I am not spending my days as a tick on Gaia's back."

Fae, for the most part, were immune to the vampire virus, along with dragons, and elementals. There were probably others that were less susceptible too, but it had been a long time since unicorns and merfolk had made themselves known. Some species, like orcs and trolls, didn't survive being infected at all, and no one understood why. The most susceptible to the virus were humans. Cross-species relationships that produced children happened often enough that nothing was completely guaranteed. Everyone was at some level of risk, regardless.

"How much time do you have left?" The virus, while it mutated your cells, caused one to develop an internal clock that synced with sunup and sundown. You could fool it if you were underground or newly turned, but full sunlight always shuts down a vampire or infected one way or another.

"Today is my last day." I watched as he moved his hand through the soft bars of light, playing with the shadows he made. "How about you?"

"Tomorrow." It wasn't like you couldn't walk out into the sun later, but it was significantly more challenging. The virus drilled an instinct into your brain, rewiring it to avoid strong light. It took a lot of willpower to stand in the sun. The other option was vampire hunters staking you to the ground, making it impossible to escape. They did that to the vamps whose loyalty compulsions they couldn't break. . . on both sides of the war.

"You have a spot picked out yet?"

He shook his head. "A vantage point from a building or high ground. It makes no difference."

That gave me a brilliant idea. "How about a tree?" Keegan looked up from his light play and tilted his head.

We left the bar with a bottle each and walked to the tree line about half a kilometer behind the camp. It was summer, so the trees were lush. There were all kinds to pick from. "Is there one that suits you?"

Keegan said nothing as we walked along the edge of the woods. I refrained from drinking so I could actually climb the tree without immediately falling. I've seen a few vamps with missing limbs and limps because their bodies fixed themselves the best they could while in a transition.

The fae started to climb a tree, and I hurried to keep up. Keegan managed like he was climbing stairs. I had to think carefully about where to put my feet and hands. About halfway up, my bottle slipped and shattered on the ground.

"Better the bottle than you," Keegan said as he reached a branch and sat, then opened his own.

"How far up are we?"

"Twenty meters? Not sure. I'm surprised you followed," Keegan said.

I sat on a branch on the opposite side of his and looped my legs around while I leaned against the trunk. I couldn't see him, but I could sense him. My vamp senses were manifesting, or maybe it was just that we were the only two beings up in a tree this early. The squirrels weren't even awake.

"And miss a chance at seeing a sunrise from an interesting location? No way."

"As a youngling, I'd often climb the trees near our home and play with the various animals that lived in them." Keegan sighed. "That was more than four hundred years ago. Those were simpler times. No magical devices, no steam-powered contraptions. One used their feet, their wings, or asked a horse to carry you. I miss those days."

He talked of home and magic he hadn't seen in some time. Celebrations he would miss, family he cared about, and some he didn't. He stopped talking when the sun was past the horizon. I moved to look at him. His eyes were open, but the color was washed out. His hands had curved into claws as his mouth gaped. The gasp he made was definitely a surprise. But it was watching him fall from the tree, bottle still in hand, that made me scream like zombies were chasing me.

My scream attracted folks from the hospital camp. They met me as I climbed down and went to Keegan. He wasn't dry husk yet, but his face was sallow, the blood that had been seeping from his wound was coagulated, and his bowels had voided. I checked for a pulse, then looked for his aura and saw nothing. I reached out and carefully closed his eyes. Others brought a litter to take his body back to the infected ward to be prepped.

I wandered camp until the bright light of midday hurt my eyes. I headed back to the bar to drink while I waited for Ian, opting not to return to the infected ward. He had promised me a bunk in the vampire quarters, and I planned to take him up on it.

VAMPIRE 101

The sunset was just as good as the sunrise, though less spectacular in how Keegan and I had greeted it. I was on my third bottle of the day when the fae in the camp built a pyre to burn Keegan's body. Unbeknownst to me, the individual closest to the fae when they died was given the honor of burning the last visage or token that represented them. The war changed the practice somewhat, so instead of adding a weapon or armor he wore to the pyre, I had the honor of burning his head.

In one hand, I held a burlap bag with Keegan's head. The other half a bottle of piss whiskey. That was how Ian found me. He cleared his throat, which caught my attention. I had a better look at him this time, more aware of things, even being somewhat inebriated. He was taller and thinner than me. Not sure if that was his age or if he'd been that way as a human. His short brown hair was styled in the latest fashion, which proved he kept up with trends. His face was clean-shaven too.

"Seems you've had a bit of a day, haven't you." Ian gave me a smile. I rolled my eyes and looked at the pyre. It was nearly hot enough. I needed to toss the head on it when the flames were blue. Fae were so particular about these things.

"'Spose the entire camp knows now, huh?"

"That you got pissed with a fae, climbed a tree to watch the sunrise, and screamed bloody murder when he fell out of it?" Ian nodded. "They're taking bets about what you'll do next."

"Oh? What's the odds?"

Ian's lips twisted slightly as he tried to keep the grin off his face.

"You going to tell me or be all smug?"

"Ten to one. You trip as you toss the head and land in the pyre."

I tried to act affronted, but I puked instead. At least it wasn't on Keegan's head.

"That shite will rot your guts out, or what's left of them."

"What do I care? By tomorrow, my guts won't even work."

Ian smirked. "Well, that's not quite true."

"Huh? What do you mean, that's not true?" His laughter made me feel wholly unprepared. "What the hell help is popular fiction good for if it's not somewhat true! I spent a good many hours reading about different species before I arrived here. So I think I know a thing or two."

"Oh, do you now?"

"Yes." Ian waited. I looked at him and held up my index finger. "One, vampires drink blood to survive. Two," I held up another finger. "Vampires can't be in direct sunlight. Three, they don't breathe. Four, they can't eat or drink human food. Five, wait, what was five?" Ian chuckled. "Stop laughing," I mumbled as I tried to figure out number five. "Oh, I remember. Five, vampires can't have children."

"That was all remarkably incorrect or inaccurate."

"What?" I scoffed. "How so? It was in a book. I read it!"

"And, pray tell, what was the name of this book?" I looked off into the distance and mumbled. "Mind saying that a little louder?"

"The Duchess and Her Vampire Duke." I looked at Ian. The surprise on his face was remarkably outlined in the firelight, which had shifted colors.

"It's blue," he said.

"What?"

"It's blue. Aren't you supposed to burn the token when it's blue?"

"Oh! Right!" I stepped away from him and almost fell. He caught me by the shoulders. His firm hands were reassuring and made my stomach do little flips. Or that might have been the booze; I wasn't entirely sure. I shrugged to gain some composure, and Ian slowly let go. I looked back, and he smiled. It wasn't a mean smile; instead, it was understanding, along with his kind eyes.

The bag in my hand suddenly felt heavy. "I know we were only friends for a day, maybe less, but I hope you're happy wherever you are now and have something better to drink than this swill. Peace unto you, Keegan." I gave the bag an underhand toss. It landed neatly in the center of the flames. The bag caught first, then wisps of Keegan's beautiful hair followed. That was enough for me. I tossed the bottle on the pyre and walked away.

"That was well done, by the way," Ian said, following me.

I huffed as we headed back toward the infected ward. "So, if everything I know is wrong, who teaches me?"

"Typically, the person who sired you, or whoever has fledgling duty."

"Oh? And who's that?" I glanced at him. "You?" I laughed. "Who did you piss off to end up with that post?"

"No one, I asked for it."

"That sounds totally unappealing."

"If you say so. I was rather looking forward to our getting to know one another."

I stopped just outside the infected ward's entry. "You, sir, need to find better things to do with your time."

"Possibly." He had a contemplative look. "Tell me, are you craving anything?"

"What kind of question is that?" I entered the ward and found my bed. Most of my clothes had been burned already, but what I hadn't worn out to the field was there, along with a few books and my other pair of boots—farm issued. "I'm not craving blood."

"That's not what I asked. Think a minute. What's the first thing that pops into your mind?"

"Apples."

Ian nodded. "Anything else?"

Plenty, and I felt my face heat at the downright randy thoughts running through my mind. I glanced at his crotch and then back at his face. His knowing smile grew to a grin.

He nodded slightly. "Come on. Let's get you set up with a cot and a bucket. I'll explain after that." I nodded as I rubbed at my face and neck to try and wipe away the heat. It was hot enough already without my embarrassment adding to it.

With all my worldly possessions shoved into my kit bag, I followed Ian to the basement hatch in the center of the hospital's main hallway. He opened it easily enough, though I knew the hatch weighed at least five hundred kilos, if not more. A dragon might be able to open it, or another vampire, but a human couldn't. At least not without a lot of help.

"Newcomers get to be near the door." Ian showed me to one of the cots not far from the stairs and the entrance.

"Why's that?"

"One." Ian held up his index finger. "Fledglings are more light tolerant than older vampires. We put you near the door so if one panics and manages to open it, then those that are intolerant won't be caught out."

He leaned over, picked up a bucket, and set it next to my bed. "Two, we don't have toilets down here, and most fledglings spend their initial waking hours evacuating. The bucket is there because gravity works, and you won't be able to make it to the latrines upstairs in time, so try to remember."

Ian gave a nod toward the stairs, and I followed. Befuddled and curious, I asked a question of my own. "So, your guts keep working?"

"After a fashion. Blood helps. Though I recommend sticking with liquids, mostly. Soup is fairly safe, and so are milkshakes, if you like that sort of thing." He shrugged. "It takes about ten or fifteen years for your body to figure out how to absorb solids again. In limited quantities, mind you. Otherwise, you'll be revisiting your dinner before daybreak."

"Do you need food after the transition?" I realized I hadn't been hungry.

"No. But it's helpful sometimes when you can't find a decent blood source. Lets you trick your body into thinking it's full, but it only works for so long."

Before I knew it, we were back in the clearing behind the hospital, heading for the trees.

"Number Three." Ian walked backward as I followed him toward the woods Keegan and I had spent the morning in. "The basement door is locked from the inside thirty minutes before sunup. So try not to be caught outside unaware. However, carry a trowel in case you are someday."

"A trowel. What the hell for?"

"Better than digging a foxhole in thirty minutes with your hands." Ian grinned as he waved his hands like some fancy showman at a traveling festival. The information was practical, but I definitely hoped I never had to use it.

"What's in the woods, anyway?"

He smiled and stopped. "Cravings," he whispered in my ear, then he disappeared. I looked around until I heard his voice echo in the trees. "Come on, Mason."

"Great." I sighed and headed for the woods.

CRAVINGS

When I reached the tree line, Ian was nowhere to be found. The smell of apples hit me as if conjured. It was all I could do not to blindly follow the scent. When I found the source, it was Ian sipping something from a glass bottle. "That smells divine. Can I have a taste?"

"Sure." He handed me the bottle. I bolted down five or six swallows until the metallic tang coated my throat, making me gag. "Don't retch. Keep it down if you can."

"What in the utter fuck, Ian?" I wiped my lips with the back of my hand in the futile hope it would rid my mouth of the taste.

He took another drink himself and then corked the bottle. "Cravings."

"That makes no sense whatsoever. I smelled apples. Apples and blood smell nothing like each other."

"No, but while your brain is sorting it out, you'll smell something you like. It's usually associated with a good memory. And that smell, that taste, will be what blood smells and tastes like to you." He held the bottle and smiled. "Now, whenever you smell apples, you'll know it's blood. Or you're standing in an orchard. The scent you associate with blood is usually so strong it overpowers everything else."

I inhaled and exhaled. The contents of my stomach stayed in place by some miraculous turn. "Oh? So what do you smell?"

"Freshly churned butter." Ian wore a smug look.

"That has to be a bit odd."

"Not really. I used to make it with my family as a boy. They still make it that way, but even if I stood next to an actual butter churn and smelled it, it wouldn't rival the smell and taste of blood. Blood tastes like fresh butter in my mouth."

Ian waited patiently while I fought the urge to panic. Blood that smelled like memories, random sexual thoughts, and the reality of my choice wasn't settling as well as my stomach had earlier.

"Why don't you come sit down?" I hadn't noticed the blanket on the ground. I followed him and sat. I even took off my shoes so I wouldn't get dirt on it. Ian dropped a knapsack on the corner of the fabric, removed his shoes, and sat next to me.

"How are you feeling?"

"A bit like churned butter myself."

He laughed, and that made me smile. "This does become easier. If you were on your own, you'd figure it out yourself through trial and error. We've found it's much better if we try to educate fledglings first. You're handling this remarkably well, I have to say."

"Oh? What's the measure, then?"

"You didn't retch up your blood. That's a good start. Your body is already shifting. Plus, you'll notice that it's a new moon tonight."

"So, what's that got to do with anything?"

"How well could you see during a new moon before?"

He was right. I could clearly see his face, the blanket, the bag, my shoes, and the wrinkles in my uniform. Before tonight, I'd have been lucky to see my hand in front of my nose, let alone in a tree line where most light was blocked out. "Okay, that's pretty neat. I won't stub my toe in the dark anymore."

"It's something your irises do to compensate for the lack of light. It might also be part magic, but no one's ever found a way to verify that. Here, I'll show you."

Ian gave me a hand mirror, and I saw pinpoints of light in my brown eyes. "How come I can see it in a mirror, but there's nothing there when I look at your eyes?"

"Because a reflection can reveal magic. Or at least that's the speculation."

I turned the mirror to see if his eyes did the same, and they were even brighter. Plus, I could see his face. He laughed at my astonishment.

"If a vampire doesn't have a reflection, something else is going on. I've never seen a vampire not have a reflection without magic involved."

"Oh." I sighed and tossed the mirror over my shoulder. It made a soft thud on the blanket. Ian laughed again, and I laughed with him. It felt good to laugh. A couple of large booms in the distance cut through our momentary ease. "Who's watching the ward tonight?"

Besides Keegan, I was the only other infected who survived. But the ward was there for a reason. This close to a front, there was always more.

"Jeremy. His bedside manner could use some work, but he does alright." That understanding smile appeared, and part of me wanted to kiss it, or bite it. He must have read the confusion on my face. "What were you thinking just now?"

"I can't really say."

"Yes, you can. Be honest. You don't have to hide from me."

Something in his voice urged me to open up, to tell him exactly what I was thinking. "I wanted to kiss you. I've wanted to do other things too since the start of the night."

"Like what?" His voice was gentle as he leaned closer.

"Sex." I blinked. "Oh, goodness. I'm sorry. That was horribly forward. I don't know why I said that."

"You said it because I gave you a slight push. A small command. It's part of the magic some vampires gain through their gaze or their voice."

"You cheated! I never would have told you."

Ian grinned. "I know you wouldn't have. Most wouldn't. A vampire's instinct to survive appears first in your sex drive. Attraction is a powerful motivator. In the living, it's linked to survival through breeding. For us, it's linked to survival as well, but more so from one night to the next. However, I've found that sex can mask a bite fairly well if you need to drink directly from the source."

"Why would I even want to bite you? You're a vampire."

"Top marks, Mason. Most people get hung up on sex and the actual biting." He clapped, and it sounded loud, so close to my ears. "It's the blood. It doesn't matter whose system it's in; we're attracted to it. Vampires can starve, but I've seen whole groups survive for a good long while, passing the same few mouthfuls between each other. They don't look pretty afterward, but they survive. At least those that don't shut down and rot away. The virus can only do so much."

"So the Vampire Duke was right! Vampires use their wiles to seduce their way into the hearts and minds of their targets."

Ian laughed. Then laughed some more. He fell back on the blanket, still laughing, and I rolled on top of him to get him to stop. "A minute ago it was funny, but it's not now. It's not like there were vampires where I'm from. It's mostly dvergar and local native groups." I shook him to stop his laughing. He reached up and grabbed my hands, then looked me in the eye.

"I apologize, Mason. It's hilarious to think about how much the pulp readers have spread so much misinformation. In this instance, the books almost have the right of it. Our biology drives us, but many of us develop a charm or mystique, if you will. Even the least social among us can generally thrive by their wiles." He grinned, and that was it. I couldn't help myself anymore.

"Since I'm already being so forward, can I kiss you? I'm pretty sure I might lose my marbles if I don't." Ian nodded. I dove in.

At twenty-five, I was certainly not a virgin. I'd had a boyfriend or two back home and one when I landed in jolly old England while I was training. I'd never been all that interested in sex. It was fun, but not what I enjoyed spending my time doing. I was absolutely not aiming to be tied down with little ones before I had my adventures.

On the verge of death, or in its throes anyway, Ian seemed appealing to me. It had to be more than the blood in his veins. I mean, I definitely wanted that, but I also wanted him. All of him, including the rigid member pressed between us.

"Uh, question. Does everything work like it's supposed to?" I saw Ian smirk as I lifted my head to see his face properly. "And don't laugh."

His lips screwed up, and he cleared his throat before he answered. "I assure you, it works."

I rolled off him and worked at undoing my uniform trousers. He kicked free of his, and I worked on my shirt while he undid his tie. Our lips found each other in the frantic effort to remove layers. We paused as the sounds of mage bombardment reached us in our wooded sanctuary. I panted into Ian's face while he looked off into the distance, then back at me. His concern was quickly replaced with need before shifting to the understanding gaze he wore like a mask. Something about him losing his composure for even one moment made me more desperate for him.

We lay naked, kissing until instincts overrode my laid-back nature. I pushed Ian onto his back and straddled him again. This time, I reached for his cock and stroked it. I marveled at the feel of veins along the shaft and how hard he was already. His pubic hair tickled my fingers. My lust won out over the newly discovered tactile response I seemed to have. "Can I put it in, Ian?"

"I think that's supposed to be my line." He chuckled.

"Yes or no, you infernal beast," I whispered, serious as anything.

"Gods, yes, please." We groaned together as I sank onto him, and my ass met his hips.

Our movements were brisk; the slap of flesh echoing around us. Ian's hand grasped my brown, braided hair as mine landed on his chest. The follicles on his chest were soft, and my fingers couldn't stop pawing through them like a cat.

The sensation I wanted was slightly out of reach. The edge was near, but never close enough. I could feel myself becoming frustrated by it as I moved, angled, and played with myself to no good effect.

Somehow Ian read that frustration and brought my head to his chest. I kissed his neck, shoulder, chest, and nipples. His taste was on my tongue, yet my orgasm never seemed to crest. Finally, he whispered one word as his hips kept their steady rhythm. "Bite."

Bite? It clicked. His neck seemed too intimate a spot. If his hands weren't pulling my hips into his every thrust, I might have picked his wrist. I turned my head slightly and bent so I could press my teeth into his chest. The left peck, to be exact. Nothing happened after I sank my teeth into his flesh.

Ian's movements slowed. "Open your mouth a little."

I did, which pulled my fangs back from my bite. The action caused my mouth to flood with the taste of apples and metal. I swallowed over and over until he came.

"Oh, fuck, Mason."

The heat in my mouth matched the warmth deposited into my cunt as he continued to fuck me. I gasped as my orgasm made me clamp down around his cock. More colorful words flew from his mouth.

All I smelled were apples and sex. Instinctively, I licked the wound, and blood stopped flowing. Ian sat up with me still in his lap, still connected for a little longer. I offered him my blood-stained mouth, and there was no hesitation as he licked, kissed, and sucked my swollen lips.

"You smell like apples," I said.

Ian made a pleased sound as he held me tight.

SURVIVAL

Except for the war blazing some distance from us, the woods were peaceful. It was like being home. I turned onto my side to face Ian while he continued to look up.

"So now that we've completely debauched each other, I have questions." Ian was, as always, amused.

"Let's hear them," he said as he turned to face me. He was a rather cheerful person considering we were in the middle of a war. Though I suspected it might be something like armor for him.

"The vampire that bit me in the field—her bite hurt. But when I bit you, you enjoyed it."

Ian smirked. "Body chemistry still works. We're just humans with protruding canines and a virus that won't let us die under the usual circumstances."

"Okay, so you're saying that it hurt because I was scared instead of canoodling?"

"Yes, exactly so. Brains work differently when experiencing fear and pleasure. Sometimes pain can become pleasure under the right circumstances."

"Oh." This was way out of my realm of experience. Why anyone would want something painful to cause pleasure was beyond me. Except maybe for childbirth? Though I'd never know it, since I was a vampire.

"Tell me a bit about home. Where are you from, Mason?"

I took a slow breath and sighed. "Well, you can probably tell I'm from the colonies. My parents were from North Carolina area until they had an offer to move out to Boulder, Colorado, to teach at the new university there. It was someone's brilliant plan to have a university in the newly formed state where everyone can exchange ideas, magical techniques, and learn from each other." I was babbling, and Ian listened, which was sweet of him.

"What do your parents teach?"

"Dad teaches English. Mom teaches botany." They also knew other things, but I didn't mention those. Some family secrets were meant to be kept.

"Are your healing skills from your mother's side?"

"Yeah, mostly, though my mom can't work magic as well for some reason. She taught me a lot about plants, and I learned more when we moved. Then I took up husbandry and animal tending, much to my parents' dismay."

"How did you find yourself doing that instead of reading in parlors?"

I scoffed. "It was reading in parlors that led me to it. We had a sick hen when I was eleven, and I read a book on healing animal ailments. Between the magic lessons and the reading, I figured out it ate something that didn't agree with it. I gave it some mint, and it was fine after that."

"Clever and beautiful." I didn't mind the compliment. Ian smiled and reached out to smooth a lock of hair behind my ear.

"I'm sure you say that to all the lady fledglings.

"The men too, or whatever they identify as," Ian said.

I blinked. Ian grinned, and there was a long moment when all I could hear were the critters around us and the occasional echoes of explosions from far away.

"You're serious?"

"Of course. Everyone deserves compliments." His nonchalantness caught me off guard.

"So if it was Keegan out here with you instead of me?"

"Pretty much the same thing would have happened, though maybe not in the same way. Fae don't really have notions about gender. Actually, a lot of species don't. Dragons definitely don't."

"Are you telling me that if Keegan had come out here with you, you would've had sex with him?" I sat up, and Ian looked at me.

"Yes. Are you telling me you wouldn't have? It would have been his choice, but I would have offered. It's one of the easier ways to learn how everything works."

I definitely would have if he'd been willing. I was ready enough with Ian. "Does that mean I might start fancying women?" I'd met others who had similar views, but hadn't really felt the need to explore any of that myself. My family wouldn't have minded. If I had chosen a partner or three, they would have been happier than when I announced I was running off to war.

He shrugged. "After some time, you realize you have more life than most. Some of life's expectations make little sense anymore. Plus, need and necessity drives us a bit."

"Are all vampires queer, then?"

"No. However, as your nature changes, it opens you to other possibilities and frees your mind of limiting social constructs. You can go places, study whatever you like, be a hermit or untethered."

"All for the meager cost of never being able to walk in sunlight again."

He reached over and touched my hand. "You're doing really well, Mason. Transitions are hard to deal with, and they take a lot out of folks. It's why we give everyone a choice, especially when someone is forced onto this path instead of choosing it for themselves."

"Did you choose?" The way he mentioned it made me wonder if his experience was different.

"Before the war, human vampires lived in coteries made up of their families. It was almost unheard of to have vampires of other species. Or have someone introduced to a coterie who was involuntarily bitten. It happens, but in those cases, the perpetrator is swiftly punished.

"In a functioning coterie, every few generations, a family member is chosen to transition. The vampire half of the family becomes stewards of the living bloodline. In return, the living family members support the vampires.

"My family is known for some magical talents, which are further enhanced when one transitions. Everyone has access to tools and knowledge they need to hone their skills. The more talented ones are given a choice. It's considered an honor to protect your living bloodline over the generations."

I knew it was rude, but now I was curious. "How long. . ."

"I'm somewhat shocked you haven't asked sooner. For most, that's the first thing out of their mouths."

"I had a lot going on."

"Quite right." He cleared his throat. "Two hundred and twenty-three years. That includes the years I was a human."

"What have you done with all that time?" The thought of that much life ahead of me made me wonder if I was choosing the right thing. Twenty-five years wasn't enough, but could I possibly keep myself entertained for a century or more? The prospect seemed daunting.

Ian used his hands to tell his story as if he were on a grand stage and not sitting on a blanket next to me, naked as a mole rat. "Traveled, helped my family, and canoodled a bit." We laughed. "Found love and lost it. I did the same things when I was alive, just bigger, better, and with more time than most." Our fingers intertwined.

The silence was comfortable, or rather, the one that we held between us was. The night was noisy. We only had a few more hours left before we needed to head back to the daylight shelter of the hospital basement. Ian pulled out the bottle and handed it to me. I drank several more swallows before the metallic taste was too much.

"Blech. Is there anything to do about the aftertaste? It's like sour apples. Maybe worse."

"You can mask it sometimes if you have someone prepare it. It's better warm, of course." His eyes lit up with mischief and desire.

I tipped the bottle and drank more, then offered the rest to him. He finished it, and we kissed. As it grew more heated, I giggled.

"What was that for?" Ian asked.

"Apples and butter. Like apple pie." Ian snorted, and I giggled more.

"I'll show you apple pie." He nudged me onto my back and moved to settle between my legs. We shared the taste of blood between us. I couldn't taste butter like he did, but I wanted to. I wanted him to bite me and taste apples. It was a ridiculous notion.

Our kisses became more urgent, more frantic as Ian grew hard again. His cock slid along my inner thigh, dribbling moisture. As I was about to ask him for more, he broke away from my lips and kissed and licked his way down my stomach.

"Ian, what are you doing?"

"Never had a bloke give you a lick before?"

"Lick what?" His smirk was lost in my thatch of brown hair as his tongue darted into me. "Oh, blessed be!"

"Liked that, did you?" He teased as I bucked into his face. Ian was undoubtedly proving his point about new experiences. At this rate, I wondered if I could reach the moon without assistance.

Ian kept winding me tighter and tighter. I was desperate to have him finish me somehow as he continued to snatch marbles from my brain with his talented tongue. It wasn't enough. I growled in frustration, reached between my legs and sunk my hand into his short, dark brown hair. Ian growled back.

"Say it," he breathed. His lips and tongue returned to the pleasurable torture of my cunt. "You know what you want, Mason. You only have to ask."

I groaned and whimpered until my tongue pushed at one of my newly elongated canines. I only needed to ask, so I asked for everything. "Bite me, then fuck me. I need you to fuck me, Ian."

It was the tipping point. Ian buried his face between my legs, and I shook with each stroke and lick. When he added a few fingers to the mix, I shook so hard with pent-up need I thought I would explode. That's when Ian struck.

I didn't feel pain. I felt the pull toward my center, sucking me into an orgasm and gushing warmth that Ian lapped at. When the feeling didn't have as much of an edge, I pulled at Ian and urged him up. His pale face was covered with blood. I lapped at his chin and lips as he slid into me. With each thrust, he seemed desperate to make a permanent connection. I was anticipating him now and let him feel my teeth as he hummed with pleasure. When he gave in, it was so beautiful.

"Please. . ." he whispered.

"Please, what, Ian?"

"Please bite me, please."

This time, I didn't care about being delicate. I wrapped my arms around Ian's shoulders, put my face in the crook of his neck, then clamped down. I didn't have to pull back much for the taste of apples to flood my mouth as Ian yelled above me, then added to our mess.

When we finally stopped and took stock, I was slightly alarmed that we were half covered in blood. "Oh sweet mother, what a mess!" I stared down at myself, then had another concern. "Does this mean we can't have sex with humans? We're infection risks right now."

Ian and his knapsack to the rescue. "No, but it means you need to be careful. Especially if you drink blood before sex. After tonight, you won't have to worry about your courses, but sometimes vigorous sex can produce blood." He handed me a cloth and a clear bottle with liquid in it. I uncorked it and smelled grain alcohol.

"So instead of blood, we'll smell like a still?"

"Infinitely better to smell like booze if you plan on spending your day in the basement." He smiled as he held out a cloth of his own, and I poured liquid onto it. "No one will harm you. But the smell would be inviting enough that some would want to see if you were interested."

Oh. Wait. "Should I be interested?" I wondered how much Ian was teaching me, or whether he was interested in more.

After a long pause, he said, "If you want to be."

"Well, that's something to figure out tomorrow night, I guess." Ian cleared his throat. "What?"

"If I were you, I'd plan on not doing much for the next few days."

"Why's that?" I poured a bit more alcohol on myself and wiped. I nearly felt clean enough to put my clothes back on.

"Remember when I mentioned the bucket?"

Evacuation. "Oh." I frowned. "Is it that bad?"

"It can be. But once it's over, it's over. Then we learn if you've retained your magic or not."

"Oh, fun." We chuckled, but mine was a nervous laugh. I tried not to think about what waited for me the following night as dawn slowly crept into the sky. We packed up the bag. Ian did a cleaning spell on the blanket, then packed it away too. No one paid us any mind as we walked back into camp and down to the basement.

Ian stopped next to my bunk. "Probably best for you to lie down now, so when you drop off, you don't fall."

"Has that happened before?"

"Sure. Fledglings' internal clocks have to sync up a bit before they can feel the line between waking and day death."

That was a new term. "Day death?"

"Rather self-explanatory, I would think."

"Right. Yeah."

He touched my shoulder as I sat on my cot. "Don't be nervous. You'll be fine. You might want to put on clothes you don't mind making a mess in just in case you don't wake up in time."

"Now you're making me nervous."

He patted my shoulder and let go. I wanted more than platitudes, but Ian seemed ready to distance himself after everything we had done in the woods. "We'll see each other tonight. My bunk is the one nearest the wall on the left. Good day, Mason."

"Good day, Ian." He walked to his cot and dropped his things. While I watched, he removed his shoes, stripped down to nothing, and covered himself with a sheet. I noticed the change immediately. It was like all the life was sucked out of him at once. The sun must have been rising outside. I quickly changed out of my uniform into a simple sleeping gown and covered myself in a similar sheet. What happened next reminded me of when my mother would come into my room and blow out the candle. One minute there was light; the next darkness, and I was dead to the world.

AWAKE

"Oh, Mother of God," was my not-so-silent plea for it to stop. It was worse than anything I had ever dealt with, including being dead. Or mostly dead. Everything was convulsing, cramping, and the only thought I had was that some folks were lucky that they were actually dead when their bowels let go.

I had eaten little in the last few days, which was good for several reasons. If I were to describe it, I'd say it felt like I had the flu, my menses, and dysentery all at the same time. The smell was horrendous. It didn't surprise me that the door was left open to air out the basement as others woke and shuffled out for the evening.

Ian appeared with a tray as I lay on my cot and thought about my life choices. He set it at the end of the cot and pulled up a chair. "I'll refrain from asking the obvious," he said with a sympathetic smile. He was gentle as he picked up a cloth and wiped my face and hands. "Considering your state, you've managed not to make much of a mess. Congratulations."

The groan I made was half from pain and half annoyance. Ian looked amused. "I've brought a few things to help. But first, drink." He held out his wrist to me, and I wasn't sure I had enough strength. Was this another test? He leaned down. "Drink now, or this gets worse."

"Worse how?" I huffed. Nothing could be worse than this, surely.

"Glad you asked. See, vampires are somewhat akin to pack animals. We maintain small groups or move as family units. We're more dangerous when we're alone with a mind left to wander and brood." His words conjured images of stories I'd read and his own story from the previous night. Small families that protected their nighttime relatives. Vampires drawn to each other formed bonds. Others created gangs. What he offered was a tether. A replacement for what, on some level, I knew was lost to me.

My parents were educated, but they hadn't approved of my signing up to help with the war. They didn't like that the adventures I'd read were things I wanted to experience. It hurt to know that I might never see them again. Not because I didn't want to or they wouldn't want to, but because it might be safer for them. I wasn't their only child, but I was their oldest.

Tears streaked down my face as I grabbed Ian's wrist and bit into it. He made a soft grunt, likely because I wasn't delicate. All the tendons and tissue made it one of the worst places to drink from, I realized, but I continued on. I swallowed several mouthfuls until Ian asked me to stop. I licked his wrist clean and let him go.

In moments, my mind felt like someone had wrapped a blanket around it. The pain in my body was distant and diffused. Ian wiped my face as if I were a child. In many ways, I was. I wondered how long this awkward second childhood would last.

"Feel better?" He reached for my hand. I felt its warmth.

I nodded slowly. "I'm cold."

Ian nodded. "It's okay. Can you sit up? I brought some hot broth and more blood. Both should help with the cold."

It wasn't a smooth motion, but I pulled myself into a sitting position, though I felt like iron ore. "You did something to my mind. I feel disconnected."

His mask of understanding slipped into place, and now, instead of being reassuring, it annoyed me. "I did."

"Why?"

"Ah, Mason. You really are clever. And willful. Most at this point don't even ask because they are so thankful that they don't feel pain any longer."

"That didn't answer my question."

"No, it didn't. Eat this broth, and I'll explain."

I took the bowl from his hands and felt the heated surface. I distantly wondered if I could sustain a burn or even feel it now. I sipped the liquid and felt my body respond to the warmth as it slid down my throat.

"We've learned a lot during the war. Most coteries of vampires have connections to one another. They are prepared for the life they'll lead because they were chosen to do so. The connection and desire to serve are already in our blood. When we're made, it seals the bond.

"With war fledglings, they have no such connection, nor are they prepared even if they've read a thousand pulp fantasies about vampires. In the early days, we let them transition if there was a safe place to do so, but no one took them in or saw to their long-term care.

"Some were lost to the enemy when they returned to the front. Some went mad and devastated camps before they were contained. It's not a lack of blood that sends a vampire into a frenzied state. It's a lack of connection. They had become individuals without a past or a future. It takes time to handle that transition mentally. The coteries knew this intrinsically.

We realized we had to make that connection for fledglings like yourself to survive."

"So you're saying that the virus makes a new vampire susceptible to mental feebleness?"

"I am." He was sincere and honest with his terse statement, but that didn't make me feel better.

"Do I seem like I'm not of sound mind to you?" I put down the empty bowl. My anger was there but distant, like the rest of the pain in my body. Ian made a good point. It was for my protection, as well as for protecting others around me. But it also sounded like I was being controlled.

"No, but that's what I'm trying to prevent. You're angry. I don't blame you. If these were normal circumstances, you wouldn't be here, and you wouldn't be a vampire. You'd be living your life back in Boulder, tending to animals and reading romance novels in your family's parlor.

"I don't enjoy making these bonds. I feel it every time one of you is hurt or meets their end. Or tortured in some cases, as their bond and mental wards are broken." He looked at his hands. "I've lost too many already. And this is nothing more than an imperfect solution to a worse problem."

He was speaking of the loyalty compulsion and how it was created, making one vampire loyal to another. I reached for his hands and clasped them in mine. "I understand. Or at least I want to." I knew he could exert a certain amount of control. He'd made suggestions using his magic that I was helpless to resist. "So, this also makes it harder for a necromancer to control me?"

He lifted his head. There was a tug at his lips as his eyes held something akin to approval. I had the oddest feeling of satisfaction, as if I'd pleased one of my parents. "It does. There are better mental wards and charm bracelets, which take time to make. Besides, those need to wait until you have finished your transition. The bond allows me to ward you against necro-mancer magic in the meantime. It's not perfect, but it's the best we can do for now."

"How long does it last?" As much as I liked Ian, I wasn't at all pleased about having a surrogate parent. I'd left home to be my own person, not someone else's burden.

"It varies. Something between a few months and a few years. It depends on the will of the individual."

Even though my anger was distant, I reached for it. I wanted it. It was my pain, anger, grief, and loss that he'd kept from me, and I'd lost so much. The more I reached for it, the more I felt a mental fog descend. "Stop. Please. Whatever you are doing, stop."

"It's instinctual, I assure you. I. . ."

"I don't care, Ian. You've made sure of that." My voice sound-ed dull to my ears. Quiet. A sad plea compared to the desire I had to scream at him, though the will to manifest such a reaction was nonexistent. All because of what he was doing to my mind.

"For what it's worth, I'm sorry, Mason." He wiped his face. I noticed a smear of blood dashed across his cheek. I licked my thumb and reached up to wipe it off his face. His surprise amused me. And in turn, I was surprised that I could be amused. So he hadn't taken everything from me. I put my blood-crust-ed thumb in my mouth. The flavor of apples burst across my tongue and dissipated just as quickly.

He looked even more surprised, if that was possible, when I pulled him to me for a kiss. Usually, I would have asked. But he didn't ask me if I wanted to be bound to him. I took, and he quickly gave in. When I let go of him, he tried to kiss me back, and I pulled away. "No. If you want any part of me, you need to let me feel things. Otherwise, you can leave."

"Mason, you don't want that."

"You didn't give me a choice, did you?" My words came out soft and wistful. If I could be angry, I would have. I sounded complacent when I was anything but.

"Listen to me. I know you're upset, but your body is still changing. If I let you feel everything, I'll feel everything, like we were going through this change together. I'm doing this for both of us." His gaze pleaded for me to understand.

"No," I said, as a quiet logic asserted itself. "You're doing this because you don't want to feel my pain. You're protecting yourself more than me. Maybe you should have thought about that before you had me drink."

He whispered, but I heard him all the same. "Don't make me feel you suffer. Please."

"Ian, so much of me has been taken away already. Don't take this away from me, too."

"Fuck." He sighed. "Okay, fine. Here's the deal. You'll need to drink when you wake up and try to keep it down. We both do. So, if you finish the bottle of blood I brought, I'll give you what you want, but you have to let me dampen it enough when we wake up so that we can eat otherwise. . ." he shrugged.

"Otherwise, you'll force me to be the way I am now." He looked pained at the way I finished his sentence. It was clear he wasn't used to someone fighting for control. I reached for the bottle on the tray and uncorked it. The smell of apples wafted out. "How many days will it take to get through my transition?"

"If we did it my way, two, maybe three. Your way, I have no idea."

I drank. The taste didn't bother me as much as the day before. Warm blood was much better than bottled, but I was thirsty regardless. I handed him the bottle, and he set it back on the tray. He seemed to prepare mentally as he rubbed his hands on his trousers.

"Ian."

"Okay, dammit." He held up his hands and sighed. When he broke the compulsion, I didn't feel it at first. Then, like a tidal wave, there were hints of something larger coming.

The feelings welled up in my throat. I turned to the other side of my cot and dry-heaved into the bucket. The cramps and pain returned, and I screamed. But it wasn't just me. Ian screamed too. I remembered feet pounding on stairs and individuals rushing into the basement. I heard Ian trying to reason with them in between our screams. Breathing hurt. Everything hurt. Something was jabbed into my arm, and the world went away for a while.

When I woke again, Ian had his arms wrapped around me with my back to his front. I didn't know what time it was, but I wouldn't be awake if the sun were up. I hurt a lot, but it wasn't nearly as much as earlier.

Ian's arm slipped away as I sat up. He groaned. "I feel like I've been hit by a dragon." I chuckled. "It's not funny."

I turned toward him. "You've never experienced this, have you? When you transitioned, you didn't know how painful it was."

He shook his head. "I was twenty-five. I had a wife and child, and my great-grandfather chose me. He didn't look any older than thirty. When he helped me transition, I felt weightless and safe. I didn't have to think about it. I know better now. He did something to make it that way so I wouldn't feel the pain of my body changing."

"Sorry for messing up your usual routine. But I know myself. And I know I'll never be whole if I can't feel, no matter how painful."

"Well, your desire to feel had half the camp down here, and we were shot with enough tranquilizers to fell a horse." He wiped his face. "Are you happy now?"

I smiled. "No, not really, but I'm satisfied."

"Why are you smiling at me like that?"

"You're miserable."

"And?"

"It's kind of adorable in a horrid way."

"Oh, do fuck off." I laughed and wished Keegan could have seen this. He would have thought us rather pathetic. Or maybe he saw from wherever he was now. Thinking about him brought sadness and then tears. Ian sat up and pulled me into his arms, and we rocked together as we both sobbed. "We're a bloody mess, the two of us."

"Maybe. But at least this way, I know I'm still me."

He shook his head and kissed my cheek. "Feel like going for a wash?"

I nodded. We grabbed our kits and headed for the showers. To save water, we shared a stall and helped each other. While I was a mess, Ian only had blood on his face. He was gentle with me the whole time, and by sunup, we were back in the basement, in his cot for the day, so we would wake together and hopefully make it through the first few hours without screaming.

THE WARD

Four days. Without Ian's mind control, my transition to a full vampire took four days to complete. Ian didn't leave my side the whole time. I don't think he could have given how much pain we were dealing with.

Our routine was simple. We got up, drank the bottles of blood Ian had fetched before we slept, washed, and then went back to the basement for the night as my guts cramped. Today was different.

I stared at my shiny brown hair as I tried to dress. Everything seemed shiny. Buttons, fabric, even the rough floorboards of the showers. I took a breath once every minute or so. My heart-beat was only a little faster than that. I turned to Ian as he pulled his shirt on. Was his heart the same as mine? I pressed my hand to his chest and waited. Slower still. He took a breath, and I could feel it as his chest rose.

"So you're one of those. Doesn't surprise me, considering you're a healer." Ian took my hand from his chest ever so care-fully, kissed my knuckles, then let me go. He continued to button his shirt as I watched, fascinated by each movement he made. My own clothes were forgotten.

"One of what?"

"A corvid." I watched as he took another deep breath and spoke again. "You observe everything. Likely related to your being able to see auras before you transitioned. Now, you'll probably see more than auras."

"I can hear when you run out of breath to speak."

Ian grinned. "Well, that confirms it, then. It might annoy you at first, but you'll learn to control it. Dampen the ability, so it doesn't drive you mad, or heighten it so that you can tune your senses to find something."

"If I'm a corvid, what are you?"

The smile on his face warmed me in its own way. I had pleased him again and satisfied myself. I knew that through our bond. It was in the background, but the magical tie was there if I reached for it.

"An apis." It was Latin for bee.

"Is that because of what you can do with your mind?"

He nodded. "It's part ability and part magic. I have to be in tune with the person somewhat, and taking their blood can ease that. But mostly, I use it to break compulsions and bonds, along with other mental talents. It's not an exact reference, but the general idea is that apis have mental abilities." It reminded me of mage mental abilities and necromancer powers. Though I suppose more than one species can have mental abilities.

"Oh, shit. That's why you're really here. You're not just a medic." The pain on Ian's face was intense. It showed in the lines his forehead made and how his lips thinned. "I'm sorry. I was so selfish and didn't understand. I didn't." Tears came to my eyes and rolled slowly down my face as I wrapped my arms around him.

He held me for a moment and kissed the top of my head. "Don't apologize for something you didn't know. I made a choice not to tell you."

"And then I made you suffer with me. After everything you've endured, Ian. You should have told me." This man used his ability to free vampires from the bonds of the enemy by breaking the compulsions necromancers had put on them. It was a painful process, and I had seen it a few times at a distance. Ian's plea a few nights ago made more sense. But it was too late now. I couldn't take it back.

"Mason, look at me." It was a simple request. He could have forced me, but didn't. This is how much power he had and refused to use, even with our bond. I looked up.

"You didn't know." He used his thumbs to wipe the bloody tears from my face while I held him. "And while I would have preferred to do things my way, it all worked out in the end."

His kindness and delight confused me. "I don't understand."

Ian smiled. "You're stronger than most fledglings at this point. You're using your abilities reflexively. Innately. It normally takes fledglings several months to a year before they develop anything useful. Sometimes longer if they had magical abilities before they transitioned."

"Oh." Sensations bubbled between us, and I smiled, feeling them. Then I frowned as I tried to distinguish Ian's feelings from mine. Ian smirked.

"Definitely a corvid. You'll get used to finding the line between yourself and others."

"But what about us? Will the bond always make that line hard to read?"

"Maybe." Ian shrugged. "If we're thinking the same thing. If we're not, it can convey images and emotions across distances. Very useful if one of us needs help."

"Or it's a convenient way to torture another vampire with the one they've captured."

Ian pulled away slightly and continued to button his shirt, pointedly avoiding the statement. "You should get dressed. We have ward duty tonight."

My nudity didn't bother me. It should have. When did I stop being modest? Or was that only around Ian? I reached for my clothes and pulled them on. Ian waited for me. As we left the shower tent, I noticed blood on his shirt. "Ah, easy enough to fix." He flicked his wrist, and it disappeared. I'd seen magic before, but I saw it more clearly now. Ian was amused at my shifting senses.

"You're going to have fun tonight. If the dragons do strafing runs, they'll mesmerize you. I understand it's quite beautiful, with enhanced senses."

"If I get distracted too much, give me a nudge, okay?"

Ian blinked. "You'll allow me to do that?"

"Yes. I don't want to lose myself on some magical trip while helping someone. I'd rather you gave me a mental poke before I'm completely useless." His face went from pleased to an outright grin. The emotions between us and the intense desire to see how my newfound senses responded threatened to make us late for our shift. "Ian," I said as I cleared my throat.

"I doubt you'll need it, but sure. I'll try to help if I can."

"Good." I smiled and walked ahead of him. His gaze was a pleasant weight on my cloth-covered backside. "And if it's a quiet night, maybe we can sneak off and indulge in a little recreation before the sun comes up." Ian laughed as I turned back to wink at him.

The night was not quiet. The infected ward had fifteen cases. Five of them died before they arrived, because of the wounds they sustained or the virus hadn't worked fast enough to help heal them from severe injuries. Bullet holes or shrapnel aren't much of a problem for vamps. Massive holes, however, were a different story. One of them dissolved to dust in my hands before I could do anything useful, which meant the vamp had to have been over five hundred years old. I dug out their tags and pocketed them to report later. Two were infected humans. They were in a deep coma; the virus working either to change or kill them. We reset one's broken leg, and they didn't even make a peep.

A gnome named Bren came in with a zombie bite that had been infected with vampire blood when his friend Gladius had her leg blown off with a magic projectile. The gnome was distracted by a zombie and hadn't shielded them in time. Gladius had knocked them out of the way, but not far enough to save her leg. They had beds next to each other in the ward. I tried not to eavesdrop on their conversation, but they were loud and adorable.

"It's my fault, Gladius. Damn zombie flanked me. I shouldn't have let my shield dissipate."

"It was trying to bite your arm off, Bren. You can't blame yourself for that."

Bren winced as I cleaned the bite. "I can blame myself all I want," he said as he grinned at her. Battlefields made strange bedfellows.

"Hey, Doc," Gladius said as I cleaned the wound. "Doc, how does it look?"

I looked between them, and Bren nodded, so I took a breath and replied. "The wound will heal. It's not severe." I knew little about gnome physiology. "We'll know in a day or so whether things will progress."

Bren grasped my arm. "Thanks, Doc."

"You can call me Mason." I smiled. "I'm a healer. I don't have formal training."

Gladius shrugged. "No one does until they get here." We all chuckled as I patted Bren's arm and moved to check Gladius' bandages. The stump was healing nicely. By the next day, she'd be fine and ready for crutches. "Let's change this before sunup, and then have you moved to the basement wing. How light tolerant are you?"

"So so. I've been a vamp for a couple of years now. Got turned earlier in the war. Been pretty lucky since I teamed up with this fine warrior." She nodded at Bren, and he scoffed.

"Until tonight." Bren was definitely sulking.

"Dinna fash yourself. If it weren't for you, I'd have been blown to pieces long before now."

It sounded like a discussion they'd had before. I made myself less of an audience. "I'll check back later after I finish rounds and set up a cot for you." They nodded, and I moved on.

The rest of the cases were shrapnel injuries, various body parts impaled with objects, or broken limbs. Some knitted themselves back together, which was promising. There was one patient Ian stayed with most of the night. They were bedraggled and smelled horrid. Their uniform was unrecognizable, but the tags around their neck were easy to identify. I brought over a chair and sat next to Ian.

"This is Kirkland. He was turned a few years ago. I helped him through his transition. They sent him to the front before he was ready. He was assumed to have been killed in action." Ian's voice trailed off. He had Kirkland's hand in his. The elongated nails were a clear sign he'd gone feral. The ones that were controlled to the point of not even being an animal, but something worse. They dug tunnels like moles and would appear behind enemy lines before anyone realized what was going on in the trenches.

"Can you help him?"

Ian shook his head. "I don't know."

He proceeded to remove Kirkland's clothes and wash him with a cloth and a basin of water. "I don't sense the person I knew."

"Will he be safe in the basement?"

I watched as Ian moved carefully. It seemed like he was preparing a body rather than cleaning a patient. "He can't go to the basement. If he's still under any control or compulsion, a necromancer could use him to kill all of us."

"Has that happened?" Ian nodded. Another naiveté was ripped from me. I hadn't paid attention to the vampires in the camp before my transformation, nor had I understood the risk. "What will you do if you can't break what they did to him?"

Ian's eyes were bloodshot. "Don't worry about that. Go fetch some more blood. We're nearly through our supply for the night."

Every ward has a specialized cabinet that could keep things fresh via a stasis spell. When the infected ward ran low, we could borrow from the other wards. Unfortunately, other wards couldn't borrow from the infected ward. Once blood was moved into our ward, it was considered infected, whether it was or not.

As I went about my chores before sunup, I thought about Kirkland and the lack of anything I felt from Ian, as if he had muted our bond completely. I wondered why. Usually, I could read him like a book. Later on, after I'd helped the wounded vamps into the basement, along with one stubborn gnome who wouldn't leave Gladius's side, I asked how he was so unread-able.

"Mental shields," he said as he curled next to me in the cot. He hadn't bothered removing his uniform. I could tell by his face he was tired, but I still couldn't feel it. I gave him a kiss and wrapped my arms around him.

"You don't have to protect me. And honestly, you can't pro-tect me forever. Eventually, I'll have to learn things on my own."

"Five days old and wiser than most of a hundred years or more."

"It's been an informative five days." I smiled, but Ian sighed and kissed my forehead. "It's okay. Let me help you, Ian."

Instead of the emotions welling up inside me, they dripped in like a leaking roof, then became a rush. I held on to Ian as he held me and cried softly into my shoulder. I had images as well as emotions. Before Ian had come to the basement, hunters had tranquilized Kirkland. They moved him to a firepit located in the field behind the hospital. Ian watched as the vampire hunters staked Kirkland down. The whole time he held Kirkland's tags in his hands. Finally, one of them came over to pat Ian's shoulder and said they would make sure the ashes were scattered, then encouraged him to go inside. Ian stayed as long as he dared before coming to the basement.

I looked at Ian as the internal clock I was slowly becoming attuned with told me the sun was nearly over the horizon. "You're safe. I'm here." Ian wiped at his face and nodded before the sun took him.

The knowledge that Kirkland was gone weighed him down into his day sleep. I held Ian close and tried to comfort his sleeping spirit with memories from home.

Maybe I was trying to comfort us both. I had no idea if I'd ever see the mountains again, and it was just as likely that I'd die a second death here as well. I didn't dwell on that, but held onto my memories of the mountains and the stars at night as I dropped off for the day.

OR DIE TRYING

The war didn't stop while vampires slept. Many of the enemy's zombie troops would scour battlefields and ransacked buildings to expose any vampires they found to daylight.

Zombies were little more than biological automatons brought to life by a necromancer's magical abilities. From what I've read, necromancer magic works in two ways. It could be focused on simply raising the dead in whatever condition they were in, or it could be focused on one dead person. With the former, you had walking skeletons. With the latter, someone could look very alive to the untrained eye, beating heart and all.

While the virus made vampires susceptible to a necromancer's control, it also rendered a vampire unable to be raised after their final death. If a vampire were pulled into the sun, no one could turn around and raise the dead husk to use as fodder.

There were all kinds of theories about why a vampire's second death kept them from being zombies. The Magical Species Pact was one of them. They assumed that the body reverts to its original species. The magic from the pact kicks in and removes any magic left in the body. Necromancers tapped into something that wasn't technically alive and, therefore, used a loophole in the pact.

While no one had seen a necromancer raise a vampire after they desiccated, they still removed their heads like everyone else after their final death. Most necromancers were only powerful enough to control one vampire or zombie at a time. What Florentine had done, controlling entire armies of vampires and zombies, was supposed to be impossible, but here we were. The precaution of removing someone's head made sense, even if the current knowledge didn't support the need for it.

A week later, Bren died. We'd moved him back into the infected ward when his lungs filled with fluid, then his body gave out. Gladius made us promise Bren wouldn't be a zombie. She stayed with him rather than come to the basement. Her dried remains were found tucked in beside the gnome's that morning, so I was told.

We couldn't figure out what Bren had died of exactly. Zombie bites are painful and a vector of infection if exposed to the vampire virus. However, the bite itself couldn't make someone a zombie. If the bite was bad enough, it could kill an individual with a strange bacterial or viral infection. Depending on one's physiology, something one species could easily fight off would be impossible for another species to fight, even with healing magic or medicine.

Ian and I attended their pyre.

"I think they were lovers." The words tumbled out of my mouth after I'd taken another drink of the horrid canteen whiskey. Turns out, alcohol affected vampires to a lesser degree.

Ian took a drink. "Really? They could have had a platonic relationship."

"I suppose." I shrugged. "I treated Bren's arm more than once. He had faint bites on his neck and shoulder."

Ian grinned. "And by that, you think they were lovers?"

"I, well, I guess I assumed." Ian chuckled. "The way they looked at each other," I gestured at the pyre, "I mean, it seemed more than a simple friendship."

He handed the bottle back to me and sighed. "I'm not mocking your assessment." I eyed him. He held up his hands. "Honestly, I'm not. I'm only challenging your assumption. Unless they told you directly, all you have is supposition."

"Maybe I need some romance in the midst of all this death." I let the rest of the air out of my lungs, sat and drank while I listened to the fire, then handed the bottle back to him.

"Well, their story certainly did not have a happy ending." Ian looked at me and corked the bottle. We had the night off from the ward. It meant more training to see what other abilities might lurk in my new state of being. "Come on, let's take a walk."

Ian slipped the bottle into his knapsack, then we stood and headed toward the woods. I glanced back one last time before turning to pay attention to the path we trod.

Eventually, we arrived at a pond. Ian unfurled a blanket and dropped his knapsack. There was a small firepit and a convenient stack of wood nearby. "You've been here before?"

He nodded, but remained quiet. There was a genuine smile on his face, rather than the calm, understanding one Ian had for his patients or peers.

Once he started a small fire, we sat on the blanket and warmed ourselves while sharing a bottle of dinner between us.

"It tastes different."

"How so?" Ian asked as he took another drink.

"Cinnamon."

"Come again?"

I shrugged. "I can taste cinnamon with the apple. It's distinct. I have no idea why. Does that make any sense to you?"

"Not really. I've only ever tasted butter. Maybe melted butter every once in a while, but it was still butter." He handed the bottle back to me, and I finished what was left. "First test of the night," he said as he rubbed his hands together. "Have you ever used elemental magic?"

I shook my head. "Everything I did before was about healing wounds or making things to heal wounds. We would invoke elements in spell work, or for ingredients, but controlling them outright, no."

"We'll try something simple." Ian muttered a few words at the fire. It dimmed to almost nothing, then sprung back to life once Ian stopped concentrating on it. "Now, you try."

"Try what? What did you do exactly?"

"I asked the fire to be quiet." He waved his hand. "It's a little different for everyone, but mostly, it's about concentration, thinking about making the fire small." He leaned back on the blanket, and I stared at the fire.

Focus and concentration I had plenty of, but fire whispering, or whatever Ian did, I lacked. I gave up after a few minutes. "You sure this is how it's supposed to work?"

Ian gestured toward the fire. "I mean, most people who have access to elemental magic usually pick it up pretty quickly. Fire's the easiest because it's mostly controlled chaos and entropy. But maybe we should focus on what you're used to."

A knife appeared in Ian's left hand. I watched as he made a slice across his other hand. The blood slowly welled in his palm. It made me want to lick it, not heal it, but I tried anyway.

I reached for his injured hand, and slowly felt for the seams of the cut. Once I pictured them, it was easy enough to knit them back together as if I had a suture kit. The blood dwindled as I worked. The skin was smooth and only had the faintest of lines. Previously, when I used my ability, it would leave behind a visible scar or scar tissue.

My fingers were still coated in Ian's blood. For a moment, I thought about licking them clean. Before I could bring my fingers to my mouth, the blood disappeared as if my skin had absorbed it.

"I forgot to make barrier spells for my hands. I never forget those." I was staring at my hands as I felt the uptick of my heartbeat. Whether it was from Ian's blood, or surprise, I wasn't sure.

"Seems you don't need them." He looked at his hand, then at me. "Try it again. Use barrier spells this time. Let's see what happens."

He made a more significant cut on his arm. I winced. Vampires were tougher, sure, but it would still hurt.

I whispered the barrier spells over my hands, and they settled into place. The knitting took a little longer because I didn't have skin contact, but it still worked.

What I didn't anticipate was the blood that dripped from Ian's arm onto my leg. It sank into my skin through my clothes, leaving them spotless. I tried not to panic. "Have you ever seen that before? I mean, why is it doing that?"

"If I were to guess, your magic originally used your life force or the life force of the person you were healing to help the magic along. If all you have access to is your patient's life force, your powers might exact a payment." My hands moved up his arm as I continued to knit the wound closed.

"Well, that makes it handy to clean things up, but it wouldn't help if the wound was serious. It could kill the patient."

"Yes, possibly, if you were allowed to work on the living."

"It's a battlefield. I'll be called up again. That's how it works. And from experience, people aren't picky when they've been wounded." I stripped the barrier spells from my hands.

Ian sat quietly for a time. "Hey." I touched his face. "Are you okay?"

"You can't go back."

"What?"

"You can't go to the front. I'll make sure of it. If you are called up, I'll make some excuse or do something. I won't let you go back out there."

Ian's anger, determination, and need to protect me slammed into my senses and threatened to overwhelm me. *Shit.* "Hey, hey. You're okay. We're okay." I gathered him in my arms, and he came willingly. Losing Kirkland was still too fresh. "They would have to be in dire straits to call up vampire medics. You know that." We both did, but it was a possibility, however remote.

I lifted his face to mine, bent slightly, and kissed him lightly. A distraction, sure, but maybe something we both needed. "Would you like more?"

He nodded, and we began to unbutton our shirts. Lips touched and teased. We laid down on the blanket as our hands worked at removing our clothing. I barely had my trousers unbuttoned when Ian's hand slipped into them. His fingers danced between my folds as he rubbed himself along my cloth-covered thigh.

I reached for his cock and caressed it. The contact made him stop for a moment, then he continued kissing and moved from my lips to my neck and then my exposed chest. I was momentarily frustrated by his cock being out of reach as he moved down my body. Then he did two things: he inserted two fingers into me and sank his fangs into my areola.

Pleasure and pain rolled over me in turns as my hips moved of their own accord. My hand grasped his hair, unable to decide if I wanted him to stop or continue. He suckled, and I moaned until I came.

Once I relaxed, he pulled away. I looked at his blood-smeared lips and smiled. His cock was still hard and pressed against my leg. I pulled my trousers off, then rolled him onto his back. He pushed his pants down to his ankles as I straddled him and took his entire length in one thrust downward. He gasped, and I bent to meet his lips to lick and kiss the blood away. The firelight danced between us while a wild energy was shared with every touch and press of our bodies. We were dead, but we were also magic. That small, vital difference made up for the life I left behind.

Ian sat up and continued to kiss me as I rode him, with another orgasm on the horizon. I threaded my fingers through his hair and pulled. He gasped, but squeezed me tighter and urged my hips to move with more alacrity.

"Ian." His name was a benediction. Possibilities and freedoms. He'd been right that first night we were together. My future was now my own.

"Mason, fuck, you're bloody beautiful. All of you. Every last part."

"I bet you say that to all the vampires that ride your cock." I was teasing, repeating something I'd said to him before, but his face was serious. It made me pause. He shook his head.

"You're unique, Mason. You always will be." His eyes held a longing that scared me a little, but it also thrilled me. It had to be the bond he had over me that let me feel and understand him intimately. More than we ever could if we were both alive.

His breathing stilled, and the predator instinct rose between us. I looked at him, and all it took was the slightest nod before

I sank my fangs into his neck and moved my hips to meet his frantic thrusts.

"Oh, bloody Christ!" Ian screamed as he came, and I fed. All the engaged parts of me locked onto him as he fell over; I came as well. Only when my orgasm subsided did I stop and lick the wounds I'd made. I settled next to him, listening to my heartbeat thump along at a more human pace.

"I'll say one thing. Sex is way better as a vampire." Ian laughed that wonderful laugh of his. The one that told me he was okay, his sadness held at bay again.

"Well, some would concur with your assessment on that one. Though I suspect it has more to do with a lack of experience, shyness, or both as a human." He propped his head upon his hand, his elbow on the ground as he rolled to look at me.

"Was I that bad the first time?" I met his gaze as his fingers caressed my breasts.

He shook his head. "No, on the contrary. But most usually are. However, you've granted yourself a bit of freedom to be who you are now. I'm the lucky bastard that has a ringside seat."

As we laughed, something moved at the edge of my awareness. A sense of panic rose in me. I glanced around. The darkness we had enjoyed was fading quickly. I hadn't realized it because of the firelight.

I grabbed Ian's shoulders. "We won't make it. Shit, Ian. We won't make it back to the basement in time. The walk back is more than an hour, and I know we don't have that long. Shit, shit, shit." He laughed as I stood and grabbed my clothes.

"Stop panicking. We'll be fine."

"No, we won't. We have to dig a hole or find some kind of cover. Fuck, Ian. What have we done?"

Ian stood, pulled his pants up to his hips, then reached for my shoulders. "Stop panicking." He conveyed a simple command through his voice, and I took a breath. "We're sleeping under-water today."

"What!?" I looked at the pond and back at him. "You can't be serious."

"To prove to you we can do it. It's another option if you're caught out. Though I recommend using cotton plugs, so things don't crawl in your ears or nostrils while you sleep." He continued to button his trousers, then his shirt. "And while it's counterintuitive, going in with clothes is much better than being naked."

I shook my head. "Ian, this," I looked at the pond and back at him, "doesn't make any sense."

He touched my face. "Listen to my voice. You'll be fine. This is Survival 101. Finish dressing. Help me pack up the knapsack. Then we'll take those two large rocks with us and sink to the bottom, just under the thermal layer. You'll know it because the water will be colder, and the light won't come through it."

"What are the rocks for?" I continued to dress as panic crawled through my nerves.

"We'll put them on our chests so we're held to the bottom until we wake."

"Oh, fuck." Ian chuckled, and the laugh I loved a few moments ago, I now hated with the fiery passion of a volcano. We packed everything and stashed the knapsack in a pile of leaves and brush. Ian used his magic to snuff out the fire. Then we wadded bits of cotton into vulnerable orifices. He picked up one rock and handed it to me. It must have been 250 kilos, if not more.

I followed Ian with my heavy rock until we hit a drop-off in the pond and sank below the surface. What air I had in my lungs bubbled out as I settled to the bottom. Ian was near. I could sense that much, but as the sun rose, he faded from my senses.

My final thoughts were that if I survived the night, I'd either give Ian a sound thrashing or fuck him again. I honestly wasn't sure. Maybe both. As infuriating as he was at times, I cared about him. I hoped we'd see the other side of the war, and then I'd have a real taste of my newfound freedom.

MAGICAL PROPERTIES

Sleeping under water was not as relaxing as one might think, especially if you woke coughing water from your lungs. If I'd thought about it, I would have tried a barrier spell. Though I wondered if it would hold while I was sleeping. I'd wondered about a lot of things as of late.

Thankfully, it was a pleasant night with not too much of a breeze. After we replaced the stones, dried off a bit, and picked up Ian's knapsack, we started our walk back from the pond.

My thoughts drifted back to what Ian had said the night before. I hadn't taken the usual path in my life. Instead of healing and reading, my parents thought a woman of my age should find a partner and raise children. When their worries and nagging proved to be too much, I'd run off to war and got myself dead.

Now that I was on the other side of life, I wondered what motivated vampires. Were vampires so different from their living counterparts? Did they only care for their families and never again make connections with the living or their own kind? Was everything Ian and I did together about teaching me, or was there more to it? I thought about how much Kirkland's passing affected him. My mind wouldn't settle. It needed answers.

"Ian." I came up beside him so I could see his face.

"Hmm?"

"In the interest of not making assumptions, may I ask some personal questions?"

"Certainly," he said with his usual understanding and carefree smile.

"Was Kirkland your lover?" That stopped him in his tracks. I turned to look at him, and his anger was apparent. I'd hit a nerve, though not pointed at me. Maybe pointed at those who took Kirkland from Ian. "I'm sorry, I thought. . ."

He shook his head. "You know that I'm not angry with you, yes?" I nodded. I didn't know what to do. His distress was clear, so I moved toward him slowly. I took him in my arms and tried to think of calming things, like trees rustling and gentle breezes. Eventually, Ian hugged me and pressed his cheek into the top of my head.

"Kirkland and I were complicated." He caressed my damp hair, his fingers tucking a stray strand behind my ear. I stayed quiet to see if he would tell me anything else. "We met at the start of the war. Spent evenings together, and enjoyed each other's company."

"Does that mean what I think it means?"

"Of course. What else would it mean?" I made a noise at the back of my throat, and he chuckled. "We were lovers."

"Before he was a vampire?" Not that surprising. I'd read romance novels that were based on such relationships.

"We spent two years together laughing and consoling each other. He was a very talented physician, but lonely, and I had no one to turn to after I'd started helping others transition or break their minds away from necromantic control." Ian turned away from me and took my hand. "We would lament, drink, fuck, cry. It was the closest I'd come to loving someone since my wife died."

"So we can love?" I asked because I wasn't sure. It seemed over the last few weeks that while I could laugh, or cry, or be frustrated, it was different. All but lust, desire, pleasure—those were intensified and honed, based on what Ian said, for survival. One could mistake that for love, but when I thought of love, those emotions didn't connect to it. Which gave what Ian had said about Gladius and Bren's relationship more weight.

Ian gave me a sad smile as we continued to walk. "Yes."

"How did he end up infected if he was a physician in the regular wing?" Ian stopped and kept hold of my hand, as if he was afraid I would run.

"I turned him."

The shock of that statement ran through every inch of my being. Ian had killed Kirkland. At least, that's what most governments thought of someone being turned, whether you had permission to or not.

"There are rules, Ian. If anyone found out…" He nodded and held up his hand to stop my litany.

"We knew that. He knew that and wanted it anyway. We dreamed of returning home. I tried to make him wait until after the war, but humans are not patient." The sad smile turned to a frown. "We made love to each other and exchanged blood. The next night, he visited me in the ward, and we made his infection look like an accident.

"The first few weeks were… wonderful. We worked side by side. Shared stories, spent time together. We both thought that we had a long future ahead of us until one night, the call came for more medics to join the front lines. Kirkland volunteered. I begged him not to go, but he insisted he'd be fine. He never came back."

"But you shared a bond. You could have looked for him." I knew the story's end already, but I was desperate for an extraordinary circumstance that tore these two lovers apart.

Ian shook his head. "I didn't bond with him, nor amid our happiness had I thought to help him ward his mind against necromantic control."

"Did someone else?" My question was ridiculous once it was out of my mouth. Of course, that hadn't happened. Kirkland might be here now if someone had stepped in to help Ian, or if the regulations that Ian explained on my first day were in place back then.

Ian looked away, then back at me. "I used a combination of drugs and gentle compulsions to get him through his transition. I loved him. We talked about the bond, but he wanted us to be authentic with each other. Whatever that means now. He never understood. Like you, he thought it would make him less than himself. I've regretted letting him talk me out of it ever since."

His anger made sense. He thought he had failed Kirkland. "That's why you pleaded with me."

Ian didn't flinch at my observation. "Most don't even realize they have a bond when they first change. They don't understand it, and they don't ask questions." He gave my hand a squeeze. "You were the first who asked me or even knew what was happening."

Ian's emotions were like a book; his face the punctuation. "You've never shared blood before. I mean, of course you'd have sex, but the whole point is to teach fledglings how to bite. That first night, you drank from me after I drank from you. And you've drunk from me the entire time."

"High marks, Mason." The understanding smile returned. "Something about you stirs me. I thought it was gone after Kirkland disappeared. I couldn't leave you defenseless. And after the next night, I couldn't bear for us not to be on equal footing."

"We're bonded to each other." I covered my mouth with my hand out of sheer surprise. There was no rule against it, but if they captured either of us, the other would suffer horrifically. "It's why I can read your emotions so well."

"That, and the fact that you're a corvid."

"Don't you think we should have talked about this first?" I wanted to be upset with him, but I wasn't, which made me wonder about my own feelings.

"After you were clearly upset with me over it to begin with, I didn't think it would matter. When you found out, I thought it would be easier for you to understand why I did it." I went to him and pulled him into a hug.

"It was foolish, you know. What if later one of us hated the other?"

"I'd live with it if I knew you were safe. Or as safe as I could make you, given the circumstances."

"I'm not helpless, Ian." Confusion and annoyance colored my voice. What were we to each other?

"I know. Stars above, I know." He sighed. "You're unique, Mason. Of all the people I've helped through their transition, even Kirkland, there's something different about you. As if you're meant for this."

He gave me a soft kiss, and we held hands as we continued to walk back to camp. His words echoed what he'd said the night before. I wish I understood what that meant to him and why, but Ian seemed unable to articulate it other than I'd been able to do things he's never seen anyone else do.

Understanding our bond gave me some emotional awareness and healing that came with a kind of bloodletting. He called me a corvid, but what did that mean exactly? Were there families that had similar abilities? Ian was an apis. What other abilities did he have besides powers of the mind? He could use magic, even elemental magic. What else could vampires do? "Do you have a book or writings about vampire magic?"

"Not here," Ian said with a sigh. "I have an entire library back home."

"I miss the reading parlors back home. I'd spend a whole day reading and drinking tea. Or what passed for tea? They were mostly wildflower concoctions."

The residents of Boulder pooled money to purchase books. Families with collections all over Boulder would open their homes at tea times to allow anyone to sit and read for a few hours. It was a way for a lot of us to make social calls or receive them, but also not bother the residents of the house. Once we had a collection that warranted its own room, one family moving back east sold their house to the local council for the purpose. There were plans for a public library, but we made do with the reading parlors in the meantime.

"It sounds lovely." Ian smiled. "Maybe when this all ends, you could come visit my home."

"I think I'd like that." I felt a pang of hunger shoot through me. "More important question: did you bring dinner?"

Ian shook his head. "Not tonight. Second lesson. Hunting. You won't always be near a supply. You'll have to find something on the hoof. Or someone who will offer a swallow or two."

My throat dried at the prospect of it. "So, how does that work?"

Ian smiled and walked off the path into the woods.

HUNTING

"Like most things, hunting requires wit and a keen sense of your surroundings." Whether he saw my frown, I had no idea, but I followed his lead.

"What about livestock? Wouldn't it be easier?"

"Certainly. Do you see any around here?"

He had a point. I'd not seen any livestock since I arrived, and I wasn't sure why. There were towns behind the front lines. Some of them had to have livestock. It made me wonder if some of the blood we had in stasis wasn't actually human. "Can you tell when the blood isn't human?"

"Not really. It might smell slightly different, but if you're hungry, it doesn't matter. Blood is blood."

I thought about when I tasted cinnamon and wondered if this was the first instance when my kind and understanding teacher didn't know everything. Maybe only some vampires developed refined tastes.

We stalked late into the evening until we found tracks that led us to a wounded deer hunkered down in the brush. Ian looked at me and I shrugged, conveying that it had a chance of living, but it wasn't likely. Back home, I would have woven a calming spell and fixed its leg. Instead, I cast the calming spell with a different intent.

The deer relaxed as we approached. I felt the leg. A bullet had shattered it. It might have been hard for me before, but now I wasn't sure if I could heal it, and the deer would only suffer until it starved and died. I did another minor spell to mute the pain. At least it wouldn't know we were feeding.

Ian fed first from behind its back like a mountain lion taking down its prey. I could feel the deer's heartbeat slow as it was drained. When he stopped, he gestured for me to take my turn as he wiped his mouth with a hanky. A lump formed in my throat. I didn't want to do it. Thus far, I'd been spared from purposely taking a life, the vampire that tried to kill me notwithstanding. It was a whole moral debate I had quietly avoided since I woke in the infected ward.

I shook my head and stepped away. Ian came over and clasped my arm like I was a child about to throw a fit. "You know it's suffering." I nodded, but cried anyway. I was here to heal, to save life, not to do this—whatever it was. "Mason, think, what would you have done if you'd found a cow or a sheep in this condition?"

The word "think" knocked the wind out of my emotional sails. Ian used compulsion to make me focus instead of breaking down. I didn't have time to be upset. I thought rationally about what I would have done. "Back home, I would have tried to mend the leg. But the leg is too far gone, and it's in too much pain. I'd have calmed it, then reduced its pain. If I were by myself, I might have cut its throat to make it quick. If I were with others, they would have done it and butchered it where it lay."

"Precisely. This is no different. It's food now. After we're done with it, other predators in these woods will make quick work of what's left. Nothing wasted, yes? There's a difference between hunting for sport and hunting for survival." He was right, but

I couldn't completely shake the feeling that this was wrong somehow. Though I didn't have that problem when I drank from Ian while we were having sex, or drinking blood recovered from the dead. I stared at the deer while it slowly breathed. Ian reached up and wiped my face. The smell of blood made my stomach growl, loud enough to startle both of us and make us laugh.

"I'm sorry, Ian," I said as my small giggle fit subsided. "I'm being childish about this. I know better, but it doesn't feel right at the same time."

He nodded. "It's a more common reaction than you would think. Which is good, actually. If you'd gone for it like it was a custard tart, I might be a bit more worried." His hand eased down my arm and took mine. "You can do this, Mason." He led me back to the deer, and I went to my knees. I did what I'd usually do back home when a domesticated animal had given its life for mine.

I whispered. "Forgive me. Your life will sustain mine, and in my actions, I hope you find peace." I sank my fangs into its neck near where Ian had. Hair and blood mixed in my mouth as I swallowed. The taste was slightly gamey, but sweet and warm. Like a tart apple. I drank until I couldn't take another mouthful. As I pulled away, Ian handed me his hanky. I wiped the hair and blood from my mouth and lips. He handed me a bottle of water, and I swished some around in my mouth, spit it out, then took a few more swallows. Vampires needed water as much as they needed blood. While our bodies didn't produce solid waste often, organs still worked to filter and use what we ingested, and water helped with that process. Vampires peed. It was usually orange because it had a smidge of blood in it. That discovery had amused me when I was alive; now it was a fact of life.

We started walking again. I looked around, and nothing seemed familiar. "Do you know where we are, Ian?"

The grin on his face said he'd had some idea when we came over a hill and saw the hospital camp a few hundred yards off. He had known the whole time. The confidence and pride he radiated through the bond were interesting. I wondered if he would be so confident if they reprimanded us for leaving our posts.

"Didn't they expect us to work tonight?"

"No, not really. I made sure someone covered our shifts before we left, even if it took longer for us to return." That didn't seem to be the whole truth, but I let it go. I didn't realize until later that Ian was responsible for me until I could survive on my own. If I couldn't, it was also his responsibility to end my suffering, as it were. Being a mentor to a fledgling was not for the faint of heart. I don't know how Ian continued to do it.

When we arrived back at the ward a few hours before day-break, we learned Ian was on transition duty again. The following night, as Ian prepared a young nymph for his transition. I officially graduated from awkward vampire child to teenager. He sent me back to my cot near the front of the basement. It made me long for the safety I'd felt in his arms. It was also the night I started having dreams about Ian.

I didn't know if dreams were normal for vampires to have during our day death. They were beautiful memories of places I'd visited, and Ian was there as if we had always been together. Walks in the park. Hikes through mountain passes. Tea at one of my favorite reading parlors. All in broad daylight. I'd tell someone if I weren't worried they might think something was wrong with me. So I kept them to myself.

THE COST

The virus seemed to like human hosts the best, and humans with magic even more. If you were a non-human magical species, but had human ancestors, it was possible for the virus to latch onto that ancestry, which caused drastic changes to a mostly non-human individual. The wood nymph, Fairdown—or that was his name in English anyway—was adamant that he didn't want to die. I was in the ward a few cots over caring for a deceased human, preparing the body so the blood could be harvested. Ian tried to be gentle with Fairdown, to explain what might happen, but he didn't seem to understand.

"I'm here to help you, and I will, but I want you to make sure this is what you want. Your beauty, your magic, even your wings could all change. You'll be a different individual. That can be hard to accept, and the virus makes it harder still to change your mind afterward."

"So you've said, friend Ian. But I do not wish to end my existence. I will endure this metamorphosis as I did when I transitioned from a wyrmling to an adult."

Wood nymphs laid eggs in ponds and shallows like frogs. When those eggs hatched, the wyrmlings found their way out of the water and onto dry land, looking for the trees their family called home. Along the way, they ate plants and insects so that when they arrived at their home trees, they would cocoon themselves in safety for their final transformation to an adult bipedal form. There were different kinds of nymphs, but they were all known for their voracious lust.

Most nymphs didn't pay attention to wars or strife unless it came near their home. For wood nymphs, the tree itself was sacred, defended by every member of the family. This one must have lost his home tree or wasn't able to find it. The third option was that he was raised away from it. Even if that happened, they usually never went much further than the village closest to where their nymph family resided.

Ian took Fairdown to the woods for his first lesson. The smug look on the nymph's face and Ian's awkward gait as they walked back told me all I needed to know about how things had gone between them. I was half curious for details, and half jealous. Though I wasn't sure if I was jealous of Fairdown, Ian, or both.

It reminded me that Ian had suggested that I could seek out others if I wanted to. If Fairdown came through his transition, maybe the three of us could explore that option.

When they came to the basement with us, Ian asked me to stay in the cot next to him since I didn't pass out immediately at twilight like he did.

Shrieks of pain brought me out of my light stupor and the dream of Ian and me having sex in full daylight. I could still see the amber and gold flecks in Ian's brown eyes as the sun hit his face. I shook off the vision and went to the nymph, who gasped and wailed as they realized their wings had detached.

Four beautiful gossamer wings lay on the cot, two large and two small ones. Blood seeped from the shriveled wing joints on his back. I put a dressing gown on and rounded his cot to face him. Others stirred.

"Fairdown, it's okay. Listen to my voice. You're safe." He keened more loudly until I used a calming spell. He was nude and covered in his own waste and vomit. I grabbed the bucket before he made a mess of me as well.

"Mason. I was wrong. This is wrong. Help me."

"I'm here, Fairdown, I'm here." When the nymph had first arrived, he'd had the most beautiful mane of brown hair, tied back in braids to keep it off his wings. His eyes were a beautiful blue that shone with a light all their own. His lithe body was well suited for flying. The light tan of his skin meant he'd spent a lot of time in the sun.

He hadn't seen himself yet, but his wings weren't the only things that had changed. Even in the candlelight, I noticed that his hair was shiny, but it was black now, like obsidian. His eyes matched—not just his irises, but the entire orb was black. Instead of glowing with light, they seemed to swallow it. His beautiful nails, which he probably had used to climb trees, were now hardened claws.

Some might have seen this as a corruption of what he was, but I thought there was a stark beauty to him. As I helped him wash, others woke and exited the basement. Ian finally arrived at Fairdown's cot. We both helped Fairdown to the shower tent and washed him up. It was then that he noticed the changes and cried into Ian's shoulder.

I stopped the water, and we all stood in the shower comforting the poor nymph. "We have you, chap. Do you feel hungry yet?" Fairdown nodded.

Ian placed a kiss on his cheek and gently guided the nymph to the crook of his neck. As Fairdown was only slightly shorter than Ian, it was easy for him to reach. Instead of a simple feed, the nymph appeared to have other ideas. He picked Ian up and took a step to press Ian's back to the wooden wall of the stall. They kissed as they adjusted together, ignoring me entirely. I moved back to give them space until my back hit the wall opposite them. My moral upbringing demanded that I should give them privacy, but instead, I watched.

Fairdown moaned softly at whatever Ian was doing with his hand. He nuzzled into Ian's neck and bit. Ian grunted with the suddenness of it, but the look on his face changed to one of bliss.

My face had to be five shades of red, not to mention my body. I'd seen various couples and groups kiss and knew it was possible for them to have sexual congress. Witnessing it first-hand made me realize my imagination was a poor substitute. Before becoming a vampire, my general disinterest had kept me from exploring possibilities, or even reading about it beyond the scientific pursuit and understanding of biological needs.

As I continued to watch them fornicate, I knew the moment Ian had slipped into Fairdown's mind. The slight pressure I always associated with Ian's presence lessened for a time, and I could feel more from him. Pleasure certainly, pain, exhilaration. Simply put, he was enjoying himself.

When Fairdown stopped drinking, Ian kissed him, tongue darting out to taste the blood left on his lips. His arm pumped at a steady pace, only quickening at the last. Fairdown buried his face in Ian's chest as they both grunted and moaned into their mutual release. The smell of sex and blood made me lick my lips. My body was tight with need. Ian's eyes were drawn to the movement. He smirked at me. Fairdown glanced over his shoulder at me, then glanced at Ian. Some wordless communication passed as he kissed Ian gently, then lowered his legs until Ian could stand on his own.

"My apologies for the abruptness of my actions," said Fairdown as he turned toward me. "I thank you for your help earlier, Mason. Might I return your kindness and offer you sustenance?" He swept his long hair back to expose his neck. Ian's gaze met mine over Fairdown's shoulder. I understood from our bond that he felt no shame or guilt in his or Fairdown's actions, while I did simply from watching. Ian implored me with his eyes to overcome my own reactions and enjoy the moment. My adventurous side brought me this far. I took a breath and braved the possibility of another new experience.

"Fairdown, do you want me to share with you?"

He smiled and turned to Ian and then back to me. "Ian said you would be cautious. While Ian has calmed me, he does not control or direct my desires." I looked between them.

"It's true," Ian said. "I did nothing more than what your calming spell did earlier."

Had Ian read my thoughts? He had mental capabilities, but I hadn't asked exactly how far they extended. My body felt feverish with need and desire. My stomach added a grumbling protest into the mix. Ian and Fairdown smiled at me. I nodded as Fairdown approached me. "We don't need to be intimate unless you prefer it," I said. I wanted to offer a choice since he was offering me breakfast. It was the polite thing to ask as far as I was concerned. I wouldn't let my libido override that.

Fairdown stopped. "Would you not like to feel pleasure, Mason? I find you pleasurable to look at." He reached out to touch my face. One finger traced my jaw, then my ear. "Your aura is entrancing. It pulses in time with your heart. If you feed, it will be glorious to watch, and I want to hear you moan from my attentions."

I rarely believed the reputation of a species, but in this instance, there was some truth to it. "Very well then. Would you like to kiss me first?" Fairdown nodded. Ian smiled behind him, cock hard already. Fairdown was too. As the nymph reached for me, head bending to kiss my lips, a tingle went through me I recognized as magic.

A Hedonistic Awakening

Ian and I had shared several experiences since I'd transitioned, but Fairdown took things to another realm. Magic hummed between us. I'd never been with another magical being. Humans I'd dated could use magic, but they didn't have access to it like I did. Fairdown was magic.

The sensation started with my lips, traveled down my spine, then centered itself right in the midst of my sex. I gasped. I'd never been so close to coming simply from a kiss. Whether that was the nymph, or some combination of him and his vampire powers, I couldn't say.

My body was still damp; my thick thighs were slick with moisture that had nothing to do with our shower. Fairdown lifted me as he'd done with Ian earlier, easily handling me, while my shorter stature presented less of a problem. He adjusted his stance and hands as my cunt slid along his solid thickness. We rocked like that for a moment or two.

I pressed my lips to Fairdown's and felt the edge of pleasure bubble between us. When he made a slight movement and I slid onto his cock, the bubble burst and I sucked in air, only to gasp again as Fairdown moved. With each press into my slick core, I felt myself wind up again. Magic pulsed under my skin. Now I understood what Ian's blissed look was about. Nymphs weren't just lustful. They fucked, licked, and kissed pure pleasure into you. It made me wonder how humans, or other species, didn't become addicted.

"Mason, you're so beautiful. You feel our connection, don't you? Take your sustenance, my beauty. Let me release myself into you. Please, Mason."

My toes curled as I pressed my heels into his back and skimmed my fangs along his neck. Cords of muscles along his shoulders strained from holding me up and being on the verge of an orgasm. The need and the frustration were all too recognizable. My vision tunneled as I felt Fairdown's cock throb and grow larger inside me. I didn't know what Ian was doing, or if he was watching like I had watched them.

As if summoned, Ian was in my mind, feeling what I felt. Jacking off as he watched from the opposite side of the stall. I realized he hadn't shared everything with me earlier. He didn't want to ruin the surprise. Now he was able to enjoy it a second time through me.

I glanced at Ian and once I caught his hooded gaze; I bit down onto Fairdown's neck. The taste of anise and apples flooded my mouth. Fairdown grunted as my back hit the wooden wall, and his rapid movements made lewd sounds as I came and drenched him. After my orgasm subsided, I lifted my head and licked the wound closed. The small action pushed Fairdown into his release. He groaned into my breasts as he pulsed inside me. We stayed that way as his spunk filled me. To my surprise, he was still hard, though slightly diminished from his release.

"You're so magical, Mason. So beautiful, inside and out." He kissed my breasts and neck. "If we had met when we were alive, I would have wanted to fill you full of my life matter and produce many nymphs with you."

I grinned. "Well, we can at least do one of those things." I gave Fairdown another kiss on the lips and then looked at Ian.

He had his cock in hand, and cum splashed across his stomach. "Ian, are you well?" He looked like a man possessed. His face held an intense need.

Ian nodded and came toward us. "Put her between us." Fairdown smiled and swiftly moved to comply.

"Ian, my friend, do you need help to ease the way?"

Ease what way? They talked in code now? What way could Fairdown mean? Ian pressed against my back, his cock still hard as it slid between my ass cheeks and bumped into Fairdown's cock, still buried in me.

"Yes, please." Ian kissed along my back and neck. I expected him to bite me at some point, but he held off. "Mason, can I fuck you while Fairdown fucks you?"

"I don't understand how that would work. Fairdown is so large already." The men around me chuckled, and I groaned. Everything felt tight and ready to burst.

"Let us show you," Ian whispered in my ear. I nodded, my lungs empty of air. I quickly sucked in another breath. Fairdown lifted me off his cock and immediately his load dripped out. It felt unseemly, but there was little I could do about it. Ian distracted me with kisses to my neck. Someone's hand gently swiped between my cunt lips a few times before I felt an exploratory finger near my anus.

"What exactly are you two doing?" was all I could ask before two things happened. Fairdown slid his cock back inside me, and Ian slid his questing finger into my ass. "Oh, blessed day!"

I'd suspected that an intrusion to such a little-used cavity at this point would have been painful. But something tingled with a cooling effect that was pleasant, and even relaxing. Without really understanding why, I rocked my hips to alternate the two penetrative objects like a water well pump. In, out, out, in. I nearly lost all sense of what was happening until the finger in my anus disappeared, then was replaced by something much larger, slowly thrusting into me.

Was there a name for this? I wondered as I squirmed on both cocks. Ian's hands grabbed my hips to still them. He and Fairdown took over with their alternating thrusts. While Fairdown was larger, Ian wasn't below average by any means. The pleasure and magic that swirled in my veins screamed for release. Any kind of release. "Ian, Ian, please, please bite me. Fuck, please. I can't stand it any longer. Someone please!"

My plea was granted, not only by Ian, but Fairdown as well. One at my breast, the other at my neck. I had no breath left, but my mouth was open with a soundless scream. Magic tore through my soul and flared inside of me, charging my healing abilities and senses. The auras we created swam in my vision. The rainbows and sparks I saw made me wonder if I'd had a catalepsy.

Waves of pleasure and magic danced away from me, carried on invisible currents. My partners were equally caught in whatever we had created, though I only registered them having achieved any pleasurable state after my consciousness returned to my body from its travels. The scream that had no breath abated, and I sucked in one lungful after another to calm my rising panic. We found ourselves on the floor of the shower stall we'd occupied, crumpled in a corner with our limbs askew and debris on top of us.

Sounds of voices calling out orders and shouts to muster seemed extremely close. A siren sounded. The one used for a pending attack, to warn everyone to take shelter. Were we being bombed? I was aware of these things, but could not move. Lights danced and magic drifted around me as someone lifted me up and laid me on a stretcher.

"Mason? Mason? Are you with me? Sweetie, say something." It was a feminine voice familiar to me. What happened to Ian and Fairdown? Were they safe? I made noises, and the voice responded reassuringly. Lights still danced, and I closed my eyes to keep them out.

That was the last thing I saw before I opened my eyes again to see Fairdown's face. "You are safe. We are in the vampire quarters."

"Where's Ian?" I coughed. My throat was extremely dry. Fairdown handed me a refilling clay bottle of water. The spring water it produced was cool, and my throat loosened in relief.

"He's in his cot. I checked. I believe we have a little time before he wakes for the evening."

"Do you know what happened?" I mean, I could estimate a guess that our collective orgasms made us pass out, but why had there been so much panic?

Fairdown shook his head. "I remember very little after I bit you. All I saw were lights and stars from the magic."

When Ian woke, he had no more of an answer. "I think it's the first time I've passed out from sex. You should take it as a compliment, Mason." He laughed, and my face heated slightly as embarrassment and hunger set in.

"Well, we should go up and find out what happened," I urged. The three of us dressed and went to the infected ward first. A few individuals stared at us, but others went about their business. Jeremy saw us and came over. His fledgling, named Christian, followed in his wake.

"Are the three of you alright?" Jeremy asked. We all shrugged and nodded. "Amazing that none of you perished when the shower tent was hit."

"Hit?" Ian asked.

"Yes. The speculation is that an enemy salvo was misdirected by friendly fire, or some magical bastard made an exceptional shot even though we're nearly twenty kilometers from the front. The record for distance of long-range ordnance was fifteen kilometers. Looks like we'll have to update our allies."

The three of us looked at each other and quickly left the ward to see what had happened to the shower tent. When we found the flattened remains, we each made various sounds of surprise.

"No one knows." Ian's voice was full of amazement.

"It makes sense. The place looks like it collapsed after a detonation. The explosion could have thrown us together," I offered.

Ian laughed. Then I did while Fairdown smiled. Explosion indeed. After that, we decided it was likely not safe for the three of us to have sex all together, but we all certainly enjoyed watching each other.

The night before Fairdown's survival training, we lay in bed talking after Ian went to sleep.

"Are you still sad about your transition?" I asked.

Fairdown shook his head. "I am settled into this new state of being. It gives me advantages I didn't have before. I will eventually return to my home tree and make many offspring so my advantages can protect the family tree."

"It still exists?"

"Oh, yes." He smiled, then held out his hand to me. I took it, and he pulled me off my cot and into his. We adjusted our clothing until he was seated to the root inside of me.

His hips made quick thrusts as I held fast to him and pressed my face to his chest to muffle my moans. We came together when he bit me, taking a small measure, then licking the wound closed.

Before we drifted off, Fairdown pulled a sheet over our entwined forms. I asked him a question I'd been curious about since he transitioned.

"What does blood taste like to you?"

He opened his eyes and blinked slowly. He took a breath to answer. "I think you call it fennel. My people have another name for it." I smiled at that answer. "But you taste different, Mason. It's something more than a simple root. You're a garden of delights." He kissed my lips, then promptly dropped off as dawn made its presence known.

I wondered what he meant, but the next evening we woke and prepared for the night as if Fairdown had said nothing unusual. By his standards, he probably hadn't, so I let it be.

After Ian and Fairdown left, I found myself with an evening free from the ward. My first stop was the canteen to see if I could find Agnes. Her voice was the one clear memory I had after they had rescued us from our explosive threesome. I hoped to buy her a drink for helping us and maybe find out how she's been. The last time I'd seen her was before my transition.

I'd avoided people I'd known in the camp prior to becoming a vampire. I didn't want to scare them with how much I've changed, but Agnes didn't sound scared. Her voice had held genuine concern, which seemed like a rarity. I had a desperate desire to know if Agnes and I might be friends, given everything that happened.

DEAR ACQUAINTANCE

Agnes wasn't a loner exactly, but she didn't talk a lot, nor did she socialize much. We'd chatted a few times, but since she was a charge nurse and I was a field medic, we'd only caught up when I came in, and that was if I wasn't bone tired. Plus, she worked day shifts mostly. Easy to catch up with someone when you can grab a few hours and eat breakfast with them. I was in luck tonight, though. I spied her plump figure perched at the end of the bar. She was alone as usual, nursing a beer. I ordered one myself and sat next to her.

"Well, look what the night dragged in. How are you, dear?" She offered a hug, and I welcomed it. It set off my senses, and the first thing I picked up was the faint whiff of apples. The second thing I noticed was that she was tired.

"I'm alright. But I feel like I should ask you the same thing."

She nodded. "Had to amputate a dragon's wing today. Damn thing wouldn't heal right and turned necrotic. Convincing the dragon it was the right thing to do was another matter. It took three other dragons to hold the poor thing down."

"Shit, Agnes. What the hell could have damaged a dragon's wing?"

"Some kind of acid ordnance, apparently. A dragon's scales can take damn near anything, but their wings are a different story, especially if it hits them in the right spot. Beautiful water dragon too." She downed the rest of her beer and ordered another. I sipped at mine, mindful of the carbonation. "Looks like you came through the shower tent collapsing without a scratch. We're surprised we found anyone alive in that mess." Her brown eyes were shining with mirth and drink.

I grinned. "Agnes, can you keep a secret?" She nodded, and I whispered all the sordid details to her. She burst out laughing.

"Oh Christ, that's hilarious. You're lucky we have mages around to put everything back to rights." She wiped happy tears from her face. It made me smile to make her laugh.

"I'm lucky my cunny didn't blow us all to kingdom come." Agnes wailed at that one and nearly choked on her beer.

She shook her head to get control of herself. "You've changed, Mason. Not the shy little church mouse I first met."

"Church mouse?"

Agnes nodded. "Aye, you'd run from one patient to the next. Squeak if anyone came up behind you. Run if people noticed you."

That assessment somewhat fit. I hadn't socialized much either, but after a night of patching up wounded folks, the last thing I wanted to do was be social. "Well, I guess I didn't run fast enough one night."

Agnes frowned. "Oh, love, I'm sorry. That was horribly insensitive of me." She reached out and patted my hand. It was warm compared to my room temperature one. "You're still here. That's all that matters."

"Can I buy you a shot? Or a few, maybe? I want to say thank you for helping us out the other night. I remember your voice saying you'd take care of me before I passed out." The smile that I got was all teeth, so I grinned back.

"Sweetheart, if you'd like, you can buy me an entire bottle."

"Done. Barkeep!" I yelled. We laughed and told stories until the canteen shut down for the night, then we wandered with our bottle between us and went back to Agnes' tent. It was small but private. We were definitely into our cups.

"How did you manage to get this all to yourself?" I looked around. She had her gear trunk in one corner, clothes hanging from one tent pole, and a good sized cot off to the side.

"I snore. And being a charge nurse has its benefits." She smiled as she lit a candle. "You probably don't need the light, do you?" she asked as she put her long reddish-brown hair into a quick braid for the night. As I watched her, I noticed her abundant breasts, wide hips, and large belly. If she were less than twenty stone, I'd be surprised. I was around eighteen stone myself. We had similar features, but I was shorter.

I shook my head. "I could certainly see your beautiful face without it."

She dropped onto the cot as I sat on the ground and passed her the bottle. "Mason, are you being a flirt?"

"Do I have a fan?" I mimicked opening one and flapping it across my face. Agnes chuckled. Folding fans were one way a lady of society could send lovers' messages in plain sight.

"If you did, what would it say?" she asked as she leaned forward. I folded my mimicked fan and pressed a finger to my lips. Which meant I wanted a kiss. I hadn't even entertained the notion until this moment. While Agnes and I were acquaintances, I didn't know what was driving me more: the faint smell of apples, or how adorable she was with her ruddy cheeks and eyes bright from drinking.

"Well, you have changed." She set down the bottle. "I thought you only fancied blokes."

She had me there. "Maybe. Then again, I'd never had the opportunity for anything else." I watched her face. Something shifted in her entire demeanor, and I barely caught it. Empathy. "You aren't a loner because you like it."

"You magical types are always reading people. Dragons are the worst, you know. They can tell things from a distance that most of us barely pick up two centimeters from our noses." She chuckled. "They also like to fuck nearly anything, so if you get the chance, take it." The laugh that bubbled out of me was contagious. Agnes laughed too, then patted the space next to her on her cot. I took the opening for what it was and moved before she changed her mind. We were nose to nose, but she pulled back.

"Promise you won't bite me."

"Are you scared I will?"

"Maybe."

"I won't bite unless you ask."

She nodded, then kissed me. Our kisses became more urgent and sloppy. She was managing my fangs just fine, much to my surprise. Maybe she had had an encounter with a vampire before? Agnes reached for my shirt, then stopped herself. "Is this really what you want?"

My cunt throbbed, and my stomach had a pang of hunger. She still smelled like apples, and I couldn't figure out why, but I wasn't about to stop whatever we started. "Yes." I unbuttoned my shirt as Agnes got up and blew out the candle. She came back to her cot, removing clothing, and the apple smell grew stronger.

I was halfway out of my own trousers when Agnes' exclamation of disappointment stopped me.

"What's wrong?"

"My courses."

Her disappointed face made me frown, though the apple smell had me licking my lips. She went to pull her pants back on, and I stopped her, then dropped to my knees. "What are you doing?" Agnes had put a hand on my forehead to keep me from my prize. "I started. We can't do anything."

I chuckled. "You smell like apples." The comment twisted her face with concern. "Vampire, remember. Trust me, I promise. I won't hurt you." She let go of my head, and I took that for permission as I pressed my mouth to her cunt. The taste of apples tickled my tongue as I tickled her clit.

Eventually, Agnes relaxed enough to let me bring her to the cot and prop her legs up at the end. I remembered what Ian had done to me several times, and repeated the lessons here, much to Agnes' moans and muffled cries of pleasure.

"Yes, shit, Mason. Right there. Make me come again. Use your fingers just like that. Christ!" I was rewarded repeatedly with more of her tantalizing flavor. Agnes breathed heavily as she grabbed me, then prompted me to move up on the cot next to her.

Agnes chuckled. "You realize your face is covered. You look like someone bashed your nose in."

"Got anything to clean up with?"

Agnes smiled and rolled out of the cot, retrieving a clay bottle and a cloth. She gently wiped my face. I still smelled apples, but it sated me for the moment. It wasn't until she kissed my neck and chest that I realized she wanted to return the favor. She caught my hesitation.

"Do you want me to stop?"

"No, but. . ."

"But what?"

"I might have a problem."

"Oh? Why's that?"

"I've only had pleasure if someone bites me."

Agnes chuckled. "Lay yourself down, dear. Let Mama Agnes take care of you."

And fuck if she didn't. Her creamy beige hands pushed me back and drifted down my wide torso as I watched her put a barrier spell over her mouth and nose. It was very smart of her. "I didn't know you could do that with a barrier spell."

"It's modified a little so I can breathe, but it keeps everything else out. I'm not trying to end up with mouth rot before I get out of this war." I laughed, then sighed as the last of my breath left me when her tongue touched my clit.

Ian was good. Agnes was talented beyond measure. I hadn't known parts of my anatomy existed until she worked her magic. Turned out, pinches, bites, smacks, basically any sharp pain did it. And when she timed it right, she'd get more than one out of me. I'd never had multiple orgasms before, but Agnes didn't let me down, and I kept asking for more as I covered my mouth with her lumpy pillow.

After I gave in, she washed me off as I lay on her cot in a fleshy pool of bliss. My eyes drooped more than once as Agnes crawled into the cot with me. We spooned until I realized it was nearly dawn and I wouldn't make it back to the basement in time. Adrenaline shot through me as I sat up.

"Fuck!" I grabbed for my clothes and pulled them on. Agnes rolled over to watch me flail around her tent.

"What's wrong?" She rubbed her eyes, clearly sleepy.

"Sun's coming."

"It's still dark out."

She couldn't sense what I did. I knew I had less than thirty minutes. Someone would have shut the basement already. Ian and Fairdown would be at the bottom of the pond, and unless I started digging, I'd be dead. I looked down at the canvas floor of Agnes' tent and whined in my despair. Maybe if I jogged for the woods, I'd make it in time to dig a half decent hole there. "Do you have a trowel?"

Agnes shook her head. "You're new, right? You only need to stay out of strong sunlight. My tent is lightproof."

I glanced at her tent and realized it was, and the only reason I even knew about the sun was because of my internal clock. "How did you get a lightproof tent?"

"Sometimes I work the night shift. I traded a couple of magic spiked pints for a blackout spell."

"Magic spiked pints?"

Agnes chuckled. "Your guy has been keeping you a little too much in the dark, Mushroom. Come, lie back down."

"How are we going to keep people out? Won't they come looking for you?"

She shook her head. "I have the day off. Why else would I have been at the canteen?" In all her nude glory, she got up and grabbed a piece of rope from somewhere and tied the zippers so it would be hard to pull the flaps open from the outside. "Take off your clothes and get back into bed, dearie. I promise you'll be fine."

To Agnes' word I was. Her mild snoring was a gentle rhythm that soothed me before I died for the day. When I woke, I thanked her using a few of the tricks she taught me the night before. We promised each other we'd catch up again on a night we both had off.

After I showered and put on a fresh uniform, I went to the ward to start my shift. We only had two patients, and both were in comas, so they likely wouldn't last the night. I washed them both and waited. Ian eventually showed up, minus Fairdown.

"Thank heaven, I thought something happened to you."

"Why?" His eyes went wide, and I remembered the bond. "Oh. Well, something happened, but nothing bad. I spent the day in a tent."

"What? Whatever made you do that?" The blush and probably the related emotions answered his question, and he scratched the back of his head and smiled. "Well then. I'm glad you're safe. The last thing I remembered before I slept was your panic, and that I couldn't do anything to help you."

"I'm sorry, Ian." I stood and kissed him. He pulled back before he realized we were in the ward alone with two comatose patients.

He kissed me back and sighed. "I'll manage. Only remember to give me something more next time than sheer panic."

I nodded and then realized Ian was blocking me from his own emotions. "What's wrong? Where's Fairdown?"

"Well, that's a bit of a long story." We sat down, and he told me how Fairdown realized the pond was close to his home tree. They went to the tree, and his family came out and embraced him. When Ian told them he used the pond to teach vampires survival, they already knew and told him they stayed away when he was there.

I started my rounds as Ian continued. "His family welcomed him, and I do mean welcomed him." Ian blushed a little, and I laughed.

"Are you saying you had a nymph orgy?"

Ian nodded. "I'm somewhat surprised I'm in one piece and not sore."

"A nymph's spunk properties—they should sell it as a muscle relaxer." Ian laughed while I grinned at him.

There was something off about my first patient's pulse. I held up a finger, and Ian went quiet. It disappeared as I listened. Ian waited until I wrote up the time of death and put the tags in order. We stood in silence for a minute. I asked for forgiveness, then tilted the cot and started the drain. Once blood started flowing, I prompted Ian to continue.

"So, magical nymph orgy, and then?"

He shrugged. "Afterward, Fairdown and I slept at the bottom of the pond. Apparently, there are nooks down there the nymphs use sometimes to store their eggs. He took me to one and held me while we slept. When we woke, we said our goodbyes. I was worried about you, so I left him with his family. He said if I found you safe, that I should bring you with me next time." Ian grinned.

Something about watching me with another individual did things for him. I'm not sure why that was, but I liked it too.

"We'll have to take him up on that." I checked the drain and then checked the other patient. Their heartbeat was slowing. It wouldn't be much longer now before we would know their fate too.

"What about your adventure?" asked Ian. "It must have been pretty engaging to make you forgo returning to the basement."

"What do you remember about the night we destroyed the shower tent?"

"Not much after you went off, though I remember people pulling us out and carting us here."

I told him about Agnes, and how I'd met her before, and that last night she was in the canteen. I'd only meant to buy her a drink, but she smelled like apples. As I continued with the lewd details, Ian's face went from a smirk to a grin so big I thought it would stay there.

"Do you think she'd be interested in a bloke like me?" It was rare for humans to want to take risks with vampires. Some were eccentric, and others enjoyed being bitten. Then there were some who wanted to be infected on purpose. With Agnes, it was definitely about sex, though I think she might have been a bit eccentric as well. It turned out that she certainly didn't mind Ian joining us the next time we all had a night off.

THE VAMPIRE ACCORDS

Drafted October 1878. Ratified June 1882 by the newly formed United Nations.

Wherein any being which wishes to become part of the Vampire species, they will first seek membership with a recognized entity that governs Vampires and is recognized by the government of the territory, country, or nation within which it resides.

An individual, upon transition, keeps the rights and legal due process of the nation or country of origin. If the transition takes place outside of the nation or country of origin, then the individual will need to declare citizenship either from the country of origin or from the country of transition.

Countries and nations have a right to refuse citizenship to a transitioned individual who was not previously a citizen of the territory, country, or nation in which they currently reside.

Coteries and newly formed Covens must register with the territory, nation, or country they reside in to be recognized as legal entities.

Under penalty of international law, Necromancers, from this day forth, are forbidden, whether inadvertently or intentionally, from controlling the species known as Vampires. To do so will violate international law and bring that individual under sanction by the United Nations, which will sit in judgment to determine the individual's fate.

International law, and the laws set forth by the United Nations, will govern conflicts between other species and the species known as Vampires. These laws supersede territory, country, nation, and local government laws when laws are in disagreement or misalignment.

The Vampire species representative, The Envoy, will moderate conflicts between other species and the species known as vampires. The Envoy will act as mediator and determine if international laws, as set forth by these accords, were violated.

An Inconvenient Life

Paris, April 2006

The motorcycle vibrating between my legs was the most action I'd had anywhere near my cunt for a while. It was certainly more reliable than partners and didn't complain as long as I kept it fueled and gave it regular maintenance.

Tonight was my regular two-week supply run to the Crossroads Coven chapter house. They gave their members enough blood to last for two weeks. Even with my status, that's all I was allotted. It was never quite enough, and what's worse, my clinic supplied a third of the blood this chapter house took in.

I parked, took off my helmet, and walked into the warehouse. The registry table had two large individuals guarding the entrance to the supply window. In the back were supplicants who had signed away their previous lives for one as a member of the Crossroads Coven. They were brought here to be infected, and if that didn't take, we drained them for the very supply the coven handed out to its members.

That was all legal, of course. Some came here to survive, some came here on a suicide mission, but as long as they could sign, made it past their transition, and then survived on their own for another twenty years, they were in. The system was brutal. I didn't have a taste for it, but it made sense. Popular fiction had stopped romanticizing being a vampire as this wonderful alternative to being human, and people didn't throw their lives away on a whim only to regret it.

"Hey Doc, how's business?" Lacey asked as she flexed her muscles. She flirted with me all the time, but I had yet to take her up on anything. I liked the flirting, though.

"Same as always, gorgeous. Keeping the blood in the right places."

Lacey and Duke laughed. "That's our Doc. Here's your number," said Duke.

I took my ticket and walked to the line at the supply window. There were only a few people in front of me. It left me time enough to notice a child hunkered in the corner nearby. Lacey and Duke weren't concerned, but the child was far too quiet for my liking. I stepped out of line and went back to Lacey.

"Hey sweetie, what's the kid doing here?" I glanced at the corner, and she followed my gaze.

Lacey sighed. "You know how it is sometimes, Doc. The sign-ups leave whoever behind thinking they'll pop out in just a few hours and pick them up." They gave explicit instructions about the transformation process. It took several days to a week before you were even presentable again. I knew from experience. I also knew that if someone was infected, and didn't make it, they were dead within a matter of hours or a day at most, if they were human anyway.

"Did whoever brought the kid make it?"

Lacey shook her head. Duke leaned over to join the conversation. "Child services were called for the little one. They should have sent a vehicle, but haven't." That made me frown.

I leaned in as if we were forming a conspiracy. Or gossiping at least. I don't know anyone that lived in France who didn't love gossip. Everything always seemed more salacious in French, at least to me. "How about this? I'll grab my lot, then take the kid to services for the night. This is no place for a child, especially one that young." I'd have slapped some sense into the adult that brought the kid, but since they were dead–dead, that wasn't an option.

Duke nodded, and so did Lacey. "You'll be doing us a favor, Doc."

"Happy to help. Besides, I've helped at the shelter from time to time, so they know me."

"Good looking and a humanitarian. We're not worthy of ya," Lacey said.

I waved their good-natured comments off and got back in line. As soon as I had my allotment, I moved to assess the child. Pupils blown wide. Catatonic, possibly. No bruises or bumps. When I reached out to touch the kid's forehead, it was cool, so no fever at least.

"Hi there." No reaction. "Do you have a name, sweetheart?" Nothing from French. I switched to English. "Sweetheart, what's your name?" A blink. Recognition. "My name's Mason."

"Dorothea." She had black hair and pretty hazel eyes that were a mix of green and brown. Her complexion was good; her skin was fair and firm; her teeth cared for, her hair combed and washed. The child's condition didn't speak of neglect or a parent who would have abandoned her. In my estimation, she was probably eight or nine years of age.

"That's a pretty name." I smiled, and the child smiled back. I frowned, and she did the same. When I stuck my tongue out, she mirrored me. It would have been fine if her facial expressions changed with it, but they didn't. It all spoke of a deep com-pulsion. The last time I'd seen something like that was over a century ago in a war I'd rather forget.

I held out my hand, and Dorothea held out hers. I took it and gently guided the girl to her feet. She came willingly. Others watched as I led us out the door. There were imagers somewhere in the entrance, so whoever was watching those would know I left with her. Between the entrance and my bike, I changed my mind about taking her to the shelter. I bent down to pick her up. She didn't protest being in my arms.

"We're going to go for a ride." I sat her on my bike and stored my blood in the rear hatch. I strapped my helmet on her head, then arranged us on the bike so she was at my back. I quickly found a hair tie to put my hair up and pulled out my amber driving glasses from a side pouch to keep bugs out of my eyes.

"Hang on to me real tight, alright?" I grabbed her hands and wrapped them around my waist. She had a firm grip, which was good.

The motor purred to life. I kicked the stand, released the brake, and we took off. As I drove through the streets, I thought about the one person I hadn't seen in a long time. I reached for the connection between us, the one I'd closed off so long ago in an effort to protect myself. It hummed to life in my chest and forced me to take a gasping breath. I knew exactly where he was, and it would take me several hours to get there if I didn't stop.

Something wasn't right with my passenger, and the only way I was going to find out was if I went to the one person I trusted to help unravel this mystery.

LINDQUIST RESIDENCE

With a few hours until dawn, I was panicking about whether anyone would open the door. I went from knocking to banging. If I started yelling, I doubt the neighbors would hear me. Ian's small estate was centered on several acres with neighbors who likely also had household members that slept for the day. Coteries were like that. There weren't many left since most had converted to covens after the war, but Ian's family was rather firm in their traditions. It was on the list of reasons I'd left in the first place.

I banged on the door again.

"Alright, alright, calm yourself," a voice said from the other side. The door opened, and a tall, handsome man with brown skin answered, wearing only a house robe. He was slightly taller than Ian and had kind brown eyes and black natural hair styled in a frohawk with the sides trimmed and faded. Plus a goatee. Simply put, he was gorgeous. "May I help you?" he asked in a polite but annoyed British accent.

"Please tell Ian. . ." I didn't get to finish the sentence as Ian Lindquist himself appeared at the door, also wearing a robe. "Hello." He had to have sensed me since I opened the connection between us. What he felt after this long was anyone's guess.

Vampires aged slowly. When I last saw him, he looked as if he were still in his mid-twenties. Now, Ian had facial hair that was well maintained, but made him look a decade older. His hair had a more modern style, but it was still short. His complexion was more pale than I remembered. Next to his companion, he practically glowed in the fading moonlight.

"Are you okay, Mason? Is anything the matter?" The concern after all this time almost made me cry, but I smiled instead. I shouldn't have avoided seeing him for so long, but once I had, I couldn't find my way back. Then again, he'd left me alone as well.

"I'm fine, but I think I need your help." I guided Dorothea out from behind me and presented her. Ian crouched down, careful of his robe, and looked into her eyes. When he frowned, I knew what I suspected was right.

"Come in," Ian said. "You were right to bring her here." We shuffled inside as Ian shut the door.

"Quick introductions then," Ian said as he clapped his hands. "Mason, this is Jason, my lover." Jason nodded and gave me a quick wave. His annoyed look had disappeared in the presence of the child that was watching everything. "Jason, this is my wife, Mason."

"Wife?" Jason looked confused. I shrugged and tried to elaborate.

"That might be stretching it a bit. Been more than a century since we've had anything close to a relationship. You've nothing to worry about from me."

Ian said nothing. Jason glared at Ian's back as the man moved down the hall. The rest of us followed.

"Mason, your room is in good order. I can bring a cot for. . ." Ian paused.

"Dorothea." I offered.

"Dorothea. Pretty name." Ian continued to move further into the house. Jason's agitation was apparent. I stopped as Ian went to retrieve the cot.

"Jason. I'm sorry. I know this is confusing. If daylight weren't nearly here and a child involved, I would give you the time to question me to your heart's content. If you give me a reprieve tonight, I promise I'll answer your questions tomorrow evening. Even the ones he won't."

Jason took a breath and then nodded. I looked at his aura. He was definitely a vampire, and a fairly young one. Fifty years at most. I found out from years of observation that the secondary aura vampires had would change colors with the primary type of magic they used. Ian's was yellow. Jason's was green. I'd seen other corvids, like myself, have blue auras. If I were a corvid, like Ian had suggested so long ago, I should have developed a blue aura myself; instead, my secondary aura continued to turn a darker shade of gray.

Ian's movements drew us to the room that used to be mine. Jason, Dorothea, and I all walked to the door and peered inside as Ian set up the cot. Ian had kept it exactly the same. Books. Trinkets I'd collected. Even the light lamp—a spelled lamp with a contained magical fire. Safer than using a candle. However, the room had modern touches, like a ceiling fan with lights, along with UV-blocking windows. When I'd last been here, we spelled the windows to block the light, which made them pitch black during the day. These windows had a combination of spells and protective coatings.

"There. We are all set for the day." Ian said. "Do you remember the sleep spell I taught you?"

I waved him off. "I've got it from here." Ian nodded. I stepped into the room, and he stopped for a moment and looked at me over his shoulder. I looked at him, Dorothea waiting patiently.

"I'm glad you're safe, Mason." His sadness hit me hard. That was definitely an emotional salvo in a long conversation we'd likely have tomorrow. Ian went to Jason, took his hand, and said, "There's a tablet with Wi-Fi in the desk if you need it. It's old, but serviceable." I nodded, and didn't explain that I had my phone. "Good day then." Ian shut the door.

"Alright, young lady, let's get you ready for bed." Dorothea crawled onto the cot without any protest. I hummed a few words, pressed a few spots on her neck, and she was out. She'd sleep until I woke her the following night. Likely hungry as hell, but there was nothing to be done about that now. I dropped the bag with my two-week supply of blood on the desk and took off my jacket.

It was easier to sleep on a full stomach, so I pulled out a liter of blood and opened it. Apples flooded my senses and not much else, which was good. Anything that wasn't just apple-flavored was likely from an individual with magic. You could drink it, but too much could cause all kinds of things to happen. Since my ability had to do with magic too, I had learned to be careful. The covens did a good job filtering the supply, but sometimes stuff got through.

I took my phone out of one of my jacket pockets and checked for messages. Nothing yet. When people showed up tomorrow night at the clinic and it was closed, the coven would know something was up. I turned off the GPS, then I slipped off my work boots and shimmied out of my jeans. T-shirt and underwear were decent enough for sleeping with the quilt on the bed.

I remembered the quilt and its familiar patterns. I ran my hand over it, and my heart squeezed with long-forgotten emotions. I'd helped one of Ian's great-great-grand-daughters make it. Maria was in her seventies by the time I met her, but she was one of my favorite people, and the only one that encouraged me to find my own way.

Good thing I didn't have any choice about sleeping during the day. If I were human, I'd have too much anxiety about being in this house again with my onetime husband and his lover.

DOROTHEA'S NIGHTMARE

When I woke, it was from the sensation of someone poking my face with their finger. I popped one eye open and saw Dorothea standing next to the bed, staring at me.

"You were dead."

I nodded. "Yes. And you're awake." She nodded. "Are you hungry?" Another nod. So was I. I slipped on my jeans, grabbed my supply of blood, and went out the door toward the kitchen. I yawned big enough to crack my jaw. My little shadow did the same.

Once in the kitchen, I deposited my supply in the fridge. It was exactly where a stasis cabinet used to be. Ian usually wasn't the only vampire in the house, and he certainly wasn't the only family member, but the house was oddly quiet. My tiny shadow hopped up onto one of the stools on the side of the kitchen island while I rummaged through Ian's pantry. I found packages of apple juice and premade pastries.

I went through a phase in the late twentieth century where I snacked on apple juice and apple pastries when blood supplies were low because of HIV.

The primary function of the vampire virus was to maintain the host at the point of transition. Aging and organ failure were arrested. Diseases like cancer were eradicated in the body. If a vampire came in contact with a disease after their transition, the virus they carried eliminated it.

There were always downsides, of course. Deformities during transition, fugue states that were worse than dementia, exacerbated mental health issues that ranged from previously unexperienced phobias to psychotic breaks.

HIV was different. When it came into contact with the vampire virus, it weakened the viruses' ability to maintain the host. Some would have flu-like symptoms until their bodies gave out years later. Other's hair turned gray for the first time. Because of the unpredictable nature of HIV on nearly every species on the planet, blood supplies were scarce for nearly a decade or so.

Then came computers. Combined with magic and innovative science, computers helped detect and filter the virus from the blood supply. Retro-viruses and antiviral meds were born. Blood stopped tasting anything like the cinnamon-apple flavor I came to associate with most vampires. There was speculation, and not too small a fear, that it might lead to a vaccine or a cure for the vampire virus, but the right combination was never found, and covens involved in scientific studies shied away from such things.

Dorothea waited patiently as I opened the box of strawberry-flavored pastries, handed her a package, and then opened the apple juice. She smiled as she ate, but the smile didn't seem real to me. Actually, there was something off about this whole situation. The house was too quiet. While I was used to waking early, it was never this bright out. When the grandfather clock in the living room struck, I counted the chimes. There were three, and then it stopped.

I looked from the kitchen entrance to Dorothea as she ate her pastry. "Thank you, Mason. You can go back to being dead."

Everything turned black. Panic. Like being in that fucking pond again with a rock on my chest to keep me from floating to the surface during the day. I fought the darkness. Reached for the bright yellow connection in my mind and pulled.

A comforting space formed, and I felt myself floating. Ian's hands reached for me, caressing my shoulders and face. "Don't panic," Ian's soothing voice said. "Darkness is your friend. It protects you. I'll protect you."

What the absolute fuck was going on? Since I had the connection closed off between Ian and me, not once had I dreamed about him. Now he had returned and taken up residence in my mind like he'd never left.

Dorothea's voice echoed in the darkness as Ian held me. "Thank you, Mason. You can go back to being dead."

As soon as my eyes opened, I sat upright, drew in a breath, and screamed. Once all the air left my lungs, I looked around. I was still in bed. The windows showed it was likely six or seven o'clock in the evening. I got up and pulled on my pants. Dorothea was in bed, a juice box in her hand. My entire supply of blood was gone.

I slammed open the door and ran to the kitchen, threw open the door to the fridge, and saw my supply. When I looked around the kitchen, I saw the open box of pastries and another empty juice box. I picked up the juice box to make sure it was real. Jason found me like that when he came into the kitchen.

"You like apple juice?"

"Blood tastes like apples to me. It's what got me through the blood shortages."

"Oh," Jason said. "You look like you've had a fright."

I crushed the box in my hand, letting it bite into my skin to ground me. "Jason, before things become extremely weird, you should probably ask your questions." Plus, I needed a distraction. I couldn't process that I might have been awake in the middle of the day, and the child I'd brought to Ian's house had somehow broken a sleep spell, woke me, then used me to help her find food, then returned me to my previous state.

"Well, then. I suppose you should start from the beginning." Jason sat down on a stool while I paced.

I explained how Ian and I met during the war, Ian's initial relationship with me as my teacher and friend. After the war, a lot of new vampires were stuck in an odd limbo because technically we were dead, and the Vampire Accords had to sort out citizenship among other things. The accords prompted the creation of covens to support the new, mostly untethered vampire population. But that had taken years. Of all the vampires Ian had helped through their transition, I was the one he rescued from temporary housing and blood bank lines.

"So you married him?"

"At the time, it was the easiest thing to do. I gained citizenship and a family. It was good for a while."

"So, what happened?"

"I happened," Ian said as he walked into the kitchen and retrieved his evening meal. "She wanted to study medicine, and I wanted her to stay here."

"You're a doctor?" Jason's face perked up. I smiled.

"Bona fide and everything. I have a clinic in a hamlet outside of Paris."

"Did you apprentice or attend one of the night schools?"

"I did both. England saw a ready workforce and skilled labor, so they started night schools for essential needs to support a population of vampires no one expected to have. They accepted me in the first year at Oxford."

"Then I told her she couldn't go." Ian's emotions came through the bond. The sadness from our separation and realizing his mistake. He had longed to explain, but I'd cut him off by closing off our bond so long ago. He had moved on, like I had. Until now.

"Ian, my dear, that doesn't sound like you at all." The lament in Jason's voice reassured me.

"Oh, it was. The house was full back then. My family provided everything we needed, and Mason had enough skill already to see to anyone's health. I thought it wasn't necessary. Until it was."

"You're being cryptic again," Jason pointed out.

"When we were together, one child who lived here, Jonathan, fell from a tree at the Lindquist home in France." I hated this memory most. The boy was always getting into trouble, but no one had expected what happened. "At first, we all thought he'd broken his arm—nothing too serious. Until his breathing became worse. Doctors wouldn't come to the house because they knew about the coterie. Public sentiment was still pretty bad even ten years after the war, though a good number of vampires fought in the war to turn the tide." I wiped away tears. It stained my hands red, and the smell of apples lingered while I continued. "I tried to do what I could, but his injuries were internal, and I'd never used my magic like that." At the time, I could only fix what I could see. The training I gained later let me fix the unseen as well.

Jason's face spoke volumes. Ian was like a steel door. I couldn't feel anything from him now, but he finished the story.

"After his funeral, she left for school. I paid for the expenses and a safe place for her to live while she studied. Though I somewhat expected that she'd return after she gained the proper experience."

"You knew I couldn't, Ian."

"You broke my fucking heart, Mason."

"I know."

The silence was absolute. None of us breathed. More than a century had passed, and in all that time, I had missed his family. Knew that they would all pass on, and we would continue to persist and watch the next generation grow up, then die. I had fooled myself into thinking it was the natural order of things until Jonathan died.

"Where is everyone?" Ian always had family around him. It was odd for the house to be so empty.

"They live on the surrounding estates. Most of them don't even know I'm related. I see to their finances and livelihoods, and a few come to visit every once in a while."

"You didn't initiate any other family members?" Someone to pass on the duties of shepherding the family, like Ian's great-grandfather had with him.

Ian shook his head. "I meant for Jonathan to succeed me."

Jason whistled. "Old man, you have some serious trauma to deal with." He shook his head at Ian, then turned to me. "So after all this time, Ian's the first person you thought of when you found the kid?"

"Ian's the only one I know who can break a deep compulsion and not kill the subject." I'd seen too many other failed attempts. Ian, to put it simply, was the best.

"Good to know you still trust me for some things, Mason."

"I never stopped."

"Fuck, you two seriously need to bang this out." We both looked at Jason, and he shrugged. "I call it like I see it. But first, we should probably see to Dorothea."

"Shit, right." I turned and walked back down the hall to find Dorothea sitting up in bed. Ian and Jason were right behind me.

"Didn't you sleep spell her?" Ian walked in and knelt in front of Dorothea.

"Sure, and yet, here we are. And so help me, if you say I did it wrong, I'll make sure you can't piss for a week."

Ian held up his hands as Jason chuckled.

"Far be it from me to argue with the doctor." Ian turned back to Dorothea and peered into her eyes. He held out his hands, and she mimicked him. When Ian gently took her hands in his, we watched as a jolt went through both of them. "There is something very elusive about how they did this. It's independent of control, though similar to what I saw in the war. Like they wanted her to be a blank slate of sorts by pushing her to be something just short of catatonic. I'm surprised she remembered her name."

Jason's beautiful face was scrunched up. "This is all very disturbing. It's why the educational covens have policies about families and children specifically."

"Oh?" I'd never heard of covens having their own rules, but I suppose it was possible.

"You can't join if you're a single parent or have living dependents. If the other covens had these policies, children like Dorothea wouldn't be abandoned to the social services system," Jason said.

"Do the educational covens have a waiting period?" I asked.

"They do. Candidates are supported in a work-study capacity. I put in twenty years as a lab and teaching assistant. It let me finish my doctorate and gave me access to facilities for my research."

I was impressed. If I'd known that kind of coven existed, I'd have been tempted. "Are educational covens a recent development?"

Jason nodded. "I was one of the first sponsored candidates when the Earlham Institute program started twenty-five years ago."

"Very interesting. We'll have to chat about this more when we get a chance." I glanced at Ian. He was still holding Dorothea's hands. "How's it going, Ian?"

"There are several layers of compulsions here. They were done over an extended period of time. If she'd been an adult, there would have been permanent damage. Fortunately, most children are quite resilient. Her brain has already started repairing the damage and removing parts of the compulsions." Ian went quiet, and we observed.

Jason wasn't wrong exactly, but he wasn't around when the war ended. I'd seen how the newly formed covens had helped vampires in the beginning by organizing blood drives, shelter, and safety. They had worked with humanity to regulate and maintain blood availability, even through scarce times.

Coteries rarely shared what they had—a ready blood supply via their living families, protection, and generational wealth. The new ranks of the covens often came with what they had on their backs. No one was turned away as long as they followed the rules.

Were covens perfect? No, the Crossroads Coven was little more than a loosely connected mob with ties to another coven above them. I chose it specifically because of the simplicity of the structure and the general lack of oversight. They let me operate my business as long as I supplied them with blood.

Anyone was welcome at my clinic, and the only thing I requested was a pint of their blood after they were healthy again. It didn't matter what species they were; I'd doctor them up. The small compulsion spell I used, which Ian taught me, made sure they would show up at some point. In exchange for the blood donations to the coven, they bought my supplies, kept up the building lease, and left me alone.

This was the first time I'd jeopardized that relationship. That fact was slowly sinking in as Ian flinched and Dorothea screamed bloody murder.

Hostage Situation

"Ian! What the fuck did you do?" I went to Dorothea. Ian tried to stop me. The second I touched her, I felt her fear, and then her control. It clamped down on me like I was a brand new fledgling. "Move vampire. I wish to leave." The words surprised me as much as they surprised Ian to hear them come out of my mouth. I looked at Dorothea and reached for her. Jason and Ian blocked my path.

"I won't let you take Mason, Dorothea. No one will hurt you here."

Ian's voice had a compulsion in it. While I knew it to be true, I wasn't the intended target.

"Don't play mind games with me, vampire." The words weren't mine, but they certainly came out of my mouth. "I want my parents, and I want to leave. You'll let me go, or I'll. . ."

"Or you'll what? Kill the only person who's cared about you in the last forty-eight hours? I doubt that seriously. You're not a murderer." Ian's gaze flicked to mine, and I tried to tell him with whatever connection we had that I was okay, and I was still in here, but scared. The slight nod told me he got the message.

A small hand turned my face toward hers. Dorothea looked me in the eye. "You're too much life; not like the others. You're like my parents." Her voice was small, but no less threatening for what she said.

"Do you know who your parents are?" asked Ian.

Dorothea let go of my face and looked at Ian again. "The Envoy and Lady Tabatha," Dorothea and I spoke simultaneously.

It was like repeating a memory. Something she heard when her parents were announced at a banquet or a ball. Some of the older covens still did things like that. An image of her parents came to my mind. They were in fancy clothes. The man was particularly tall, with long black hair and a very nice tan. The woman was a mage, which is why she had the title. Magic flowed around her. She had long brown tresses, kind brown eyes, and rose-pink skin with a dash of freckles across her face. Dorothea was a miniature of the woman, except she had her father's black hair and hazel eyes instead of her mother's brown.

"The dhampir? Your father is Lennix Creighton?" Ian asked. Dorothea nodded. If I'd been allowed a reaction, it would have been disbelief. "How old are you?"

"I'm eight."

The dhampir wasn't part of Crossroads or any other coven. Once declared, they were considered outside of the coven structure, supposedly. If the Envoy's partner and child were left at the chapter house, it was most certainly some kind of retribution. Plus, if Lacey and Duke were right, Tabatha was dead, and Dorothea was meant to be lost in a vast system of social support that spent most of its resources caring for individuals, but had very few figuring out where those individuals came from or why.

There were always covens waiting in the wings to offer a dhampir, but that individual had to be above reproach, and because they were alive, but mutated by the virus, dhampirs usually exhibited a natural immunity to vampiric powers.

All of that tumbled through my brain and circled back to what Dorothea had said earlier. She compared me to her parents.

I looked at Ian. What could that even mean? He gave a slight shake of his head. Something to talk about later when I wasn't the puppet of an eight-year-old. *Well, now at least I know her age.*

"We'll help you find them, but you have to let Mason go. You know what you're doing is wrong, yes?"

"How is it wrong?" my voice asked for Dorothea.

"You're a necromancer, Dorothea. Necromancers and vampires aren't supposed to hurt each other. If your father were to find out, he would be very cross. You love your father, don't you? You wouldn't want to make him cross."

Dorothea did the first child-like thing I'd see her do since I'd taken her from the chapter house: she burst into tears. The powerful emotions broke whatever hold she had over me. I walked us to the bed and sat down with her curled in my lap.

"Shhh, I've got you, little one. You're safe." I rocked her as she wailed her pain and loneliness into my shoulder. Ian backed out of the room, and Jason closed the door behind them.

Fifteen minutes later, I met them in the kitchen. "She's asleep." Likely exhausted from Ian breaking her compulsion and then from controlling me for so long. I went to the blood fridge and pulled out one from my supply, downing half of it.

"Did you know she could do that?" asked Ian.

I shook my head. "She could barely tell me her name when I found her."

"I must have triggered something when I removed the compulsions," Ian said.

"Maybe." I glanced at Jason and Ian. "I think she woke me during the day. I'm not completely sure, but I remember coming to the kitchen and feeding her apple juice and pastries, hearing the grandfather clock in the living room chime three times, then I noticed it was too bright. After that, there was darkness, until I woke up in bed. Maybe something was triggered with the sleeping spell?"

"It's possible," Ian said with a shrug.

"If she's a necromancer, she's proof that necromancers and vampires are related. Many suspected, but studies have been lacking on anyone with a necromancer lineage because they refused to be genotyped. Dorothea might represent a missing link." Ian and I both stared at Jason. "I'm a geneticist. Mostly, I work with plants because of my magic, though I can't help but be fascinated by this development."

I smiled at Ian. "You always did have a thing for doctor types. Especially if they were witty and handsome."

"Oh, he does? I guess that explains you too, then." Jason grinned. I shrugged with a grin of my own. Ian blushed, even though I don't think he'd eaten anything yet.

"So I have a type." He shrugged and walked over to the fridge, pulled out two units of blood from his own supply and handed one to Jason. "Her powers are fairly effective, but I think they rely on direct contact or she wouldn't have waited until you touched her. Plus, Jason, being the youngest of us, would have been easier for her to control."

"Oh, thanks," Jason sighed.

Ian moved closer to Jason and cupped his face, then kissed him on the lips. "I did not mean it as a slight. She tried with me too, but I was too old for her. It's why I tried to stop Mason from touching her."

"But she only had control of me physically. I was still me, but I couldn't do anything."

Ian nodded. "Like she said. There was something about you that made it hard for her to control you, though she's powerful. I hate to think how much more powerful she'll become when she's an adult." The fear in Ian's eyes was real. The ghosts of a war we had survived, which had left deep wounds, spoke volumes between us. If the covens had known, they wouldn't have let the child exist.

"But something isn't adding up. Whoever did this to Dorothea had access to her more than once. They stripped her mind down to a compliant child, then finally took the rest when they intended for her to be lost. She was basically a two-year-old in an eight-year-old's body. If anyone else had tried to dispel the compulsions, it's likely Dorothea and the person doing so would have died." Ian frowned as he thought and stared at the liter of blood in his hands.

While Ian seemed lost, Jason circled back to his previous topic. "If she's half mage, and half carrier of the vampire virus, one could have possibly suppressed the other, or remained out of reach until they fucked with her mind." Jason's theory was plausible. "Genetics and magic are tricky like that. I'd have to run tests to even narrow it down."

"I think discovering your genetic holy grail will need to wait, Jason. The bigger problem is that someone dumped that kid and likely put her mother under a compulsion to have her agree to a transformation. The guards at the chapter house told me her mother died."

"Shit." Ian paced the kitchen. "We're definitely in a pickle." He sighed while I tried not to laugh at his turn of phrase. "I don't know how to reach out to the Envoy without lighting a beacon that would attract attention."

"We have some time. They don't know I'm here."

"Why wouldn't they? Our last names obviously connect us."

"I didn't use my married name when I joined Crossroads."

Ian looked at me. "Why not?"

"First of all, since our license expired, my married name hasn't been valid for seventy-five years. Second, I didn't want to risk your family being inadvertently drawn into the coven. You sign over everything you own when you join or transfer. I can leave, but it's hard to move resources from one coven to another. You either have to be well off or really old, and I'm neither."

Ian gave me a look that said I could have been. I knew I had an account with my married name that I could have used. Ian left it there for me. I checked to make sure it still existed from time to time.

Ian took a breath and then sighed. "Fine, we have time. But that still doesn't solve the problem of contacting the Envoy and letting him know his daughter is safe."

"I have an idea." But I wasn't sure it was any safer than the covens.

FRIEND OF A FRIEND

"Hello darling, how are you?" I called the only person I could think of who might be able to get us in contact with Tabatha's mage family. The guys hadn't liked the idea, but we didn't have any other covert options at the moment.

"Mas? Oh lovely, how are you?" Hilda's sultry voice tickled my ear with her French. She spoke sweet words, but her mouth, specifically her tongue, was dirty as fuck. While I tried to avoid magic users, Hilda was pretty harmless as a hedge witch. Plus, she had connections.

"Not going to lie, Hildy. I'm in a bit of a bind."

"Oh? Well, that's no fun. I'd rather you be bound up for me to deliciously torture than be in a hard spot."

It wasn't lost on me that Jason and Ian could hear everything, even though I didn't have Hilda on speakerphone. Jason chuckled, and Ian looked surprised. I gave Ian a look that said he could keep his provincial thoughts about my sex life to himself, and that I'd learned a few things along the way. It wasn't the same-sex partners, obviously, but rather the hint of BDSM that he shied away from. A little slap and tickle were fine. More than that, and he clammed up.

"Hildy, I need some contact information for the Lafayette mage family. Someone discrete, if possible."

"I thought you didn't dabble with laced stuff." By that, she meant blood laced with magic. Often, the best sources were from mages. Nice enough to get you high, but not make you explode if you drank too much.

"No, I don't, but I have contacts that do. They said they'd help me out with upgrading my ride if I could get them a source."

"Oh, for heaven's sake, Mas. I think you love that bike of yours more than physical contact."

"You can't go wrong with a well-oiled machine and two hundred fifty horsepower between your legs."

Hilda cackled. "I suppose not. Give me a day or two to find someone for you, mon amour. Is the number that came up the one you're using?"

"Yep, give me a ring when you've got it."

"Will do, Mas. Ciao!"

"Ciao!" I hung up while Ian and Jason shared stunned looks. "What?"

"Nothing, darling." Ian said with a chuckle. Jason snickered.

"Fuck you both."

"Is that an offer?" Jason asked.

Ian smiled. "I imagine it could be, depending on whether you could speak French."

"Oui," Jason said.

Ian could speak French as well, so mostly he was fucking with me. I couldn't help that I had a thing for accents that weren't wholly from the States. I made a noise at the back of my throat and shook my head. The appearance of Dorothea rubbing her eyes saved them from a scathing rebuke.

"Hello there, little one. How are you feeling?" I knew she was sad. For once, her emotions matched her face and body language.

"Sad. Hungry. Is there anything besides pastries?" Dorothea asked. It was nearly midnight.

"There's an all-night petrol station close to here. I can pop down and pick up some things," Jason offered.

"You can take my bike if you'd like."

Jason chuckled. "Be careful offering me your ride. If you think it's that good, I might not give it back."

"I can share." Jason and I exchanged a look that was full of interesting questions, especially when he glanced at Ian and then back at me.

"I'll keep that in mind." We both knew I wasn't talking about my bike.

After Jason left, I took Dorothea's hand and walked her over to the couch to sit with me. Ian popped up from his chair and grabbed a book off his shelf, then came to sit with us. I recognized the children's book of short stories. We used to read it to his family's children before we sent them to bed.

Ian smiled as he cracked open the book and started. "Once upon a time. . ." Dorothea was instantly drawn in.

When Jason returned with several warm pasties—basically the British version of a panini—along with milk, cereal, bread, meat, a large selection of cheese, and a bottle of wine, we took a break from reading and snacked while Dorothea ate. Ian took a bite of cheese, moaning at the taste.

"After all these years, and you still like anything to do with milk."

"Of course, why wouldn't I?"

"I've found myself sick of apples sometimes."

"Apples?" Jason asked. "Oh, right."

"What does blood smell and taste like to you?" I asked Jason.

"Banana splits."

"No way. That's such a complex flavor!" I'd never heard of anyone having an entire dish as a craving before. Not that I asked all that often. We considered it somewhat personal information.

Jason shrugged. "It was my favorite dessert. My parents would make them for my birthdays, and there was a place I'd take dates to that would make the best ones in the area I grew up."

"How did the two of you meet?"

There was a complex look between Jason and Ian. I could almost read it. The memory, the smile shared, the history, and then finally, who would tell me. Jason took point.

"We started talking on a dating app a few years ago. Then met at Ian's local and hit it off. I moved in recently and work in a lab space Ian renovated for me in one of the outbuildings he has on the property. And I keep Earlham apprised of my progress."

I looked at Ian and then Jason. "That's very efficient." I was smiling because I knew Ian. For him to have gone to all that trouble, he must have been serious about Jason.

"Quite satisfying in other departments as well," Ian added, confirming my suspicions while giving Jason a rather salacious look. I doubt we'd be as guarded about the topic if it weren't for Dorothea being amongst us, carefully watching and munching away at a hot ham and cheese pasty. Though it made me curious about something else. "What about coven membership?"

"I'm part of the Earlham Coven. Mostly scientists, and it's mostly hands off. We're shipped allotments wherever we're located. Part of the employment package as well." So the large blood supply in the cooling unit wasn't only Ian's, or maybe it wasn't Ian's at all. The proud look on Jason's face and the mild blush on Ian's actually sparked an odd pang of jealousy. They were equals in their relationship. It was something Ian and I never had other than through our bond, and that was dubious at best, in my opinion. Though Ian never saw it that way.

Chitchat continued until Dorothea looked sleepy in her chair. I reached over and touched her gently. "How about we have a bit of a wash-up, hmm? I'll send these two off to find some clothes."

Ian cleared his throat and nodded. Jason smiled and followed him out of the room. I led Dorothea to the guest bathroom and drew a bath. She stripped out of her clothes as I pulled various products from the cabinet. Once she was in, I handed her a washcloth and soap. "Would you like me to help wash your hair?" The sleepy nod made me smile. Her hair was beautiful, but matted from sleep. It would take time to work out the tangles.

"Once my friend calls back, we'll figure out how to contact your parents from there." I didn't know if she knew her mother was dead yet. I didn't want to put that stress on her. However, she caught on to something.

"You're lying."

"About what?"

"My parents."

"We're going to try to contact your mother's family. I'm hoping they can contact your parents."

"Oh." The clarification seemed to calm her. I continued washing her hair while she cleaned the rest of herself. Once we were done, I helped her wrap her hair in a towel, and found another that we wrapped around her in lieu of a robe.

Back in our shared bedroom, Ian and Jason had left clothes on the bed. A variety of dresses and small shirts, along with a pair of child-sized coveralls. Dorothea went for those with a shirt and got dressed, then crawled into bed with the tablet. After a few minutes, she was asleep. I gently pulled the tablet from her hands and covered her up, then I picked out similar clothes from the pile of adult clothing and returned to the bathroom to clean up.

HELPING HANDS

I was waiting for the bathwater to drain when Ian and Jason appeared at the bathroom door.

"Little one all tucked in?" Jason smiled with his arm wrapped around Ian's shoulders. Ian had an odd look on his face.

"She'll be out for a few hours at least. I'm not sure what happens later when she's awake during the day and we're all dead."

"I left out some cereal and fruit if she wakes before us." Ian shrugged. "And I asked one of my relatives to come over and check on her in the morning."

"I'll make sure to leave out the tablet. Hopefully, that will keep her entertained." I sighed. "Best we can do at this point besides make sure we spell the doors shut."

"Easy enough. I'll leave a key for my relative. It will get them through the magic wards."

The guys stood there and stared. "Well, if there isn't anything else, I'm going to take a shower."

They exchanged a look. "Would you rather take a bath… with us?" Ian offered.

The smile that formed on my face must have been comical because they chuckled. "Is that a yes?" Jason prompted.

"That sounds lovely."

Ian came into the bathroom and offered his hand. I took it. He led me past Jason. I grabbed Jason's hand, and we all went to the other wing of the house, which I hadn't seen in quite some time.

When we arrived at the main bedroom, there was a banked fire, three robes on the bed, and three glasses of wine already poured. I heard what sounded like whirlpool noises coming from the ensuite.

"You two were rather sure of yourselves."

"Oh please, you've been giving us 'fuck me' eyes most of the night. We'd already be here if we didn't have to worry about half-pint. She's cute, but a handful." Jason's bluntness made me laugh, and Ian blushed. I missed that blush. Ian handed me a glass, then handed one to Jason.

"A toast?" Ian asked.

We held up our glasses. "To odd circumstances, old lovers, and new. Here's to new memories together," Ian said.

The glasses made a soft clink as we tapped them. I didn't have the heart to tell them I'd be gone after I'd figured out how to get Dorothea back to her father. No sense in ruining the mood. Ian reached over and rubbed my shoulder. When I glanced at him, he gave me a slight nod.

Our connection. He knew this was temporary for me. It might be why Jason agreed to it, or wanted it. Ian always wanted me, which was nearly the only thing that was consistent with our relationship. It wasn't a bother, because I always wanted him, too.

I took another drink from my glass, and then Jason tried to take it from me. Instead of giving up the last quarter, I drank it off. "Well, okay then," he said as I set the glass down. He took my hand and led me into their bathroom. Ian followed close behind.

A mass of bubbles were foaming in the jets of the steamy water. I couldn't even remember when I'd had a bath like this. I'd dreamed about it once or twice. But life on a non-existent budget meant budget accommodations, which were mostly showers. A warm bath was a luxury.

Jason reached for my shirt. "May I?" I smiled up at him and nodded. He slowly slipped my shirt over my head.

Ian's hands came around to my jeans and landed on the button and zipper. "May I?" I nodded again, and Ian opened the fly of my jeans slowly, then slipped his hands around my hips and under the band of my panties. He pushed both to the floor, where he lifted each leg to remove the articles completely.

Jason reached for my bra next and removed it with ease. "Go ahead. We'll join you shortly."

"I don't get to help?"

Ian shook his head. "No, you get to watch."

My lips formed a silent 'oh' as I crawled into the hot water. As I settled, they carefully folded my clothes on a nearby vanity, then removed their clothing, one after the other, with fervent kisses in between, until they were both gloriously naked. Their hands drifted over their bodies as they kissed. Ian fondled Jason first until Jason reciprocated.

A burning desire shot through me as I sank up to my chin in bubbles and my fingers drifted to tease my clit while I watched. The guys didn't acknowledge my voyeurism. Ian knew I liked to watch, and I knew he liked an audience. I only hoped Jason was okay with it. It's not like the three of us talked about what would happen.

As Ian dropped to his knees, I drew in a breath and almost choked on water since I was in total peeper mode with my nose barely above the waterline. The sounds of the whirlpool must have covered up my gasping, because it didn't deter Ian. In one smooth move, he put his hands on Jason's hips and took him into his mouth all the way to his base. This was no small feat. Jason was as well off as Ian, if not more so, and hard. Vampires, because we're mostly dead, had little gag reflex, which came in handy sometimes.

Ian's hair was just long enough for Jason to thread his fingers through and yank. He came off Jason's dick with a loud pop as both men looked at each other. Then Jason turned to look right at me. I slowly sank below the bubbles, moaning as my fingers furiously worked toward the orgasm I so desperately wanted.

Hands descended into the water, not to pull me out, but to play with me, like I was a fish. I felt caresses on my breasts and ass, my sides, and face. I floated in warmth and tenderness until I was gently pulled to the surface for a kiss. Hands roamed and played, while lips and tongues teased any place they could reach. It honestly surprised me teeth hadn't come out yet, but we'd all fed earlier, so the emotions driving us weren't from hunger.

We took sponges and washed each other's backs and fronts. We touched and fondled each other in the process. But I didn't want to fuck in the whirlpool. I escaped their capable hands and extracted myself from the warmth. I grabbed a towel and crooked a finger at them. "Come on, before my skin grows cold." Jason laughed as he climbed out, and Ian followed with a grin.

The king-size bed we fell into was large enough. Our limbs tangled, with me in the middle at first, and then the guys situated me to be on the bottom. I watched as Ian propped himself over me, and Jason kissed and caressed his face.

"You start while I get the lube," Jason whispered. Ian nodded.

Ian's attentions turned toward me as his lips touched down on mine. I was so distracted by kissing him I didn't realize I'd wrapped my legs around his waist while he pushed into me until he bottomed out. The slap of his hips against my thighs was a sharp noise echoing around the room. Jason came back into my field of vision and put a hand on Ian's hip. He stopped and gave a small grunt as Jason removed an anal plug from Ian's ass, wrapped it in a washcloth, and tossed it off the bed.

Laughter bubbled out of me. "Shit, you two were serious about tonight."

Jason looked over Ian's shoulder. "Someone was getting fucked." I laughed again until I groaned as Jason shoved himself into Ian, which shoved Ian into me. Jason certainly knew what he was doing as he fucked us both into the mattress.

The sounds we made as we kissed, grunted, and humped each other were glorious. My body relaxed into the sensations until Ian grabbed my legs and looped them over his shoulders. Somehow, that was a signal to go slower and deeper. Every thrust built upon the last. Jason leaned over and sucked my big toe, which shot a sensation right to my clit as my toes curled.

"Oh shit, fuck," Ian whispered as my whole lower half tightened toward my orgasm. Jason picked up his pace, which meant Ian groaned more.

"Someone bite me, for fuck's sake, please." I needed it. Though it didn't always have to be a bite. Something like a spanking, to the point it covered my ass in welts, worked too.

What I didn't expect was both of them obliging me at nearly the same time. Ian's teeth hit my breast while Jason's sunk in above my ankle with hands clamped around my right leg. I writhed as much as I could, pinned as I was. My orgasm washed over me and forced the air from my lungs. I lay there for a time, wondering if the world would ever be as beautiful as the two men on top of me.

Ian pushed up, which gave me a marvellous view of his cock still buried inside me. Jason moved, keeping hold of my leg as he wrapped his arm around Ian's shoulders. He nuzzled at Ian's neck before he clamped down. Ian spasmed in response, unloaded in me, then pulled out and splashed me with more. He kept coming until Jason stopped drinking. I don't remember the last time I saw something so fucking hot. I reached for my clit again and began working myself toward another orgasm.

Jason noticed my hand motions and gently moved Ian to lie next to me. Ian and I kissed and shared what was left of my blood on his lips while my fingers toyed with my swollen nub. It distracted me from where Jason's head ended up. His tongue touched down on my clit, and I moaned into Ian's mouth. Ian chuckled as he continued to reward me with kisses for every moan and sigh I made.

I didn't have to tell Jason to bite when I was on the edge of my second orgasm. His talented tongue drew soft punctuated whines until he bit and I came in a flood of blood, Ian's ejaculate, and my own juices.

If I thought that would be it, I was wrong. I giggled from my orgasm high as Jason helped me roll to my hands and knees. He slipped into me with hardly any resistance and filled me full. I groaned from the sensations as Ian repositioned himself so his dick was near my head. I sucked him as Jason fucked me from behind. Ian made pleased noises and pushed my hair out of the way so he could see my face. He always did like watching a good blowjob.

"She doesn't always need a bite. Sometimes you can give her what she needs in other ways," Ian offered as his hand landed on my ass. It didn't sting, but it made a loud smack.

Jason smirked. "That's helpful," he said as he used his thighs to nudge my legs wider, then a hand to press my back into a more sloped position that offered my ass up like a serving platter. Jason's hand came down as he thrust into me. I whined and moaned at the same time. "Oh, fuck yes. I'm gonna make this ass so red."

I stopped sucking Ian's dick long enough to encourage him. "Yes, do it. I want your hands imprinted on my ass." The shit that came out of my mouth. Ian snickered, then groaned as I kept working his cock. Jason's slaps were measured to keep the pain endorphins going, but not push me over the edge. Ian squirmed slightly, but lost it when I pushed two fingers into his ass.

As Ian came into my mouth, Jason amped up his thrusts and slaps. As my ass truly began to burn, and the pain was a blanket of throbbing heat, Jason reached between my legs and rubbed at my clit while he fucked me. My orgasm swept through me, making me shake. Jason kept the wave going until I slumped forward onto the bed, slipping off his cock.

I hadn't realized Ian had moved until I turned slightly to see him swallow Jason down. This time, Jason wasn't gentle. He fucked Ian's face until he groaned with his own release, which Ian swallowed with a satisfied moan. He was skilled at keeping his fangs out of the mix, unless his partners wanted them.

As dawn fast approached, we'd turned ourselves into a blissed-out mess of bruises, bites, and fluids of various kinds. The three of us lay in bed, Ian in the middle, Jason spooning him and me snuggled into Ian's front.

"We should clean up."

The guys made odd noises. "If the kiddo comes in before we're awake, I don't want her to think we murdered each other." If I knew Ian, he likely still spelled the door to lock between dawn and sunset as a precaution. The house had UV windows, but he didn't risk his safety, especially when he used to have family members living here. However, none of us knew the extent of Dorothea's magic.

"Fair point. Come on, old man, move your ass." I laughed at Jason's comment as he moved to the bathroom.

The shower started, and I smiled at Ian. "You two seem very happy together."

Ian kissed me and gave me a pleased smile. "We are." He didn't have to say why, nor did I list all the things that I saw. I kissed Ian again, then got out of bed. While we still had feelings for each other and our bond, Ian and I were ancient history. Fun to visit and talk about, but best put back on the shelf until the next reunion or party that prompted one to stroll down memory lane.

As Ian rolled out of bed, there was a knock at the door.

MIDDAY VISIT

I grabbed a robe and tossed it on as Ian slipped into the bathroom and closed the door while I opened the one to his bedroom. Dorothea stood there with a stuffed monkey. I knelt to be at eye level with her. "Did we wake you?"

She sighed. "No, I had a bad dream. It woke me. Then I ate some fruit. I found this monkey, and then I found you, but the door was closed. My parents told me to knock if the door is closed."

"Such a smart girl." She smiled at the praise. I wondered how often she heard something like that from an adult.

"Can I sleep with you for the day?"

"Are you sure you want to? We'll be dead. You won't be able to leave the room if you wake up." It was one reason I had my own room. I woke earlier than Ian, and disturbing spells while someone slept was risking a catastrophe. Though I was pretty sure I'd sleep in late, or take another dip in the tub if I didn't. The tub certainly wasn't here the last time. Ian had done more than upgrade a few outbuildings.

"That's alright. I brought snacks." She opened her arms and revealed that the monkey was covering a banana and another juice box.

"Tell you what, let's get a few more supplies and the tablet, just in case. I'll let Ian and Jason know so they can tidy up a bit. How does that sound?"

She nodded her head, and I quickly ducked into the bathroom and told the guys while they were in the shower.

"Hurry, Mason. There isn't much time before dawn. You can take a shower after I shut us in for the day." Ian was clearly nervous.

"We'll hurry." I closed the door and quick-stepped to Dorothea, taking her hand as we dashed playfully about the house to gather the things she needed to stay with us for the day. By the time we were back in Ian's room, the sheets were changed, and both men were dressed in boxers and shirts for bed. Dorothea and I settled all her loot on the rug in front of the fireplace.

When I came out of the shower, Dorothea was snuggled up with Ian, who was already dead. Jason smiled at me as I dried my hair. "Did Ian set the door?"

"Oh yeah. Like a timer." I grinned at Jason's comment. "He actually locked me out of the room one morning when I wasn't quick enough. He apologized profusely for it the next day. But I didn't hold it against him. He hits a certain part of the morning, and it's like watching someone go on autopilot. He literally spells the door, crawls into bed, gives me a kiss, then he's out."

I nodded. "That sounds familiar. I'm surprised you didn't want your own room to sleep in for the day."

"I might not pass out at dawn, but we wake up about the same time, so it didn't seem necessary."

"Oh? Maybe I'm the weird one."

Dorothea scrunched her nose up. "You're not weird, Mason. You're not dead."

An odd smile formed on Jason's face, and I likely mirrored it. "What do you mean, sweetie?" She wiggled out of Ian's embrace and crawled to where I was perched on the end of the bed.

She pointed at my heart. "It beats all day now. Never stops." She looked up at me, and I shook my head.

"I don't understand, Dorothea."

"You're like Daddy. He sleeps during the day sometimes, but I can wake him."

Well, that made sense. Her father was a dhampir. Dhampirs were born of vampires and humans. Sometimes you could have dhampirs from vampires and other species, but that was rare. What made them interesting was that they weren't dead, could tolerate light unlike vampires, but had a lot of the benefits of a vampire—such as access to magic.

"Your father's a dhampir, sweetie. It's not unusual for him to be awake during the day."

"But his heart beats like yours. Mama's beats fast like mine."

Jason and I looked at each other over Ian's body and shrugged. "Well, that's a mystery for another time, I think. Ready for bed?"

Dorothea nodded. I got into bed, and Dorothea crawled between Ian and me. Jason reached over Ian and gave Dorothea a kiss on her forehead, to which she responded with a quiet giggle. She snuggled into me as I wrapped my arms around her. Jason took a breath and then another, then was out, or dead rather. I could feel the sun at the edge of my senses. It was past dawn, but not by much.

I kissed Dorothea's head and smoothed her hair back. "Sleep tight, little one."

"Sleep tight, Mason."

My world stopped until I gasped from Dorothea's hand on my face.

"Mason, Mason! Wake up. Someone's trying to get in."

She wasn't wrong. There was someone rattling the door. My body pulsed with adrenaline as I got out of bed and walked to the door. "Is there anyone there?"

"Oh, dear me. You scared me, ma'am. I was checking the door to make sure it was locked like it should be. Mr. Lindquist asked me to come check on his niece while he was out for the day." There was a pause. "Is she in there with you?"

"Oh, yes. She wanted to stay with us for the day. I'm sorry we didn't contact you to let you know before you came over."

"Oh no, no worries, ma'am. I didn't expect anyone to be awake in Mr. Lindquist's room. Will the two of you be alright in there?"

"We'll be fine. Unfortunately, we can't open the door. Ian spelled it closed for the day."

"That's his usual way. Alright then. Mr. Lindquist asked me to fetch some groceries. Is there anything special you'd like to have?"

I looked at Dorothea, and she lit up. "Hot chocolate."

I nodded with a smile and turned back to the door. "If we could have some more fruit, apple juice, and hot chocolate with marshmallows?" I looked at Dorothea, and she nodded enthusiastically. "That and whatever else Ian gave you for the list, we would be extremely grateful."

"Certainly dears. I'll make sure to leave everything in the kitchen."

"Thank you, miss?"

"Maria, you can call me Maria, ma'am. I've known Mr. Lindquist my whole life, and he's been nothing but a treasure to our little community. Even if some of us don't remember how he's related, I do. My mother made sure of it. They named me after my great-great-grandmother."

I covered my mouth as tears sprang from my eyes. "I knew the woman they named you after, I think."

"Are you Mason perhaps?"

"Yes." I never wanted to open a door more. Her voice sounded so like her namesake, I could imagine that she looked like Maria as well.

"I've heard stories about you. Mr. Lindquist went through some sad times after you left. Any time anyone asked after you, he'd only say that you were away and that you'd be back someday."

I wiped at my face. Dorothea came up next to me. "Don't cry, Mason. It's okay." I patted her head.

"It's okay to cry sometimes, Dorothea." She frowned but nodded. I didn't want to give her some kind of false platitude. She would think it was a lie if I did.

"I'm sorry, Mrs. Lindquist. I didn't mean to upset you."

"It's alright, Maria. Thank you for stopping by today and helping us out."

"Think nothing of it, ma'am." She took a step away from the door. "Sleep well."

"Thank you, Maria." After Maria left, I looked for my phone or something that would let me know what time it was, but the grandfather clock sounded through the house, and the low-toned chimes indicated it was only ten in the morning.

I went to Dorothea and sat next to her on the bed while she played a puzzle game on the tablet. "How am I awake right now?"

"You're not dead."

I sighed. "I know that since I'm awake, but how?"

"Mason, you're not dead. Like not at all. I can't make them not dead. I tried." She pointed at the guys. "They don't have sparkles."

"Sparkles?"

Nothing made sense. I half wondered if I was having some blood fever dream.

"The sparkles mean you're alive. So I can wake you up. No sparkles mean you can't wake up right now. Uncle Marceau doesn't have sparkles, nor do Ian or Jason. Daddy and Mommy have sparkles." She rattled off these facts as if she were used to saying such things while she played games or skipped rope.

Maybe Dorothea wasn't a necromancer. If she could only control people with sparkles, as she put it, was it possible she could control certain kinds of magic users? Or death magic? I shook my head. I had no idea what road my mind was wandering down. One thing was for certain: she only had to touch you to use whatever it was.

"Dorothea, when you controlled me the other day, was that because of the sparkles?"

She shook her head. "Nope, that's because you were dead."

My head hurt. There were three things I noticed when I crawled back into bed: I was warm, I was breathing at a human rate, and my tears were clear as water. I put two fingers up to my neck, and my pulse was human-like, too. For the last hundred-twenty-eight years, I've never had a human-like pulse, as far as I knew, but today it thumped along as if it had always been there.

"How long can I stay like this, Dorothea?" She shrugged. "Great. Okay, well, put me back to sleep. If you need me again before sunset, wake me up."

Her grin made me smile, and that was the last thing I saw before she touched my face. "G'night, Mason." Then I was dead to the world.

LIFE'S HANGOVER

The guys stared as I went through three liters of blood.

"Thirsty?" Jason asked.

I nodded. Yeah, I was thirsty, like I hadn't eaten in days. I remember the feeling from the lean times, but this was a whole new level of thirst and hunger. As if I wasn't only running low, but had used up my body's abilities.

Ian glanced at Jason, then me. "Did something happen?"

"Fuck. Ian, stay out of my head."

"You're quietly freaking out and drinking way more than you've ever needed. It's very alarming, Mason."

Dorothea offered the answer I wasn't willing to give them. "A nice lady came over and rattled the door. I was scared, so I woke Mason up so she could talk because I didn't know she was a nice lady. Mason sparkles. That's why I can wake her up. But I couldn't wake you up because you don't sparkle. Mommy and Daddy sparkle. Mason is like Mommy and Daddy. So that's why I can wake her up while she's sleeping."

We all stared at her, and Dorothea giggled.

"Nope, that's it. This is all too weird. I need samples. I need to understand what's going on." Jason stood up and waved his hands as if the samples would suddenly appear from thin air.

"I'm good, but you'll have to ask her if she wants to share."

Dorothea perked up. "Share what?"

Jason came over to her. "I have a stick with a cotton swab on the end. It scrapes the inside of your cheek and takes some cells. Then I put them in a machine and look at them."

"Can I see the machine?"

"Sure." Jason held out his hand. Dorothea took it, and we all made the short trek to Jason's lab.

I whispered to Ian as we walked. "He's great with kids. You should have your family around you, Ian. They want to be part of your life if you'll let them."

"I couldn't leave like you did, and I stopped being able to watch my family grow old and die, generation after generation. Some of them know I'm here, but they are all echoes of people I knew. I see faces I remember, but they aren't the people I loved."

"Ian, you're being too hard on yourself."

"I'm old, Mason. Maybe I have a few hundred more years in me, but I don't want to spend it watching those I care about die over and over again."

"So travel, go see places with Jason. Take some time. No one said you couldn't take care of your family while you're doing things. The world is different now. You can literally do both. You don't have to be here all the time."

Ian chewed on his lip and shook his head. He could be stubborn, but not this stubborn. I wonder if he'd take it more seriously if the suggestion came from Jason instead.

Once we arrived at the outbuilding that was now Jason's lab, we waited for Jason to unlock the door with his thumbprint. The outside wasn't much to talk about, but inside was state-of-the art.

Jason picked up Dorothea and plopped her on a chair next to his workstation while he set up sample kits.

"You have the latest blood chem machine." I swooned over it. The machine I had in my clinic was at least thirty years old and secondhand.

"Jealous?" Jason caught me caressing the coveted machine, and I snatched my hand back. I turned to him and smiled.

"Professionally, yes. I'd give a fang for half this equipment."

"The Earlham Coven is very well funded because of the researchers it cultivates, and the university chips in, especially for the biomedical sciences. Or biomagical. I've had access to advanced equipment for a while because of that, and write-ups I make for the manufacturers."

"Now that's seriously hot." Jason laughed. "Would you be interested in a washed-up doctor for a partner?" I offered as I sauntered to where Jason and Dorothea were sitting.

Ian cleared his throat. His possessiveness came through clearly in our bond, which made me turn to look at him. "Oh, so you can be jealous."

"I never said I couldn't." Though his eyes were on me, he moved closer to Jason. It wasn't about my making a pass at Jason. He wanted me to see them together, so I could picture the three of us together. There was a plea in his gaze. When Jason looked up with a smile and covered the hand Ian placed on his shoulder, I knew they had discussed it. Probably before they had sex with me. What I meant as a jest, they actually wanted. It was flattering and confusing. They deserved better than me. They had to know I wasn't the type to stay.

Dorothea rescued me from my internal drama. "Mason, you go first."

"Okay." I looked at Dorothea and offered her my hand. She took it. "Ready, Doc!"

Jason grinned as he pulled out three swabs. "Open." He gestured toward my mouth. I did as asked while glancing at

Dorothea. It took longer for Jason to arrange and label the samples than it did to take them.

"Me next!" Dorothea was getting into this. Maybe we had a budding scientist on our hands. Jason repeated the procedure with her and she watched as he labeled Dorothea's samples "Dainty C." while he labeled mine "Mama L." It was a clever way to code and age the samples, though I hadn't been a Lindquist in quite some time.

Jason took one of Dorothea's swabs and prepped a wet mount slide, then put it under a microscope with a monitor attached. Even that seemed a luxury. My eyes weren't bad, but staring down into a microscope for evidence of bacterial infections was always a pain in the ass.

"These are your cells." Jason pointed out different parts of the cells on the screen to Dorothea while Ian and I watched. He really was amazing with kids. "Do you want to see more?" Dorothea nodded enthusiastically.

"I need a different kind of sample to do that. Do you want me to show you?" Jason got another nod. He turned to pull out a butterfly needle kit with five vials. "Should we make Mason go first?" Another nod. I chuckled and sighed like I was being put out when I offered my arm. Ian remained a silent shadow throughout the entire process.

With five vials of my blood and then Dorothea's, Jason seemed like he was set. When I offered my hand this time so we could leave Jason to work, Dorothea didn't take it. "I want to see how it works." The young girl's plea melted my heart, and Jason's too, apparently, because he nodded.

"It's all right; she can stay with me. It will give you two a chance to talk." Jason's subtle smile indicated he knew it could be more than talking.

"Call up to the house if you need anything, or to let us know you're headed back." Ian understood Jason's meaning. Ian turned to Dorothea. "Do you need anything? Snacks or water?"

"I brought snacks!" Dorothea pulled an apple out of one pocket of the overalls she wore, then a banana out of another.

"The kid's a magician." Jason chuckled. "We have water. Go Ian. We'll be fine." Ian nodded, then leaned over to give Jason a kiss. Ian was stalling. I couldn't blame him. We were going to argue or fuck, and it was a toss-up as to which one. Knowing us, it would likely be both.

PHYSICS

As we walked back to the house, I thought about what they were offering. I knew what he and Jason wanted, and it scared me. Not because I didn't want it, but because I could see myself having a life with them. In only a few days, we had settled into an easiness between each other, where our glances and thoughts effortlessly translated.

Ian was the most stalwart person I'd ever met. After all these years, he'd remained here, like a beacon in the dark. I didn't deserve either of them. I'd broken Ian's heart, and now Jason was willing to risk his, too. I was afraid I wouldn't live up to their expectations, but even more afraid I wouldn't live up to mine.

I turned to face him after he locked the door and turned toward me.

"Ian. . .I'm—" He cut me off.

"Shhh, no apologizes. I knew your spirit when I met you, Mason." He took a step toward me. "My adventurous, blunt, caring lover. I knew I couldn't tame you. I wouldn't ever want to. But I panicked when you wanted to leave."

I looked up as he stepped close enough so that my chin touched his chest. "You almost tamed me. I was happy here until I needed to be more."

"Could you be happy here again?"

"I want to say yes."

"Then say yes."

"It's not that simple."

"It could be."

"Until it's not."

"Then say yes for now. Say yes until you can't say it because it would be a lie. Say yes to the possibility of being happy with Jason and me."

"What about my coven?"

"We'll figure it out."

"What about Jason?"

"We've already figured it out." Ian smirked and wrapped his arms around me. "Are there any more excuses buried in that brain of yours?"

Nothing came to mind. I shook my head, but dropped my gaze, then looked back up at Ian. It would be nothing to close the distance between our lips to stop us from talking. For once, I didn't choose the easy path.

"I never stopped loving you." Through our bond, I imagined Ian knew as much, but it was important for me to say the words. "My anger kept me away for so long that when I felt it less, I didn't know how to come back."

He sighed. "No matter how far you go, for how long, you'll have a place here and in my heart." His gaze caught mine. "Say yes, Mason."

Ian the knight, ever vigilant, ever waiting, rescuing vampires in distress. I returned and rewarded his patience with not only with my mind and heart, but my body as well. The three of us would be tied together if I agreed to this.

"Yes."

All the emotions we had fell out of their neat boxes and fornicated in our minds. He glanced at my mouth, and I gave him the slightest nod. His lips caught mine as passion tried to drown us. He scooped me up. I wrapped my legs around his waist as we continued kissing. Ian's hands fondled my ass as we moved. I didn't know where we'd end up, but I hadn't expected it to be my room until he put me down on my bed and I felt the quilt under my hands.

Once we were naked, time stretched around us. Ian kissed every centimeter of me, from my lips to my pussy. He buried his nose in my damp curls while I played with my nipples. His tongue made lazy strokes like I was an ice cream cone in his favorite flavor.

As my senses narrowed to what Ian was doing between my legs, my thoughts spun a fantasy of the three of us living together. The sex would be amazing; there was no doubt about that. I could open a new clinic and stay with Ian's coterie, or maybe find a job with the Earlham Coven, like Jason, and do medical research. Go back to uni to learn more, or travel with Ian and Jason.

When I first met Ian, vampires traveled by boats in holds that you hoped wouldn't be opened to sunlight while you slept. Cautious people traveled in sealed coffins that put them into a stasis until someone opened them again. When planes became more prevalent, traveling as cargo was faster, but still dangerous and boring as hell. These days, regular travel by mass transit was pretty effective. Traveling across the ocean was done mostly by plane as a passenger in a light-proof sleeping bag. You could enjoy the flight while you were awake, and they even had a timer to make sure you weren't caught out by the sun. If you landed during daylight hours, they stored you in a specialized lightproof mini-hotel room until you woke. Or in a morgue if you flew economy. If you knew fae, they could transport you in a box or coffin through their tunnels, but those only worked over land masses, not vast oceans.

My travel fantasies were interrupted as Ian's fingers slipped into my vagina, eliciting a moan from me and a satisfied sound from him. I played with Ian's hair as he continued to lavish his devotion around my labia and clit.

"Watching you and Jason together does things for me," I said. Ian paused, then continued playing with a questioning hum. "I'd love to fuck you while he fucks me, or the other way around." He chuckled and lifted his head while his fingers continued to tease, which made me bear down on them, creating a delicious resistance.

"The last time we did that, we flattened a shower tent."

It was my turn to laugh. "That was magical overload. I doubt we'd have the same result this time unless Jason's more than a vampire."

Ian kissed and teased. "I don't think so, but he is rather talented."

"So I've seen." I smiled down at Ian. "But I wasn't talking about you penetrating me."

Ian's gaze locked with mine for a moment. "Fuck, you're so bloody beautiful. What did I do to deserve you?"

"You waited for me. Though that makes me a shit person. I shouldn't have stayed away so long."

His fingers slipped out of me. As I watched, he licked them, then put the tip of one against my anus. I squirmed as he slowly pushed the digit into my ass. "I want to mark you. Shove every bit of myself into every opening that will take it, then watch Jason do the same. I want us to claim you, heart, body, and soul, so no matter how far you wander from us, or whoever else you fuck, you'll know you're ours and we're yours until the end of our days."

Tears pricked my eyes as the smell of apples wafted between us. I didn't know what to say. I gasped on a quiet sob. Ian continued.

"Maybe after that, after we claim each other, and mark each other inside and out, you'll know that you can come home and we'll be here."

Not only Ian, but Jason too. Because we'd all shared blood. The bond Ian and I had strengthened, and the one with Jason was growing. Jason's admiration and affection came through. It wasn't only for Dorothea and Ian, but for me as well. He had to know what we were doing. If he were bonded to Ian the same way I was, then Ian would feel the same from Jason.

Maybe this little dream of ours was doomed, but even so, it was a dream worth living while we had it. My answer to Ian was to pull him up my body and fiercely kiss him. He nudged between my legs and sank himself into my pussy with practiced ease.

The methodical slowness drove me to the edge; my vision blurred, and my frustrations mounted. I was wound too tight, but that delicate edge was where Ian wanted me. He kept me there with each push, burying himself deep, then lifting his hips and ever so slowly dragging himself back out, only to slowly push in again, or slam into me to elicit moans and grunts from my throat.

"Turn over," Ian whispered. I complied, desperate for everything he wanted to give me.

I heard a packet open, then cool liquid dripped onto my ass. "When did you grab lube?"

"Pocketed some this evening on a bit of wishful thinking. I can't get enough of him." Ian pushed back into my cunt as his finger lubed up my asshole.

"He's fucking gorgeous and talented in all kinds of ways. Fuck Ian, you two are so fucking beautiful, it hurts." I moaned as Ian pushed his finger in up to his knuckle while he pushed as deep as he could go into my pussy.

"Fuck, I love your voice. The things you say." Ian continued thrusting and playing with my other hole. "Do you seriously think we haven't fucked in his lab?"

"How could you not?" Ian's hand came down on my ass as the fingers from his other one worked further inside. All this talk of Jason and Ian amped the edge I was riding up to epic proportions. I wanted another round between the three of us as soon as we could manage it.

As Ian leaned over me, he teased, letting me feel the tiniest prick of his fangs across my shoulders. It was a distraction from the momentary empty feeling I had until he repositioned and slowly pushed his dick into my ass. If I had needed to breathe, I might not have been able as Ian's cock was so fucking perfect, and filling, that I wanted badly to come right then. However, he had other plans.

Ian wrapped his arms around my waist, then picked me up. We changed positions, and my ass sank even further onto his cock as he sat on the bed and I on him, facing the door. It gave me thoughts of Jason walking in and joining us, but those would have to wait until Dorothea fell asleep. We would need to make it up to Jason later for missing out.

I leaned back and caressed Ian's face. The position had me open, wet, and needy. "Ian, fuck, please."

"Yes, my love, not much longer. I promise."

I moved, raising my hips and slowly dropping down to relieve all the pressure. I nearly wept again for everything I felt. Ian reached between my legs and rubbed my overstimulated clit as I thrust myself onto his cock repeatedly. "Ian, please fucking bite me, please."

"Do you want me?"

"Of course I want you." Even without his dick in my ass, I would have answered the same.

"And Jason, too?"

"Yes, absolutely. I want you both, Ian. Jason is beautiful, brilliant, and I would be as lucky as you to be his partner. I want you both so badly I can't think of anything else." I hadn't stopped fucking myself on Ian's cock, but Ian's fingers made slower and slower circles around my clit. It was maddening.

"Would you have our children?"

I didn't even hesitate. "Yes. Yes!" I panted.

When Ian bit me, I screamed until I didn't have any air, then soundlessly screamed some more. His cock pulsed in my ass as I shook, and he held me until we both finished. We flopped like rag dolls back onto the bed. I laid on his chest staring up at the ceiling as his cock softened and slipped from me. Time and reality reasserted themselves.

"Would you have our children?" I repeated with a questioning tone and a soft laugh. "It's been two days, Ian. I'm as much about the fantasy as the next woman, but. . ."

Ian held me. "It was more about having you admit the possibility. I know you fancy Jason. He feels the same. Besides, it might be a reality now because of Dorothea, right? Because of what she discovered about you. If that is something you'd want. If it happened."

I carefully slipped off him onto the bed and rolled over so I could see his face. "If by some long-shot miracle it happened, I'd want it."

"Even if it kept you here?"

I nodded. "Even then." He kissed me gently, urgently, as if to contain the words between us. "I'm scared, but I want this. I have my doubts, but I can't deny what I feel for both of you."

Ian kissed me again, then kissed my forehead. "I'll take it. I'm not asking for perfect. I only want you to be happy, and I learned a long time ago that standing in the way of your happiness was one of the gravest mistakes I ever made."

"I might be a stray cat, but out of everyone I've ever known, I've always trusted you. You've never given me a reason to believe otherwise." I snuggled into him. "Trust is even more important than love in the world we inhabit. I'm happy I have both with you."

"Are we getting more sappy in our old age?" Ian looked at me with a smirk on his face.

"If that's the case, I'll embrace it wholeheartedly."

A few hours later, Jason rang the house intercom to let us know that he and Dorothea were returning for lunch. Ian made grilled cheese and tomato soup. Jason returned to his lab while Ian and I entertained Dorothea with different coloring books, stories, and games until it neared dawn.

When Ian locked his bedroom for the night, we were all piled in the bed, me with Dorothea in my arms, Jason on one side of me, and Ian on the other side of Dorothea. We were as safe as any of us could be as the dawn stole us for the day. When the evening returned, Dorothea woke us all with kisses on our faces.

I'd put away the idea of ever having a family or children when I became a vampire. Now I suddenly had both, and I would do anything to protect them.

ETHICAL DILEMMA

A few weeks turned into a few months, and no one came look-ing for me or Dorothea. I hadn't heard from Hilda, and I was reluctant to follow up with her in case her poking around raised suspicion.

Crossroads Coven was known for vampires that were tran-sient. It hurt somewhat that no one had contacted me about my absence. Or they were biding their time. Covens were un-predictable like that. Maybe they got someone else to run my clinic. They owned the building after all. When I signed up with them, I knew I was a cog in their machine, but it stung to have that particular reality front and center.

While my solitary days seemed to fade into the past, joy and predictability replaced them. Our little family developed a routine. Jason continued to work on my unique biological mystery, and we all took a hand in teaching Dorothea whatever we knew.

She was naturally drawn to math and science, which delight-ed Jason and me immensely. Ian, as much as he tried to teach her English, French, and World History, was less successful. Dorothea grew bored with it unless the stories were fantastical, or about mages or vampires.

Having relationships around a child's schedule proved inter-esting. Dorothea and I slept in my old room most days. Sometimes she would wake me during the day if she had a bad dream, but often I'd wake with her snuggled into my chest. It was on those evenings that what Ian said came back to me.

Dhampirs lived longer than humans, but only half as long as vampires. Even so, that was still a long time. If that even explained what I was to begin with. I was alive during the day and dead at night—or rather, vampire-dead. Whether it was a recent development, something Dorothea did to me, or something she had discovered, Jason was still figuring it out.

I had little hope that any of my reproductive organs were still working after all this time, but I wouldn't crush Ian's spirit. Vampires could have children with living hosts, which was how dhampirs were created. Jason was indifferent to the idea, but not opposed to it. Frankly, Jason thought my unique biology wouldn't allow it. Based on the evidence so far, I tended to agree, though Ian held out hope. The idea of our impossible child encouraged Ian to visit with his family members that lived nearby. Jason and I both thought this was a positive thing. Ian became less melancholy and more like the man I remembered.

When Jason asked me to come to his lab, at first I thought it was for one-on-one time, which was nice, but it turned into something else as I pressed into his back and gave him a kiss on the cheek.

"Hi, sweetie. How's work going?"

He turned to give me a proper kiss, and I wrapped my arms around his broad shoulders as his wrapped around my waist. "Pretty good, actually. You wanna see?" I nodded. When he started his computer playback, a pang of disappointment shot through me. Jason smirked, our bond conveying my emotions. "Patience, love. Though I like it when you're in the mood."

"I know you do." I kissed him and then sighed. "Okay, show me what you have."

Jason started the holo, and it showed cells floating in a medium. "These are yours. I can now confirm you are not a dhampir, or well, not exactly. If your healing abilities would have been any less, you would have died from the virus."

He waved his hand, and the images moved forward. A bright light shone, and the cells ate themselves from the inside out. "That's what happens if your cells are exposed to a burst of UV light—at night." Jason's face was excited, which meant he had made a serious breakthrough. "Since Dorothea can wake you up. I set up a timed experiment with your cells during the day." He waved his hand again. The images moved forward. The clock kept count, and when the cells were exposed to ambient light at sunrise, we watched as they changed.

Vampires have more deoxygenated blood because we don't have to breathe as much. Blood from vampires usually looked purple if kept in a sealed vial. It's more important that we have blood and water to keep things moving. The cells—my cells—looked purple then turned bright red, almost pink, as if they were suddenly absorbing nutrients like a human's would.

"Did you see it?" Jason asked in a whisper. I nodded. We kept watching.

The UV light passed over the cells this time, and nothing happened at first. Then they glowed softly. "My healing ability."

Jason grinned. "Yes. Not as powerful outside of your body, but while the cells are still alive, they are still doing what your magic programmed them to do, which is to protect you from foreign bodies."

"If that's the case, then why do I still pass out?"

Jason shrugged. "Sunflowers track the sun. Magic skips generations. Dragon scales are impervious. It's just who you are. If you had infected yourself during the day somehow, your body would either have destroyed the virus or killed you trying to kill it off. Maybe your powers are weaker at night, and just maybe the virus exploited that."

"But when I was going through my transition, I spent my last day in the sun."

"How long was it between the time you were infected and your last walk in the sun?"

"Four days, based on what Ian told me."

"Were you inside the whole time?" I nodded. "It rarely takes that long for someone to transition. I would bet your ability was fighting it off. It's possible that when you took your walk outside during the day, instead of destroying the virus, it forced it to become dormant. Which made it more like a cancer than a virus."

"Shit, so you're telling me that my ability mutated the virus?"

"It's happened before, but usually we've seen deformities or people gaining abilities they didn't have previously during the transition process. Once the transition period is over, the virus does its thing to maintain a body far beyond its initial capabilities. I think that's why it's extremely hard for vampires to become infected with other bacteria or viruses, and why some people don't survive being infected." Jason smiled at me. "Somehow, your healing ability made the virus mutate or adapt to sunlight. It's very possible you're the first vampire that can walk during the day without it killing off the virus, and therefore the host."

I was dubious. "When Dorothea wakes me, I feel okay, but after the sun goes down, it's like I've fought off a cold or the flu. My whole body aches."

"Do you eat during the day?" I'd never thought about eating during the day. I didn't think it was all that important, and I was never awake long enough to eat. "Next time you're up, eat something. See if that makes a difference. Start with soup or juice."

"You think I could train myself to be human again during the day?"

"I think it's possible. I also think your particular mutation could provide a vaccine for vampirism." Jason looked over his notes and paused the holo playback.

The information was a shock at first because people had tried, but there was no known cure, magical or otherwise. "You're chasing ghosts. Actually, ghosts are more tangible than a vaccine for vampirism."

Jason laughed. "Maybe. But I think it's there. Something in the way your biochemistry works literally flips a switch between day and night." He shrugged.

"What if it's not a vaccine but something that makes vampires day walkers?" This entire line of inquiry made me nervous. If this information got out, it could either destroy a whole species or mutate a dangerous apex predator into a new one. Not to mention, it put me at risk of being hunted by every coven on the planet.

"Predators have limitations for a reason. It keeps them in check. The sun keeps us in check. Besides, I wouldn't even know I could be awake during the day if it weren't for Dorothea. If you tell the Earlham Coven about this, they'll want to know how you discovered it and why. Can you keep those details out of it?"

"Well, not really. Science means the details are important," Jason said.

I gave him a long look. But he wasn't looking at me; he was looking at his holo displays and the information coalescing there. "Would you really put Dorothea and me in danger to make an advancement?"

"No, of course not, but if this is a key to a vaccine, just think, Mason. People can really choose whether or not to become vampires. Our human partners wouldn't have to worry about being infected. If they had had this during the war, you might not have transitioned. People wouldn't have died needlessly from an infection that could have been prevented."

He finally looked at me when I put my hand on his shoulder. "I get it. But vampires aren't the flu or HIV. It's a species—granted it's one mutated from a virus, but still. It could wipe vampires off the planet, or take away their one limiting factor. There's too much risk."

After a long moment, Jason sighed. "Yeah. It's not worth it, especially not right now." He smiled. "Besides, I'm mostly speculating based on one experiment. There's no point in making wild guesses. I'd need more data to test my hypothesis."

"Please promise me you'll keep your research here and not share it with the coven."

He nodded. "I promise I won't share." The grin on his face grew three times bigger. "Now," he drew me into his arms, "how about we get back to the original topic?"

I'd just crawled into Jason's lap with my hand over his cock when the house intercom buzzed. "Sorry to interrupt, but your phone is ringing, Mason." Ian's voice sounded amused.

I gave Jason multiple kisses, then hopped off his lap. "You and I aren't done yet, so don't wander too far." Jason propped his elbow on a nearby workbench and smirked.

"Don't make me wait too long, or I'll come find you," he said. I had no doubt he would do exactly that.

CONTACT

The handoff was less than graceful as I swept into the kitchen and Ian tossed my phone to me. He was in the midst of making spaghetti, which was Dorothea's favorite. The three adults ate the sauce, and sometimes the noodles if they were mushy enough. It might make a good test meal if Dorothea woke me during the day again.

I found a quiet spot in the living room and took a seat.

"Hey Hilda, I didn't expect to hear from you."

She laughed, though there was a slight lisp, as if she were missing teeth. She was trying hard to cover it, which meant something serious had happened. "It took much longer than I thought. The Lafayette's are somewhat aggressive. Finding the right connection took time."

It was code, and it meant she was fucked, and so was I. Whatever happened since I had talked to her last, it wasn't good. They were using her to get to me. So either they knew who I had, or something even worse was going on.

"Well, safety first, like you always say. But I've been a bad girl recently. I'm sorry if that made it harder for you to find what I needed."

"Actually, it made it easier. Your reputation precedes you. You're not the little girl everyone thought you were." Hilda sighed as if she were tired. "If you think you'll find what you need, I have a place you can meet your contact."

"Should I come alone?"

"They'll be disappointed if you do. They like parties. You should bring your friend, the short one."

Which meant I absolutely should not bring Dorothea unless I wanted her to end up in the same situation I'd likely walk into. "Well, I like a party as much as he does, so I'll try not to disappoint."

"See that you don't." She gave me the information. It was downtown London, which meant they tracked me that far. "Oh, and Mason," she said.

"Yes?"

"Don't darken my door with this bullshit again. Ta love."

"Ciao."

I turned off the phone, removed the comms crystal, then broke the thing into as many bits as I could. I ran to the bathroom to dump it all in the sink and turned the water on the exposed insides. One advantage of biodegradable tech—water in the right places slagged a device fairly quickly. Ian appeared at the doorway. "Everything alright?"

The shrug rolled off my shoulders. Ian frowned. "I have a contact I'm meeting to see if they can put me in touch with Dorothea's parents."

Ian nodded. "And you had to destroy your phone?"

"Precaution. Mages are pretty sophisticated with technology these days." Based on what Hilda told me, who knows if they were tracing the call. Whoever she found had definitely roughed her up enough that she was pissed off. I trusted her to deal with the situation. Hilda was made of stern stuff. Our friendship was a casualty that I couldn't worry about while Ian was looking to me for answers.

Ian looked more frustrated by the minute. "Maybe one of us should go with you."

"No. You and Jason should stay here with Dorothea until I know everything is safe."

"Mason." Ian knew something was wrong. I walked past him into the hall, then headed to the kitchen. Jason was scooping sauce into a bowl for himself. Dorothea was already slurping noodles. "We should talk about this."

"There's nothing to talk about. I'll see what I can find out, and we'll go from there." I wasn't about to risk all of us, and I was the most expendable.

Ian grabbed my arm. His gaze pleaded with me. It reminded me of the first night I went back into the field after I'd transitioned. He was scared. That night, the vampires advancing on the trenches suddenly stopped and screamed in terror. It was like strings had been cut. A lot of strings, all at once. When ordnance stopped flying, we realized something had changed. Vampires from the enemy either dropped to the ground and cried or ran away. Zombies dropped in piles around them.

We directed or dragged the newly freed vamps to shelter where we could find it. Basements that were still intact, buildings with interior walls and no windows. I'd stayed with a group, seeing to our wounded before we all died for the day. The bond between Ian and me was a living thing. I tried to reassure him I was safe, but scared. Ian did everything short of using his mental abilities to force me back to camp. Thankfully, my self-preservation and fear of sunlight stopped him. The next night we were too busy with wounded to talk about it.

The same feeling came through our bond now. Ian's distress threatened to choke me. It wasn't until Jason intervened that Ian gained control of himself and shut down.

"Love, you're hurting her without permission, and we have an audience." Jason's voice was a gentle balm on the situation. Ian gasped and let go of my arm. "Good, now come have some of the sauce you made. I put the Parmesan you like on it." Ian took a slow breath, then walked away, likely to his study. I looked at Jason, and he nodded. "It'll be fine. He knows he's overreacting."

"You've seen this before?"

"Sure, every time I go to Earlham for a week, he acts like I'm never coming home again."

It was my turn to sigh. "I'd hoped it would have subsided after all this time."

"How do you mean?"

"He lost someone in the war, and he's never quite gotten over it."

"Oh, that makes sense." Jason glanced at me. "To be honest, I thought it was you who made him react that way."

"I certainly didn't help matters." I shrugged. "But he knew I wasn't a bird that could be kept in a cage, no matter how lavish."

Jason rubbed my shoulder. "Come have lunch with us. He'll come out later when he's done sulking." I followed Jason to the kitchen island and pulled up a chair. I took a bowl and slurped up the sauce. For someone who didn't eat all that often, Ian knew how to make a decent tomato sauce. The Parmesan was a nice touch.

When Ian still hadn't returned after we had finished lunch, I went to his study and found him staring at ledgers. I closed the door behind me and waited. He finally set his pen down as I approached his chair. "You know I'm right."

"That doesn't make it any easier." He looked up at me, and I opened my arms. He reached for me and buried his head in my stomach. "Things were going well. We're happy. Why does that have to change?"

"Nothing lasts forever, Ian." I brushed my hands through his hair and caressed his head. "Not even us. We only last longer than most."

"Will you come home?"

I tried to calm the doubts in my mind, because they had nothing to do with us. "Wherever you and Jason are is home for me, no matter how far I go. You know that. We've said as much. You have to trust that I'll do everything I can to come home."

We wanted to protect Dorothea above all. However, the one person we forgot to mention anything to about my impending trip was the one person we were trying to protect. It was during the day, and we were in our room when Dorothea discovered I was leaving. She was sitting on my chest when she woke me.

"Mason, you can't leave. No one wants you to go."

It took me a minute to register her words. I gently pushed her off me and sat up so I could look her in the eyes. "I have to, so I can find out how to contact your parents."

She cried. I wrapped my arm around her shoulders and held her tight. "Kiddo, things change all the time. You've been so brave. Your parents have to be worried sick about you."

"But what if they hurt you? What if they make you all zombified, and we can't find you? Ian and Jason will be sad. I'll be sad." It was definitely a risk, given how I'd found her. Whoever had done that to her, I hoped with all my soul it wasn't her parents or family. If it were, they would certainly never see her again. I'd make sure of it.

"Part of growing up is dealing with the sad. People disappoint each other all the time." I kissed her forehead. "I'm going to try very hard not to disappoint everybody, but sometimes it happens and there's nothing I can do about it."

She cried until she passed out, which left me awake. Apparently, Dorothea could wake me up and put me back to sleep, but if she didn't put me to sleep, I stayed awake. That was a new development. I didn't know if it would help Jason or not, but I looked forward to telling him when he woke.

I tried to go back to sleep myself, but no amount of lying in bed worked. I remembered Jason's comment about eating something during the day, so I tucked Dorothea in and went to the kitchen for leftovers.

The spaghetti was magnificent. When I had eaten something during the night, it wasn't as if it was bad; it was just dull, uninteresting, not what I wanted. Of course, that was mostly bread and apples, not something with this much flavor and spice.

Once I devoured a whole bowl, I went to the blood fridge and pulled out a liter. There was a faint smell of apples, but nothing like I was normally used to. When I tasted it, the metallic flavor was more prevalent than apples, though it was still there. I slowly sipped the pint throughout the rest of the afternoon, then went back for pastries. When the sun dropped below the horizon, my stomach hurt, but I wasn't hungry.

Later, I spent most of the night in the bathroom. Jason took care of me, mostly feeling guilty about having me experiment with food. He handed me a bottle of electrolytes. I drank it and frowned.

"I know. It tastes weird, but it should help. We should try to get another liter of blood into you after your guts stop."

"I've eaten pastries before, so maybe it was the spicy sauce. Or the noodles? Fuck, I don't know. I haven't felt like this since I transitioned."

"That makes sense. Since Dorothea left you awake, you're feeling the effects of a transition. It probably happened every day at dusk. This is probably the first time you have been awake to feel it. I wouldn't have believed it if I hadn't seen the results myself," Jason said as he stayed near the bathroom door.

"Well, I much prefer the idea of remaining a vampire instead of something constantly mucking with my insides."

"I don't know, Mason. You have to admit, it's pretty interesting. You could, in theory, stay awake through the day and maybe even walk around in the sun."

"Not interested. I've been part of the nightlife for a while. I rather like it."

"You should try to understand it. It's part of you." Jason paused for a moment. "And it might help with whatever you're walking into." Another pause. "When do you leave?"

"Tomorrow night."

LONDON TOWN

I took the train in from Birmingham and left London Central to head toward Hyde Park. It was famous because royalty lived around it, along with ambassadors and diplomats. When I'd first arrived so very long ago, I went straight to a pub, found a decent guy, and snogged him right here in this park after three pints. But that was when I'd had a pulse, and a shag had consequences if you weren't ready for it.

Tonight, I was meeting some very pissed off mages, or pissed off vampires. The spot they had designated was fine, and even in the open, but that meant nothing at midnight on a Friday.

Five minutes past midnight, and I was ready to leave. Either they were spooked or something else was up. When something whizzed past my face, I knew they weren't here for a friendly chat. I ran toward the shot, then veered left when I heard yelling and ducked into the tree line. A fence came into view, then another. I climbed them with little thought. Adrenaline and panic ran through me as another projectile flew past my face. Whoever was after me was a horrible shot.

I made a dash for the edge of the park and dove into a nearby pub. A game was on, and only a few people noted my hasty entrance. Everybody resumed watching the holo as I walked up to the bar and ordered a pint, as if that had been the plan all along. With a fresh pint in hand, I sat where I could watch the street to see if anyone might be following me. The pint was for the headache I'd have later from staring at auras in the hope I could spot possible foes before they spotted me. My new phone interrupted my viewing session by vibrating in my pocket.

"What the fuck is going on with you?" Despite the thread of panic in his voice, Ian sounded pretty calm. Neither he nor Jason were shielded from my emotions because of our bond. I've never been good at blocking things out. That was Ian's department. I'd asked him to ward me before I went on this adventure, but he refused for exactly this reason. Our connection was my only failsafe. Before I could answer, Jason's voice, infinitely more calm, tickled my ear.

"Interesting night already, Mason?"

I laughed. "You could say that. Had to give my guests a bit of a slip, but now I'm in a pub with a pint." A glance at the old clock over the bar told me it was nearly two in the morning. If I left now, it would take me the rest of the night to get home. "I'll find some place to hole up, then be back tomorrow night."

"We're not that far away. We could drive down." Jason's offer was a sweet gesture. If things got serious, I wasn't about to lead whoever chased me right to the very people I cared about, so I changed the subject.

"How's the kiddo?"

"She's coloring, though she asked about you. Wants to know when you'll be home."

Jason had his hands full. "Glad you're able to keep her busy." I made kissy noises over the phone. "Tell her I'll be home soon. I owe you."

"You owe me many, and if you get your ass back here in one piece, I'll show you."

The sultry sounds of Jason's voice were an incentive to ditch this fantasy of contacting Dorothea's parents and go home. "I'm looking forward to you showing my ass exactly what you mean."

Jason sighed. "Just be careful, love."

"I will. Give Ian a tranquilizer or something. He's too anxious." The silence over the line told me exactly what they thought about that idea, but I could feel Ian winding himself up. "If he's a wreck, then I'll be one, and that's not a good idea right now."

"I'll see what I can do. No promises."

Ian's soft voice, full of frustration, muttered, "I never should have let the two of you near each other." Amused that he was miserable, I felt nothing but love for him and Jason all the way to my toes.

"Too late. You like it, and we know it." We both worried about him in our own way. He felt seen and protected, which was usually his role. He'd been the one to take care of people for so long, it was hard for him to allow anyone to see to his needs. Jason was the first individual in a very long time Ian had allowed so close to him, and because of that, so had I.

I flipped the phone shut and watched the street. It was another hour before I gave up on reading auras and called it a night so I could find a place to crash.

With the pubs closing, it was easy to lose myself in various small crowds and chat people up for ideas about places to stay. Had a couple of offers from interested parties and thought better of them. I didn't want someone else pulled into this mess.

As the first hint of daylight touched the city, I could sense it waking. Bakeries were opening, and the smell of coffee was in the air. I gravitated toward a shop, intent on grabbing a cup, then booking myself into a hotel for the day. My brain was screaming at me to find some place dark, and I shivered with the anxiety of it. It was still early. I had about thirty minutes—plenty of time.

However, others had different plans. They grabbed me from behind as I passed an alley. The stench of the ogre was intense, which probably wasn't his fault, but more pronounced because I was huffing coffee fumes a moment before. The mage—I guessed by how fancy he was dressed—stepped into my field of vision and whispered a few words, then drew some symbols in the air. It was a variation of a sleep spell, and I didn't have my arms free to counter it.

When I woke, it was in perfect darkness. A gentle hand caressed my face. In French, a soft voice said, "Darling, I need you to wake up and tell me what you know."

Darling? I focused my senses to take in as much as I could in the all-consuming darkness. To my sheer amazement, the woman with me was Tabatha, Dorothea's mother. I remembered her from when Dorothea had controlled me, and I'd seen images of her parents in my head.

"You're dead. Am I seeing dead people now?" I replied in French so the ghost would understand me.

"What gibberish. I'm not any more dead than you are." She shook me as I tried to keep the world from spinning by closing my eyes. "Wake up. I need to know who you are and why they've brought you here."

"Lady Tabatha. You keep shaking me like that, I'm going to puke, and I'm not completely sure what will come up."

"How do you know who I am?"

"Oh, well, that's a bit of a story." I looked around and all I saw were stone walls with no visible door. "Where are we?"

"It's an oubliette." I looked around again, and it certainly fit the definition of one.

"Really?" I asked, curious. Tabatha made an exasperated noise. I kept glancing around to see if I could find anything that might resemble a door.

"Yes, likely on my family's estate somewhere."

"In France?"

She nodded, then said, "Oui."

"I can see you just fine. Can you see at all?"

"No, and how, for the love of all things, can you see? It's pitch black in here."

"I'm a vampire." She backed away from me, which confused me since the Envoy was her consort. "I won't hurt you."

She cried, and for the life of me; I wasn't sure what to do. I reached for the mental link between Ian, Jason, and me, and found nothing. "Hey, hey, do you know if this thing blocks magic?" She whimpered and mumbled. "Speak up, lady."

Tabatha's voice trembled as she spoke. "That's what it's designed to do. Like a magical Faraday cage. You can use magic in it, but it can't get out, and nothing can get in without the right key."

"Fuck." I wouldn't hear the end of this one when—if—I managed to get home.

THE OUBLIETTE

I paced, Tabatha cried, and I still didn't know why. She had her shit together when I got in here, so I wasn't sure where the breakdown came from other than "I'm a vampire."

As the wailing shifted to sniffling, I broached the subject. "You're in a relationship with a dhampir. Why in all the world would you be bothered by another vampire?"

"First off," she said as she sucked in some air, "he's alive, not dead, like you." I wasn't about to dispute that second part, since I wasn't completely sure what my status was at this point. "Second, they put you in here to punish me."

"Oh? Because from where I'm standing, your aural assault with all of your dramatics is doing way more harm to both of us." It was possible my frustration with this whole situation was making me lose my cool.

I wasn't even sure how I'd been taken from London, near dawn, and transported to wherever this was in France to begin with. Maybe they had a lightproof trunk? Or a portal? Could mages do that? Or they had help from the fae and used the tunnels? But if that's the case, then I was in a much worse situation than I really wanted to think about. The social fabric of the covens appeared to be falling apart. Maybe it was already corrupt, and I hadn't noticed until I was caught up in it.

Tabatha gulped and simpered. "When was the last time you fed?"

"I don't know, a day or two ago?"

My mind flashed to the twenty minutes I'd spent fucking Jason in one of the many spare bedrooms before we joined Ian and Dorothea for breakfast. The guys had wanted to make sure I had more than my usual liter before I left for the night. They had even worked out who would be with me and who would watch Dorothea. Ian and Jason had stepped up in ways that I hadn't predicted, but definitely appreciated.

Jason's bite on my inner thigh itched a little as my whole body tightened from the memory. I was licking my lips as I thought about it when Tabatha's voice intruded.

"How long can you go without blood?" She still had a bit of a whimper in her voice. I tried to be nice.

I shrugged, not that she could see it. "A week, I guess. But by that point, everything hurts. Anything tastes good, especially if it's apples."

"Apples?" For a woman who lives with a dhampir, she was amazingly unknowledgeable about vampires.

"Doesn't your partner have some kind of craving?" Maybe dhampirs didn't need blood? That seemed weird, but I'd never met one in person. In the plethora of species you learned about in med school, dhampirs were generally left out because of their rarity.

She shook her head. "I'm not sure what you mean. We only see each other when he's not traveling, or for official functions, and that's not very often."

The current topic wasn't helping much. "Do you know any light spells?"

She straightened. The soft wobble had almost left her voice. "Yes, but I've been using my magic to create food and water. My energy is nearly depleted, and I need sunlight or something that stores energy to recharge."

"Who's they, and can they hear us if we talk?"

"My family and I'm not sure."

Shit, shit, shit. I kicked the wall. I could do a silence spell, but my magic was only as good as how much blood I had in my system. In a few days, I wouldn't be able to do magic either. "Tabatha, we need to talk, and I need to be close enough so I don't waste energy. Are you alright with that?"

"Not really, but what choice do we have?"

I sighed. "You have a choice, but not if we're going to help each other get out of here."

"That's just it. We're not leaving this place until we're dead. No one leaves an oubliette. You're here to make sure I don't leave."

"How's that?"

"Well, either you frenzy and kill me, or I starve and die, and they blame my death on you either way. Then they'll take you out and stake you in the sun, or leave you in here to starve too."

"Your family is absolutely delightful." I paced the distance between the walls again. I figured if she wouldn't let me close, maybe we could talk about things that wouldn't matter to her family. "Why are you down here? Do you know?"

"I'm being punished because of Lennix." Her voice had a bitter tone. "No one was really that forthcoming, and I was too distraught to ask. I had hoped this was a scare tactic using me to bring my consort in line. Your presence here means it's not."

I leaned against the wall and kept looking for an opening. I thought it was night, but the oubliette could be fucking with my senses. I had no idea how long it had taken to transport me, and I wasn't awake when they put me in here. "How did you and the Envoy meet?"

"It was a political alliance between the Dalton coven and the Lafayettes. Everything was normal for the last decade or so. We attended functions, conceived Dorothea, and even settled on an estate in England. I raised our child, and Creighton went here and there to settle disputes between vampires and other species."

It sounded as though there was no love lost in that relationship. "I didn't realize political relationships were still a thing."

"We weren't wed. Creighton courted me, of course. His coven allowed it, and my family thought it was advantageous. But Creighton was only ever considered a consort. It allowed my family to claim our child. He's not my favorite lover. Until recently, he's always provided for Dorothea and me."

"Political arrangements can have consequences." The irony of my statement was not lost on me. My marriage to Ian was an arrangement of sorts. Though Ian never wanted to throw me in a hole and forget me—quite the opposite. I slid down the wall and sat across from Tabatha. Now that I had her talking, she was less upset and more frustrated about everything she'd lost.

"My family acts like he's my only provider. I have others, and I can take care of myself. I don't understand why they didn't remove his status as a consort. They could have barred him from Dorothea and me. It's apparent I don't matter all that much given where they put me. While he was kind to me, Dorothea was the one he'd spent time with between assignments. I never understood it. That's what the younger family members are for, but he only ever let them take care of her if he was away or if we were at functions. It was very odd."

I didn't think it was odd. Creighton sounded like an active parent. It explained why Dorothea responded to disappointing her father so strongly. "Who was normally with Dorothea?"

Given Tabatha was here, and Lennix wasn't, I had a horrible hunch.

"Oh, one of my younger cousins, a lovely girl by the name of Marion. She took care of Dorothea most days. Made sure she attended class, had her meals, accompanied us on play dates so I could talk with the other parents. Dorothea especially liked her, and so did Creighton. He would bring her a present as well when he visited, to reward her for how well she did with Dorothea."

So, Dorothea ended up at the Crossroads Coven chapter house as a way to tie up loose ends and punish her father. Marion was likely the woman who died. Either the Lafayette's had put her under a deep compulsion like they had Dorothea, or the Daltons had, and used Crossroads as their dumping grounds. As far as I knew, Crossroads wasn't associated with the Dalton Coven. The next coven above Crossroads was Garden Delights. They weren't looking for me; they were looking for Creighton. This trap was for him, but when he didn't stick his head in the noose, I looked like a suitable substitute.

"You really think your family will let you rot down here?" And by extension, me as well, since I hadn't figured a way out of this place.

"I'm down here, aren't I? And so are you. They are punishing me to get to Creighton, and he's going to leave me to rot." She huffed.

"What about Dorothea?"

"What about her? Mage families covet children. Not that Dorothea had shown any talent for magic, but that's no matter. She could have learned some things and helped raise other children, even though she was a peculiar child."

It was my turn to be upset. "Peculiar how?"

"She likes bugs and nature. She would bring flotsam into the house all the time that we'd have to throw out." Tabatha laughed, amused at her daughter's curiosity. "You'd think she was building a den of some sort with all the rocks and leaves she'd tuck away."

"Aren't mages attuned to those kinds of things?"

"Maybe some are, but my family practices alchemy, or transfiguration. We only need sunlight to recharge." That explained how she made water and food in this place where there were only stones and dirt.

I tried to keep my calm about her dismal opinion of Dorothea. I don't know what kind of father Creighton was, but clearly, Tabatha hadn't known her very well. While the thought pissed me off, I knew I had to get Tabatha to work with me to get us both out of here.

As much as I didn't want to admit it, Tabatha was right. After some indeterminate time, possibly a week or more, I couldn't really tell, no one had checked to see if either of us was still alive. My weakening system was on the verge of collapse. Tabatha was barely making enough food and water to sustain herself. We were running out of time, and all we had left were desperate measures that neither one of us wanted to take.

WHISPERS IN THE DARK

It could have been the impending doom after so long in the dark. The need to unburden my soul made me open my mouth.

"Your daughter is safe," I whispered. My throat was parched, and drawing in the stale air made it hard to speak. Tabatha wasn't faring any better.

We'd slowly migrated toward each other in the dark. Her shoulder leaned against mine, propped up in a corner because we'd fall over otherwise. I heard Tabatha swallow three times before she answered.

"How do you know my daughter?"

"I rescued her. She was at my coven chapter house. She's safe, I promise." I didn't want to put Ian and Jason in danger with my last breath if someone was listening.

"What happened to Marion? Dorothea was with her when. . . when. . . they took me."

"I don't think she's alive any longer."

Tabatha sighed, which probably would have been a sob if either of us had enough moisture between us. Which brought me to my second-worst idea ever.

"Listen," I said with a raspy voice. "We have to survive. If I infect you, you'll turn. Then we can share blood."

"That's. . . a horrible idea." She tried to move away from me, and I tried to laugh, but choked instead.

"It's the only one I have. No good ideas left." I didn't know how long we had. My senses were fucked, and I couldn't reckon time at all. It made me wonder if I could even infect Tabatha, given I was so weak.

"Is it painful?" she asked in a soft voice.

"Yes, death is always painful."

"No," Tabatha sighed. "Your bite. Is it painful?"

"You've never let Creighton bite you?"

She made a sour face. "No. I'm the mother of his child, not a blood bag."

I cough-laughed. "Wow, you're a prude."

"I am not." The indignant tone made me smile.

"Are we really going to argue about sexual experiences in our current predicament?" If she wanted to, I was fine with that, but I figured there were more important things to talk about. She made a noncommittal noise, which I took as acceptance. "Why are you asking about vampire bites?"

"I'm dying. One of us should survive."

"We both could if you let me infect you."

"Then where would I go? With you? Out there without my magic?"

"Sometimes your magic follows you. It can change a little. But you'd still be here. Doesn't that matter, for Dorothea's sake?"

She moved closer. "I don't want to be a vampire." As much as I could, I looked her in the eyes. I knew she was serious when I saw her face.

"Fine. Then you don't have to be one, and we'll die together."

She shook her head. "No, someone has to survive and let Creighton know what happened."

"He'll figure it out on his own, won't he?" Based on recent events, either he was trying to gather resources to figure out what happened to his family, or he knew he was up against some incredible odds and was in hiding until he could do something. I realized there was a third option: he was already dead and none of this mattered.

"Creighton gave me a way for him to find me." She took a labored breath. "If I were ever in trouble."

"What's that?"

"Micro things in my body. They send signals."

"Nanites?"

She nodded. "Tap my skin in a pattern, and they activate and send a message with my location. He warned me that because of his work, someone might take me or Dorothea. If we were ever in trouble, we could send this signal." She reached over and tapped my arm: three short taps, three long taps, then three short taps. SOS. I laughed, or tried to.

"What?"

"It's Morse code. S-O-S. Help. Why haven't you activated them?"

"The signal would never get out of this damn room."

"Oh, right." Magic, conventional signals, light. It was worse than a tomb. At least those had exits. I closed my eyes for a little while until I was nudged awake.

"You can drink my blood, and when you get out, activate the nanite thingies."

"We don't even know if that will work."

"Do you have another idea?"

"My first one."

"No." Tabatha was adamant. She reminded me of Keegan for a moment, though less fae and more posh. "If you bite me, could you put me to sleep first so I don't feel it?"

"First you're scared of me and now you want me to bite you? Make up your mind."

"You don't understand. I'm supposed to die. They put me down here to die. When that happens, they might come fetch you to make an example of you. Say you killed me so they can legally exact justice."

"If I drink from you now without infecting you, I will kill you." Infecting her would do the same thing, but at least she'd be around to talk about it.

"But you'll have a chance, with the blood, and the nanites. They'll come for you, and that's when you can use the nanites."

"What's supposed to happen when I use them?"

"I don't know." Tabatha took another labored breath. We weren't long for this world. My body was shutting down. Tabatha had stopped being able to make drinking water. Humans didn't last long without water. Vampires could last a little longer without blood and water, but not much.

"We're full of bad ideas." I closed my eyes again, and this time I felt a kick to my leg. It surprised me she had that much strength left.

"Wake up!" I opened my eyes and looked at her, surprised she knew I was falling asleep. "What's your name?"

Oh, now she asked after all this time. If I'd had any energy left, I'd feel insulted. "Mason."

"Mason, I need you to take care of Dorothea and tell Lennix what happened. You need to drink now, before I die."

"Why?" That was a silly question, and I knew the answer somewhere in my fogged brain.

"Because of the Magical Species Pact, if you drink from me after I'm dead, the blood will lose its magic, and I suspect the nanites won't work either. Unless you're a vampire, magical stuff stops working after death." She moved to straddle my lap, and it shocked me awake. I don't know where this sudden burst of energy came from. Maybe it was that last surge of adrenaline for survival before we expired. I saw that enough during the war.

She took my head and brought it to her neck. We smelled of muck, mud, and impending death. It was my turn to whimper. "I don't want to kill you."

"I'm dead already, Mason. We both know it. At least this way you'll have a chance to make it out of here." She hugged me closer, and I lifted my arms to hold her. "Do it now, before I lose what's left of my nerve."

"Fuck. Fuck!" I growled, and she held me tighter. I wrapped my hand around her neck and hummed while I pressed the nerve clusters that would send someone into a dreamless state. Tabatha went slack in my lap, and I screamed my frustration into her sleeping body before I struck.

I've never been so overwhelmed by apples and the hint of clove in my life, and never had the taste been so welcome. I gulped and felt my limbs and body buzz from the nutrients.

When her heartbeat slowed, I pulled away. There was still time to infect her. If we got out of this place together and she saw her daughter again, she could be mad at me all she wanted.

I used my fang to pierce my lip and smeared my blood into the bite. Figured if it worked on me so long ago, it should work on Tabatha. I didn't lick it closed until I was sure I'd coated it. Then I took her head in my hands and kissed her. In her sleepy haze, she swallowed.

Once I had her on the floor, I made more of an assessment. She had slow respiration and a heartbeat. I tried to wake her up by reversing the sleep spell. It didn't work, so I tried again, and her heart stopped.

"No, no, no. Don't you die. Not now." I began compressions, pinched her nose and gulped down enough air to breathe into her lungs. I went on like that for what seemed like ages, alternating between chest compressions and breaths. If she'd been infected, her heart would have slowed and stayed that way. It wouldn't have stopped.

Tabatha never woke up.

It wasn't long after Tabatha died that her family opened the oubliette. My system immediately corrected itself, and I knew it was less than an hour before dawn. Tabatha had been right. I tapped my arm and hoped the nanites worked. No one bothered with a ladder. Someone with advanced telekinesis took hold of my arms and lifted me out of the oubliette. I watched as Tabatha's body followed. They zeroed in on the bite mark.

A man full of vengeful anger and vitriol walked up to me. "As is our right, based on the evidence presented, your life is forfeit, vampire. You will be staked in the sun, and your ashes scattered." Whoever the pompous overgrown jackass was, with his perfect suit and coiffed hair at too-early o'clock, I hated him. I hoped it wasn't someone important to Tabatha or Dorothea. "You murdered my daughter, and by law, I have a right to claim retribution." Given what they had done to us, I shouldn't have been surprised.

"I also have a right to a tribunal." Another man slapped me in response.

"We are your tribunal, vampire. Your kind will understand that the Lafayette family is not to be trifled with."

"Oh, goodie." Another goon punched me. It would have dropped me if not for the invisible force keeping me in place. This was going to be a fun morning.

SUNRISE

The aggrieved father was the telekinetic one. I noticed it when he used more magic to keep me suspended, floating along as the group moved. They left Tabatha's body on the ground like a dirt-stained broken doll.

We stopped in an open field. There was a scorched hollow in the ground with rocks around it about the size of an average biped. Exposing me to the sun wouldn't make me catch fire. My desiccated corpse, however, would be easy tinder. I was certain I was not the first vampire to have been staked in this place.

Tabatha's father threw me down into the dirt. It hurt after being suspended off the ground for so long. The goons that escorted me approached, and I noticed they had stakes in their hands. Staking a vampire wasn't pretty. You had to hold them down, or they had to be unconscious. I wasn't planning on letting them stake me without a fight. Unfortunately, I had no experience combating telekinesis. I tried to get up and found that I was helpless to do anything but writhe on the ground as the men approached me.

"No, no, don't do this! Please! I'm a physician with healing abilities. I tried to save Tabatha, but we were too weak. She was too weak. Her heart gave out. Please!" When the first stake slid into the space below my wrist in my right arm, I screamed. The second one went to the same location on my left arm as the hammers pounded the fancy marble nails into the earth.

As that happened, my boots were removed, and two more marble stakes were driven into the top of each foot. The pain was excruciating, and I found I couldn't take a breath to scream anymore. Blood, smelling of apples, dripped from the holes they created.

Mages surrounded me as I remembered a similar scene from Ian's memories. The hunters during the war made sure the subject died. Usually, they would stake the vampire through the heart to render them unconscious if they weren't already. They considered it a mercy, especially if they were under the compulsion of the other side and had no control of themselves. My captors gave me no such thing. They wanted to watch me suffer as the virus drove me mad with the need for shelter and darkness.

It was then that my bond to Ian and Jason came back. I tried not to panic. Ian wouldn't be awake much longer. Jason cried. Soon, I would be dead. I only hoped that whatever Creighton discovered, it would be worth it, and maybe he'd be able to find his daughter again someday. I knew Ian and Jason would keep her safe, and those were my last thoughts as the sky lit up.

In what anyone considers their last moments, or their last breath, we rarely have the chance to say something profound. At most, given a situation, many say, "Oh Shit" and the end drops on them like curtains at a vaudeville show. As my doom came ever closer to touching the horizon, I relaxed.

My memories of home comforted me. The mountains in all their beauty. The chill spring air, and the winters that tested everyone's will and skill to survive. In my mind, I listened to the sound of a brook rushing with spring water as the runoff from the mountain snow cascaded its way across the landscape. All of this I saw as if I'd seen them yesterday instead of over a century ago.

The continued peace I felt as the sun kissed my skin caused me to realize things were not happening as expected. Astonished sounds came from the mages. I felt warmth and heard my heart beat more rapidly in my chest.

"Why the fuck is she glowing? I've never seen any of them do that."

"What's going on?"

Tabatha's father yelled at me as he backed away slightly. "What fuckery is this? What magic are you using, vampire?"

I turned my head to look at my arms. The exposed skin glowed yellow-white, then slowly shifted to crimson red. I took regular breaths, and the pain I felt from my limbs being pinned like an insect specimen increased tenfold.

Great, instead of desiccating, now I was going to bleed out.

But that didn't happen either. The glow grew stronger. The marble pins crumbled as if they had been attacked like a foreign entity as my flesh it knitted itself back together. I sat up and then pushed myself off the ground. The men surrounding me were afraid and curious. I was like no vampire they'd ever seen. When the sun rose to its full glory, that's when my magic lashed out.

Men screamed as they bled, their blood rushing like streams directly into me. As each fresh wave of blood touched my flesh and was absorbed, my sheer magical power increased. Their mage blood, full of magic itself, fueled me.

Amidst this, I lost Jason's connection. Ian's was gone long before. Maybe Jason would have stories for him tomorrow night. It amused me, and I knew that no matter what happened in this field, I would need to reach out to them when I was able.

My oath as a doctor warred with my desire for revenge. Not only for me but for Tabatha, Marion, and Dorothea as well. Hell, maybe even Creighton. The thought of what they had started by sacrificing their own family lit a rage in me. It wasn't anything to see each beating heart in the chests of my captors, the outline clear within their auras.

They were all in a sorry state, with blood dripping from their eyes, ears, and nostrils. I approached each one, put my hand to their chest and drew out the rest of their blood as I crushed their hearts. I left Tabatha's father for last.

"You left your daughter to die in that hole," I said in French as I approached him. "You and your collaborators tried to destroy a family, and you nearly succeeded. By whatever grace the universe has granted me today, you are found wanting. Rest assured that I will not mourn your death. And when I'm done here, no one will find your bodies. Just as you intended for me." The pompous ass screamed as he died.

Guilt was a distant thing as the energy under my fingertips glowed. It was my healing ability, supercharged by the dormant virus and the mage blood I absorbed. Tabatha's sacrifice had saved me. Her blood was the catalyst. There was no other plausible explanation.

To keep my promise, I moved from body to body and made holes. Tiny holes that replicated across bloodless flesh and bone, dissolving them into so much sludge. That feat brought the power coursing through my veins back to tolerable levels. As the sun rose higher in the sky, my skin glowed with warmth, and my wounds healed completely. I still had too much power.

The warmth began to burn, and I wondered if the magic would burn through me, seeking its own retribution for my actions.

An intruder from the direction of a wooded area was nearly in front of me when I lifted my hands to defend myself. "Do you mean to harm me?" I called out in French. He didn't run but continued to move closer to me with a device in his hand. "I warn you, stay back."

The box in his hand beeped out a signal. I recognized the pattern: three short, three long, three short. S-O-S. The person holding the box shut it off. "What the fuck are you?" he asked in accented English.

That was an extremely good question.

SURPRISE GUEST

"Were you sent for Tabatha?" Magic thrummed in my veins. If this person wanted to start some violence, I wasn't above obliging. I'd had enough of being another's plaything.

"Yes." He eyed me and reached for something at his side.

"Stop. If you're pulling a weapon, I won't hesitate," I said, as I tried to keep my hands up. My clothes were grimy from the oubliette and splattered with blood from the men I killed. Somehow, the violent deaths hadn't neutralized the magic in their blood. It should have; instead, it had turned my healing power into something more. Why wasn't I affected by the Magical Species Pact? It was a problem I'd have to think about another day.

"What happened to Lady Tabatha?" The person testing my patience wore jeans, a black t-shirt, and sensible shoes. His short, light brown hair matched the light tan of his skin. His eyes were interesting. He had central heterochromia. Both eyes had a ring of blue around the iris and then an outer ring of green. When I looked at his aura, it had the duality of a vampire. His accented English led me to believe he was European, though where from I couldn't say. We continued speaking in English.

"Are you a vampire?"

"Dhampir, like yourself."

"Ah, no. I'm not, or at least I wasn't before today." I stood in the morning light, transfixed between the stranger before me and the heat of the sun that warmed my body for the first time in more than a century.

The stranger gave me a quizzical look. "Fine. Not my problem. Where's Lady Tabatha?"

"Dead, unfortunately."

"How do you happen to have her nanites?"

"That's a long story, but there is a short version that hopefully means you'll help me. We were stuck in a hole together. One of us needed to survive to tell Creighton and assure Dorothea's safety."

"Do you know where Thea is?"

I nodded. "Look, we should go. We might not have much time before someone comes looking for Papa Lafayette and his goons." Not that they would find anything except more burns in the grass, but with magic, you never knew what people could discover.

"My vehicle is this way. You'll tell me the entire story on the way while I take us somewhere safe. And you'll wear these." He pulled out two magical restraints. I hadn't worn something like that since the war and my transition. It wasn't an unreasonable precaution, given everything that happened.

"Fine. Lead the way." He tossed me the restraints, and I put them on. My arms were still free, but the power I held muted immediately. He turned back toward the tree line, and I followed until the world tilted. The last thing I remember was face-planting in the dirt.

When I woke up again, it was to the gentle sway of a vehicle hugging curves and winding around mountain roads. The sun was high overhead, much to my surprise.

"Oh good, you're not dead," the driver remarked as he returned to watching the road in front of him. "Are you okay?"

"I haven't the faintest idea. Based on everything I know, I should be dead."

"Well, you're not, so you should start talking."

"Why don't you explain how you were able to find me so quickly?" He glanced at me with a stern look. I was happy to talk, but I wanted information first. Was this man really my rescuer, or was he here to finish what the mages started?

He sighed when I wouldn't say anything. "I've been watching the house and surrounding areas since Tabatha went missing. I followed the group as best I could, expecting that they would lead me to her. Instead, what I found was you."

"If she had survived, you would have found her too. The lady was stubborn." My driver glanced at me with an amused look in his eyes that didn't reach his face.

"You seem to have that trait in common."

I smiled. "We seemed to, yeah."

"How did she die?" I explained our last moments together and wiped my face as guilt filled me. Not only had I taken a life, I'd killed Dorothea's mother and Creighton's partner. It may have been an act of survival, but Creighton would certainly want retribution, whether he was close to Tabatha. She was the mother of his child.

The silence that greeted the end of my story was getting to me. I asked a question and prepared myself for the answer. "What do you think Creighton will do when he finds out?"

The guy shrugged. "I'm not sure. He and Tabatha weren't close, but he cared for her."

Something in the way he said that pricked my senses. There were layers there. "Do you have a name? Mine's Mason."

"Ethan." He didn't turn to look at me when he said it.

"I would say it's nice to meet you, Ethan. Though given the circumstances, I suppose that's not exactly true." He didn't respond, so I kept talking. "You're the first dhampir I've ever met."

"We keep away from vampire politics unless it involves The Envoy. We're valuable to the families and the covens we belong to. Some of us strike out on our own."

"Are you and Creighton related?"

"No. My family agreed to let me be his understudy. Given the current circumstances, they'd rather I returned home."

"Or take his place?"

"As long as Creighton is alive, no one can take his place. That's by their own rules. The fact that one coven has enacted retribution on him and involved a mage family will probably start a war."

Shit. Murdering a large portion of a mage family didn't lead to quieting hostilities. They couldn't touch him without causing an all-out war, and yet the coven involved might have started one. Covens have argued before. Arbitration was usually the preferred way to handle them. Vampires had long memories; they tended to bide their time, planning for the long game instead of the quick win. Something had changed. It's not like I paid all that much attention to vampire politics. Right now, I was way out of my depth.

Ethan and I fell into a comfortable silence as he drove. When we arrived at a small cabin in the mountains, I had the morbid thought of it being my last resting place. I took in the smells and sounds, determined to enjoy the moment. It had been a long time since I'd spent time in the woods. Places like this always reminded me of Ian. Hopefully tonight I could let Ian and Jason know I was safe.

As Ethan led the way, he explained the precautions. "Communications are limited to things that can't be hacked or traced. If you have a bond with someone you don't trust, I suggest leaving the bracelets on to keep you from reaching for it."

"My bonds are trustworthy. They'll be rather distraught when they wake up. I'm not sure how much I'll be able to communicate, depending on where we're at." The closer you were, the easier it was to communicate.

Ethan ignored my subtle prod for our location. "You'll have to make do. Mages can track all kinds of things, and you just lit up half a family. The only better trackers on this planet are dragons, so you'd better hope the Lafayettes don't have ties to any or we are truly fucked."

"Tabatha never mentioned dragons. Would Creighton know?"

"Can't contact him until later."

He escorted me into the cabin after he disabled the spells and wards around the place. The cabin was a studio affair. The bed was in the back left corner of the room with a nightstand and headboards made of wood grown from the floor.

In the back right corner was a small kitchenette, which contained an island counter, two chairs, a small cooling unit, and a hot plate. There was one cabinet on the wall that likely contained more goods or cutlery and dishes. A small sink below that completed the kitchen.

A magical fire stove occupied the front corner across from the kitchen space. Once lit, it wouldn't go out. You only needed some kind of tinder or magic. Near that was a loveseat and a plush rug.

To the left of the front door, under the only window, stood a claw-foot tub. A cabinet hung above the end of the tub, and under it were water temp fixtures. There was a curtain frame that started on one side of the window and looped around the whole tub until it met the right wall, blocking the window and the rest of the room if necessary.

The cabin, which was a mixture of composites and grown materials, like the bed frame. The care and design made me wonder if Ethan had contracted ents to construct it. If this were to be my final resting place, I'd have to admit, it was pretty nice. Much better than a field or an oubliette.

Ethan started a fire, lit candles, and replaced the ward around the cabin. "If you'd like to clean up, there are spare clothes along with towels in the cupboard next to the tub."

"This is much more posh than I thought a safe house could be."

"Why do you say that?"

"I figured we'd be in a shack somewhere with barely anything, waiting for whatever happened next. This place is stocked and rather lavish. It's obvious you've been here before." It was a private hideaway if I ever saw one. Ethan's familiarity with it told me he likely met someone here from time to time.

Ethan stared at me for a moment. "You're a corvid, aren't you?"

I nodded. "Do dhampirs have classifications like vampires?"

"Sometimes. Regardless of whatever abilities we have, they tend to manifest to a lesser degree or are completely different based on our parentage."

"Your aura reads the same as a vampire. I thought it would be different." Ethan's primary aura had a deep red color, likely related to determination. His secondary aura, related to his magic, was the color of clay.

He shrugged and walked over to the kitchen area. "I can't read auras, but I have arcane talents. I can use basic spells and magical tools, and sometimes read spelled text, which would make me a lepidoptera if I were accepted in those circles. Creighton has a calming ability with his voice. If he was a full vampire, he'd be an oscen. They all have oratory skills of some kind."

Ethan took food from the small cooling unit, and I watched as he made a sandwich. "You want one?"

"No, thank you. I'm good. Though if you have soup, that might be helpful."

"All full up on blood, are you?"

"For now, yes." While the bracelets dampened my magic, it was there, and so was all the blood rushing around my veins. Ethan moved to a cabinet and pulled out a pouch of tomato soup and handed it to me.

"It heats when you open it."

I'd seen such things, but it had been a while. "Do you need blood?"

"Only when I'm wounded. Otherwise, no."

"Convenient. Well, I'm going to take my soup and sit in the bath for a few."

"When you're done, try to get some rest. We might have to move again at sundown. It wouldn't do to have you completely off your feet if we need to leave. You can take the bed." It was a king-size bed. I supposed Ethan was trying to be gallant, or maybe just vigilant. We didn't exactly trust each other.

Before I could take a step toward the tub, images came to mind of the peaceful evenings spent in bed with Jason and Ian, and sometimes the mornings with Dorothea. The four of us, content and ready for rest as we all wished each other a peaceful sleep. Dreams of us taking in the countryside during the day while we watched Dorothea play with a kite. Or evenings spent at the theater watching the latest film. I had missed dreaming. I hadn't realized that closing myself off to Ian would end them.

Being in the Oubliette did the same thing. If I made it back to him, I'd ask about what he knew.

"Mason. . ." Ian's voice and his smiling face shifted to a frown. "Mason?" He reached for my arm, but it wasn't Ian's touch. "Mason?" Ethan's voice brought me back to reality as his face swam into view. The room was too bright by half, and I felt disoriented. Ethan grabbed my other arm to steady me. "Mason, are you okay?"

Daydreaming was new. Then again, so was being awake for this long during the day.

"Yeah, yeah. Sorry." I grabbed Ethan's arms to steady myself. His strength was tantalizing. I had a moment where I imagined draining that strength, the satisfaction I would feel as it wilted under my fingers. I shook my head. This was why I didn't enjoy drinking blood laced with magic.

Besides the side-effects, it gave me impressions of who the person was and what they enjoyed doing most. I've heard the high was nice. Sucks that it never worked like that for me. Being blitzed would have been nice right now.

Images rushed through my mind of perverse things. Most of them were of tormenting people or sexual fetishes. My stomach protested, and I let go of Ethan and stumbled to the sink. The dry heaving didn't help.

"Is there something I can do?" Ethan asked as he touched my back. The magic flared, and the bracelets heated, burning my wrists. "Mason, talk to me. What's happening?"

"Cleansing spell. Do you know one?" I blurted. I tried to stay calm as emotions and images bombarded my senses.

"On you?" I nodded. "It's not meant for a person," Ethan said. The surprise in his voice was interesting. He cared.

"Thankfully, I'm a vampire. The mage blood is fucking me up. I need to do something big with it, or get rid of it somehow." He hesitated while I lifted my shirt and exposed my back. "Do it, Ethan."

He listened then and used both hands. My veins felt like they were on fire as the cleansing spell lanced through me. If I screamed, I didn't remember it. When I woke again, it was late afternoon, and I was curled on the loveseat. I had burns on my wrists where the bracelets used to be. I turned my head and found Ethan propped up against the small sofa near my feet, napping.

I sat up, and Ethan woke. His gaze met mine a moment before he asked, "Feel better?"

"Other than the massive headache, yes. Where's the toilet?"

"Out the front door and about twenty meters at the back of the cabin."

"Quaint." Ethan shrugged. "Will I trip anything going back there?"

He shook his head. I moved and eventually found the composting toilet. Once I'd emptied my guts and bladder, I went back into the cabin. The sound of water cut off as I entered.

"I drew you a bath. I've added some salts for the headache."

Whatever I did that garnered this odd kindness was a mystery to me, but I wasn't about to turn down a fresh bath with healing salts. "Thanks."

Ethan pulled the curtain around to cover the window. "I'll check the perimeter, and the wards. Take your time." He walked out and closed the door behind him. I quickly stripped and sank myself into the piping hot water until only the top of my head and my knees broke the surface. Given how long I'd been in that hole with Tabatha, it did not surprise me when the water quickly turned a murky shade of gray. It wasn't as bad as it could have been. The cleansing spell had taken care of more than the excess magic. I washed up with the tray of products nearby. As

I got out and toweled off, I found a T-shirt and a pair of shorts. Ethan returned as I crawled into bed.

"Will we need to worry about daylight tomorrow?"

"I don't know. I guess we'll find out."

He gave me a concerned look but moved the problem further down his priority list. "Get some sleep. We'll talk to Creighton later tonight."

It was as good as any command Ian could have given me. I was out the second I closed my eyes.

SOMEONE SCRYING IN THE NIGHT

Ethan nudged me awake. It surprised me that I was even close to functional. You lose many people working in the medical field. It didn't happen often after the war, but you remember some of them. They stick with you like ghosts. I'm sure some of them were ghosts, even if I couldn't see them. I hoped Tabatha wasn't. I'm not sure I could handle it if I knew she was lingering around me.

"What do we need to do to contact Creighton?" I felt nothing from Ian or Jason yet. If Creighton wanted me dead because of Tabatha, I'd rather get that over with before the guys came to and realized they were losing me all over again.

I watched as Ethan reached under the bed and pulled out a large bamboo box. Inside was a large silver dish that had a nearly perfect mirrored surface. I'd heard about these things before, but I'd never seen them. There were crystals you could take mental images with, or leave messages for another person to read. Scrying mirrors, like the one Ethan had, offered two-way communication that couldn't be tracked.

The spells on the mirrors were very hard to maintain. At some point, you had to bring them back together to redo the original enchantment. I'm sure there were many mirrors that had become regular household objects simply because their current owners had no clue what they were before they came into possession of them.

He tapped the mirror, which created rhythmic tones. As this was the first time I'd ever seen one used, I giggled. "That's remarkably similar to a dial tone." Ethan looked at me as if I'd lost my marbles.

Ethan shook his head and repeated the tones on the mirrored surface. The surface wavered and made similar tones in return. He gave another series of tones, and the mirror lit up, then resolved into the face of a person I'd heard of but never met.

"Do you have her safe, Ethan?" Creighton asked, eyes bright with worry. His face looked tired, and his shoulder-length black hair seemed dull. That might have been the mirror, but I doubted it. If Creighton was in hiding, stress would definitely be a factor.

With a glance at me, Ethan shook his head. Creighton's face fell. I could see him wipe his face with his hand, then he glanced at Ethan. "There's something else. What is it?" For Creighton to have read Ethan's impassive features meant they knew each other much better than Ethan let on.

"Love, for the sake of night, tell me what's happened," Creighton pleaded. The wince on Ethan's face said enough, and that's when all the pieces of the puzzle clicked into place for me. I put a hand on Ethan's arm and gestured for him to move. I wouldn't have Ethan be the one to tell his lover and friend that Creighton's other partner was dead. It wasn't fair, and certainly not his fault.

"Hello, Creighton. You don't know me. But I knew Tabatha, and I've had the great fortune of knowing your daughter, Dorothea." With that introduction, I explained myself. Ethan and Creighton wore the same expressions throughout the story I told, and when I finished, only Creighton spoke.

"What's your name and coven?"

"I'm Mason Lindquist. Depending on who you talk to, I'm part of the Lindquist Coterie, or part of the Crossroads Coven. But there I go by 'Doc.'"

"And you're a vampire?" His accent was British, and the doubt in his voice was interesting.

"I'm something. I'm definitely infected, but what I am exactly, I don't know yet."

"Be that as it may, we have little time, and I've arranged for transport for—" There was a pause where I knew he wanted to say Tabatha, but stopped himself. "I've arranged the transport for Ethan and Thea."

"Within the next seventy-two hours, a plane will be waiting at this location," a map showed on the mirror, and we studied it before it disappeared again. "Then Ethan, you and Thea can meet me near my current location. Your safety will go a long way toward figuring out my next steps in resolving this rather distasteful action." Which definitely included Ethan. I saw his eyes light up at Creighton's words. It made me smile, which made Ethan blank his face.

"We'll work to make that happen, Lenny. I promise." Ethan's response was earnest, regardless of what obstacles might be in our way. He didn't want to disappoint Creighton. I knew how that felt. I'd been that way with Ian once.

"I know you will, Ethan. Be safe until I see you." Creighton spared a glance at me. "Mason."

The mirror returned to its smooth state, and I frowned. Creighton didn't know what to do with me. I was too many things to him, and the largest one was that I murdered the mother of his child.

As I wondered if there was even a way to make up for the damage I'd done to Creighton's family, thoughts of deep grief and sorrow entered my mind. I gasped in pain from the emotions and reached for the two threads in my mind connecting me to Jason and Ian. I conveyed my existence to them. It broke through their grief as they reached back, first with joy and wonder, then with confusion, since their last memories of me were gruesome. Their thoughts and feelings were overwhelming. I cried happy, bloody tears of relief that whatever happened to me hadn't destroyed our connections.

"Ethan, I need to talk with my family. They're worried. And I can't give them some vague mental image for us to meet up somewhere." I wiped at my face while desperately trying to figure out a solution.

"You don't have any location that's a fallback?"

"No, I don't think. . . Wait. Ian did. Or at least he had one once."

"Can you get us there?"

"Sure, but the real question is, can I get them to go there?"

"What do you need?"

"I need to concentrate and relax. This might take some time." I walked over and hopped on the bed, crossed my legs, and then closed my eyes. If Ian and Jason understood where I was trying to have them go, then Ethan and I could travel during the day while they traveled tomorrow night.

I pictured Ian's summer house in France. We'd been there a few times before I left. It was near a lake. He would hire staff, open the house and Lindquist's from all over would come and spend time there. It was a fairly grand affair.

Once I had that in mind, I repeated an image of us on the porch swing, together, over and over, until I caught their attention. Jason noticed first, then Ian. They focused. Good, that was good.

The next image was of Dorothea playing in the backyard of Ian's home in Birmingham. I repeated that until there was an acknowledgment. They both cared for her and expressed that she was safe by sending me bits of joy and astonishment at how fast she was learning. Ian returned an image of Dorothea reading a poem she wrote out loud, and it threw me. The sticky wetness of blood tears streamed out of my closed eyes. I shook off the image and tried to recenter myself.

Then I added the image of Ian and me at the house, then the image of Dorothea, and repeated it. Another affirmative came through the bond. I gasped at my success so far. I added another image of Jason and Ian walking with Dorothea. We'd taken to the habit of walking around the estate after breakfast. Jason and Ian would point out stars. Dorothea would dash between us as we walked down the path. Together. That's the message I wanted them to understand. All of us needed to be together at Ian's summer home in Narbonne.

Jason and Ian sent their own versions of the images from their perspectives to explain that they understood. I sighed with relief. The last thing I focused on was safety and protection. They returned the sentiment.

I hung my head as I let go of our bonds, exhausted from the mental strain. I looked up when Ethan pressed a wet cloth into my hand. The warmth was pleasant on my face as I used it to wipe away the blood.

"Did it work?"

"I think so. We'll see soon enough."

Ethan nodded. "If you can stand it, we should travel during the day. Make sure the place is safe for them when they arrive."

"That's if my whole daylight episode wasn't a one-off."

He sat next to me on the bed. "We'll find out in a few hours." He pointed at the window. "That's not spelled to block light."

Of course, why would it be? He and Creighton were dhampirs. They lived in the light without issue. "Well." I looked around. "I suppose you could shove me under the bed." I folded the cloth in my hand and wondered if this would be my last night. It seemed like I'd had a lot of those lately.

"The better option would be to wrap you in blankets and flip the loveseat to block the rest. It stays in the shadows when the light comes through the window."

"Okay, so if I scream, shove me under the couch." Ethan almost smiled. If I lived past the morning, I'd make it my mission to see his face crack a grin. "In the meantime, is there anything to drink?" He nodded and grabbed a very nice bottle of wine out of a storage space I hadn't noticed near the kitchenette.

As Ethan opened the bottle and poured, I figured I should get to know him better if I was planning on leading him to my family. "So, you and Creighton. Did Tabatha know?"

Ethan almost smiled. "Not only did she know," he said, as he finished pouring and handed me one, "Tabatha told me once she was glad Lennix had someone he could be intimate with."

"They weren't intimate?" That struck me as odd, considering Dorothea and all.

"They are. . . were business partners, more or less. They cared for each other like friends might, and indulged when they were lonely, but they wouldn't have classified their relationship as more than that. Before this whole mess, Tabatha was supposed to marry into another mage family. Creighton would have retained the status of consort for Dorothea's sake, but he wouldn't have seen much of either of them afterward."

"I've never understood mage families and their need to broker and arrange all their relationships. I have nothing against polyamory, but I also don't feel the need to tie myself up with obligations beyond a personal connection."

"Being part of the Lindquist Coterie means you were part of the family or you married into it." I blushed and drank my wine. "Hmmm, I think the lady's protests might be for naught."

"I tried it and discovered it wasn't for me." I shrugged. "Nothing wrong with that."

We sat on the loveseat and drank. I told stories about the war, how I became infected, and the interesting patients I'd treated over the years. When the first rays of light came through the window, I stopped breathing. I went so long between breaths that Ethan looked at me with concern. Dhampirs breathed like humans. I was something in between. Or something more.

When the rays solidified, my lungs burned with the need for air. I gasped. It was a sensation I hadn't felt in more than a century.

"Are you alright?"

My pulse beat faster as the sun rose. "I'm breathing without thinking about it, and my heart rate is up."

"Your flesh has more color as well. I thought that might have been because of the magic yesterday, but maybe not." Ethan peered at me like a specimen in a dish. He reached out and touched my hand. "You're warmer." I gave him a curious look, wondering how he even knew that. "When I woke you up earlier, you were room temperature."

"Dorothea started waking me up during the day whenever she had a nightmare. She explained the ability as 'seeing sparkles.' We've been trying to figure out why, but nothing makes any sense."

Ethan took my empty glass and stood. "There are tales among vampires that the older they become, the more power and magic they can access. Maybe this is a natural manifestation of your age."

He washed the glasses as I turned to look at him. "Did you just call me old?"

The near-smirk was there while he dried the dishes and put things away. "If you're not going to desiccate, we should try to get some sleep, then travel to the meeting location."

My steps were tentative as I moved toward the window to open the curtain. I felt it warm my face once I stood in the full sunlight. Maybe Ethan was right, and it was a manifestation of my age. Whatever it was, like everything else in my life, I embraced it.

As I got into bed and pulled the sheets up over my face, Ethan pulled the curtain, muting the light. When I felt the bed move, I opened my eyes.

"Would you mind if we shared? My neck and back would appreciate it."

That made me curious. "How old are you, Ethan?"

"Fifty-five." He certainly didn't look fifty-five. It made me wonder how dhampirs aged. If I were to guess, I would have said he was barely thirty. Laughter bubbled out of my mouth as I watched him.

"Sure, old man, plenty of room."

Ethan sighed and rolled his eyes. "Thanks."

I threw back the covers, and Ethan moved to lie down. "Don't mention it."

SAFE HOUSE

My eyes had not adjusted to being in sunlight. Ethan stopped to buy me a pair of very dark sunglasses so my eyes would stop tearing, and we purchased supplies. I marveled at the variety and kinds of food available. The last time I'd even thought about solid food was during the lean times, and even then, things were mostly apple related, to calm the hunger pangs. Now, there were things I wondered if I could eat at all or should attempt to try, given how bad the spaghetti experiment went.

"Don't take this wrong, but maybe we should try some blended things. Make them the consistency of soup until your body adjusts." Ethan said.

"You sound like Jason. That was his suggestion, and I went all in on spaghetti." I described my evening in the bathroom.

He grimaced. "I can't imagine what that must feel like."

"Stomach spasms are no joke." I smiled. "Have you ever been sick?"

"No, not even a sniffle."

"Interesting."

"Why's that?" Ethan sounded curious. I wondered if he'd ever thought about why that might be.

"The virus we carry is the same, but the effects are different."

"Huh, I've never thought of it like that."

When we turned off onto the dirt road that led to Ian's summer home, I spared a thought for my family. The four of us were an unlikely one, but we made it work. We would be sad to see Dorothea go, but it had opened other possibilities. After so long without progeny, the idea of having a child appealed to some recessed part of my psyche. Ian was a natural parent. It was one reason I was so surprised when I found out he'd cut himself off from his living family. Maybe with help from Jason and me, that would change after all this was over.

The vehicle came to a halt in front of the grand French cottage-style house. The smell of the water from the lake and the surrounding trees was pleasant.

"There should be a key that will let us through the wards." I got out of the vehicle and headed toward the back of the house. The porch sloped a little too much. Not enough to fall over, but it had seen better days. The key was not in great shape when I found it. Not only was the old iron key embedded in the branches and trunk of a bush close to the porch; when I grasped part of it, the key snapped. I groaned in frustration.

"Mason, I don't sense any wards. Do you?"

I approached the back door slowly and touched the handle. Nothing. No pushback or confusion. This house hadn't been used for a while. Jonathan, Ian's beloved great-great-grandson, died here. I wish I had remembered that before I pushed Ian toward this location.

The sigh that escaped my lips didn't go unnoticed. I leaned back while holding the door handle and then pushed with my shoulder. Once, twice, then the door gave with a loud groan. Dust flew as we walked inside. Some things were still in good condition, like the kitchen dining set, but other things were moth-eaten or rusted through.

"Taking our chances with the mages might be better. This place is no better than a death trap."

"It's not that bad." I looked around. "I've lived in worse."

After we checked the basement to make sure it was lightproof and not flooded, we started cleaning. The kitchen turned out to be mostly salvageable. The living room, not so much, even though there were covers on the furniture.

"I should have brought camping supplies. A sleeping bag, or a tent."

I glanced at Ethan with a smirk as I used a bit of magically enhanced cloth to scrub the counters. "Have you never slept rough? What are they teaching children these days?" Ethan scoffed and shook his head. I kept cleaning the counters until my eyes blurred and my balance left me.

"Mason?"

That was all I heard before I hit the grimy tile floor. When I woke up again, I was lying on a moth-eaten couch with a cool rag on my forehead.

"Can you stop doing that? The last thing I want is your family showing up to find you incapacitated, or worse. I'd rather not have to explain that you keep overexerting yourself."

Ethan's concern made sense. With everything that had happened, I knew I should take it easy. "Sorry." Ethan frowned at my apology. "I don't know my limits right now, so it's hard to figure out what the problem is before something happens."

"Do you even have a guess?"

"Well, if it were a human patient, I'd check if their blood sugar was alright. Electrolytes and such. If it was a vampire, I'd suggest not using magic or exerting themselves too much until they can feed again."

Ethan held out his arm. I blanched. "No, I'm not drinking from you. I've done enough to Creighton's family already. He finds marks on you, he'd be a fool not to retaliate."

Ethan smirked. "You don't know him."

"You're right, I don't. If it's all the same to you, I'd rather not give him one more reason to hate me."

"Mason, you're clearly in need. Your people won't be here for at least another day, depending on how fast they can make arrangements. I need you upright and functioning."

"Ethan, you didn't plan for any of this. You don't have to keep paying for my misfortune. I'm probably dehydrated. That's all." That probably wasn't all, but like hell if I was going to admit it.

The pounding in my head turned into a throb as Ethan stood and put his hands on his hips. "You're infuriating. Has anyone ever told you that?"

The laugh bubbled out of me, though it hurt my head. "Many times."

He went to the kitchen and returned with a refilling bottle of water. "If you die on me, I'll find a necromancer to raise you long enough to tell your loved ones you're the jackass that refused blood when it was offered." The clay and glass bottle was cool in my hands, which told me that either I really wasn't used to having a regular human body temperature, or I was spiking a fever.

"That's if they could raise me. Vampire, remember?"

Ethan gave me a hard stare, shook his head, and walked away. I opened the bottle and drank. Why all the men in my life saw me as some sort of fragile object mystified me.

Others in my life hadn't, certainly not the women I'd been with over the years. Stout women with large breasts and kind eyes, especially when you touched them in all the right places. I'm not a small woman, but definitely had a weakness for larger women. It was something Ian never minded. When we traveled as a married couple, we'd often find others to spend an evening with. I hated corsets personally, but bless me if I didn't immediately find them entirely too attractive on other women after my transition. Ian was right on that front. As adventurous as I was while I was alive, I really hadn't discovered myself, nor let myself actually live. It took dying on a battlefront to open my eyes.

"Mason, open your eyes. Mason. Damn it."

How long had Ethan been yelling at me? Did I pass out again? Maybe it was worse than I thought. Or the cleansing spell took too much out of me? I noted that for future reference, in case I exsanguinated six mages and overdosed on their magical blood.

My body moved, but not by me. "If you fucking die on me, I swear I'll find your ghost and make some witch use it for nefarious purposes." I laughed. "Oh, now you come to your senses. Damn it, Mason. Please drink so your family doesn't kill me and start a whole other host of problems we can't afford to have."

I opened my eyes and oriented myself to the situation. Ethan had me cradled against him, my head on his shoulder. It was a much easier place to strike, but infinitely more dangerous to the donor if they were human. I didn't know if dhampirs shared a similar weakness or not. His steady pulse was tantalizing, but I held myself back.

"Don't be stubborn. Drink, Mason, please."

His plea broke me. It reminded me of when Ian had said something similar, and I had resisted until I couldn't any longer. I prayed I wouldn't hurt him.

When I sank my fangs into Ethan's neck, he trembled. I moved to straddle him as I drank. He wrapped his arms around me and held me tight and whispered my name like a benediction. That's when I pulled away, licking the wound to make the flow stop. Since it was still daylight, the metallic tang overrode the taste of apples.

He loosened his hold on me as his eyes dropped to my lips, then to my breasts, framed by the large V-neck T-shirt, then back up to my eyes. Magnets couldn't have come together faster than his lips meeting mine.

He tongued my fangs with each kiss and grabbed my ass to press my hips closer to his. His jean-covered bulge nestled between my thighs. I rocked against him, desperate for ⊠plea-sure as Ethan's blood worked its way through my veins. We only stopped kissing long enough to draw a breath as I ground myself down on him. When he came, he pulled away from my lips with a groan and buried his head in my breasts. I tried to move my hips again to see what other sounds I could elicit from him, but he grabbed them and held me still.

As my senses slowly returned, I tapped his shoulder, and he let go of me long enough so I could stand. He reached out to ⊠steady me, but I squeezed his hand to reassure him, so he let go.

I mustered my courage. "Are you okay?" He laughed, and it was a throaty, rough sound. I blinked. I'd broken him. Creighton was going to murder me.

He reached up to touch the bite mark on his neck and smiled. "I'm fine, Mason. Truly."

Part of me wanted to dissect why he was smiling; another wanted to leave it alone. I listened to the more sensible version of myself for once and nodded, then headed for the back door, grabbing the water bottle along the way.

It was near the end of the day, and the sun was sinking below the lake's surface. I'd always wanted to see it when we'd visited, but back then, Ian never woke before full dark, and I thought it was still too much daylight to even risk it. The closest I'd ever seen was the space between sunset and full dark. That was pretty, but it wasn't the same.

Clouds with purples, pinks, and dashes of blues were reflected in the gently rippling water. My eyes watered from the beauty of it as tears streamed down my face. I wiped at them, realizing they were still clear.

Ethan found me, and I tried to give him a smile. He looked concerned. "Are you upset?"

"No, not at all. Though if it was going to happen, I would have wished it involved less dire circumstances. I've had too many close calls the last few days, well weeks, actually." I liked Ethan, but I couldn't help feeling I'd taken advantage of him.

"Would you like a hug?" He stood patiently next to me while I debated if that was the smart thing to do. He tilted his head and held out an arm. I curled into him and tried not to cry too much. "You're a lot like Creighton. He puts up a brave front, keeps people at arm's length, until he can't. The only person who ever brings down his defenses is Thea. She's his heart."

"What about you?" I looked up from Ethan's shoulder to meet his gaze. "He cares for you, that's for certain, and he trusts you."

Ethan nodded. "We have a camaraderie, and we're able to relax around each other. We don't have to be Envoy and protégé in private. He confides in me, and I in him." He paused for a moment. "We've been together for fifteen years. I was there when negotiations began for his consort status with Tabatha. When Dorothea was born, I was with him. I've assisted him with more investigations than I can count."

I waited out the pause in Ethan's story. The sounds of the lake and the buzz of the coming night filled the air.

"I believe we love each other. Neither of us ever said we were exclusive, but I kept to him and never once thought that it made sense to want someone else. Our lives were too complicated, and trusting someone outside our circle was dangerous at best." He glanced away. "Creighton and I have never shared blood. While we have fangs, they aren't the best for biting. It's considered a taboo to drink from one of us, so no one in my coven has ever touched me like that. I would suspect it's the same for Creighton."

Shit. Well, that was now added to my growing list of offenses and mistakes. "I'm sorry, Ethan. I didn't know."

"Really? I thought that might be why you wouldn't drink from me in the first place. I have to confess, I've always been curious about it." He smiled. "It hurts, but in a good way?" The oddly light and curious tone suited him. I liked this Ethan versus the stoic one.

I gave him a smirk. "I think it takes a certain kind of person to enjoy it, unless you're a vampire."

His eyes widened, and his eyebrows went up a little in surprise.

"Thank you again for saving me from myself. When Jason and Ian arrive, you all can exchange 'I rescued Mason' stories."

He grabbed my arms and abruptly turned me to face him. "I couldn't make you drink, Mason. You rescued yourself. I suspect you always have to some extent." He rubbed my arms, then let me go. "Do yourself a favor and let your family help you more often. No one should be alone, especially not someone as remarkable as you." He kissed my forehead, then walked away. It left me a little baffled. He made good points of course, but I wondered how much of that was really for me, or something he wanted to say to Creighton.

BLATANT DISREGARD

As the night wore on, Ethan made wisps of light to help navigate the house. While I could see fine, I appreciated the light. Being in total darkness really sucked. By the time we were done, the basement was in decent shape, along with the kitchen area and the small sitting room.

We had a quiet dinner while seated on a pile of furniture coverings on the sitting room floor. Ethan had some sausage, cheese, and an apple, while I had some kind of pumpkin squash soup. The soup tasted all right, but the smell of apples was pervasive. I salivated and watched Ethan take a bite of the fruit.

"You're drooling." He looked at me with a small smirk on his face as something appreciative settled in his gaze.

I blinked and shook my head, then wiped at my mouth. Fuck. "Inadvertent response. Blood tastes and smells like apples to me. The scent is so strong that it more than rivals real apples."

He tilted his head, glanced at the piece of fruit, then at me. "Does all blood taste like apples to you?"

I nodded. "Yes, unless the blood came from someone who is magic or heavily uses magic."

His eyes widened. "What does it taste like with magic?"

"Like... spices. That's the best way I can describe it. And from what I understand, it's unique to me. No other vampire I know can discern different kinds of blood. They can get a high off the magic that's laced in it, but they couldn't tell you if it came from a fae or a mage." I should have suspected his next question, but even when he asked, it still threw me. No one had ever asked.

"What do I taste like?" Was it my imagination or had he leaned closer?

"Cinnamon with apples." I smiled at him. It was the most common flavor I'd come across because of how blood was harvested from infected folks that didn't make it through transformation. The cleansing spells they used on it didn't always work. "I think it might have to do with the virus in our blood, but that's a guess."

"You have more senses than other corvids I've met. Even older ones tend to have more developed hearing or sight. I've never heard of one having taste as well." He took another bite of his apple and caught me staring again, then held it out to me. I didn't know what an actual bite of apple would do to my guts, so I wrapped my hand around his and held it still as I licked the pulpy flesh. The taste conveyed pleasure and gave me the nice little dopamine hit I needed to stave off hunger for a bit longer. I even licked my lips, desperate for another taste. When I opened my eyes, Ethan had moved closer. "You're hungry, aren't you?"

Yes! "No. What gave you that idea?"

"Mason, I've lived near vampires most of my life. Your face looks like you'd been in the desert for too long, and I gave you my last drop of water."

"When there are lean times, vampires can use food to calm hunger pains. Especially if that food is what they taste when they drink."

Ethan set his apple down and reached for my hand. "You're cold."

"I'm mostly dead now. My heart and breathing have slowed too. I can change that with blood for a bit." He tugged on my hand, and I followed until I was straddling his lap.

"If you're hungry, you should drink, Mason."

"Ian and Jason will be here with Dorothea soon. I can wait." I tried to pull back until Ethan bit his lip and a drop of blood welled up. I drew a large breath, and the smell of apples flooded my senses. The scent lit up my insides as the sensation dropped right to my pussy, making it clinch. I licked my lips and squeezed my hands into fists, trying to resist the impulse to lick him. "You did that on purpose."

He nodded. "Kiss me, Mason. Please." Shit. The 'please' was too much. I knew how Jason and Ian would react. We didn't hold each other to a monogamous standard. I had to trust that Creighton wouldn't do the same based on what Ethan said.

I stuck my tongue out and traced his lips. The taste of apples, sweet and juicy, coated them. I swallowed the first drop, then went back for more. Our lips met, then opened for each other. Ethan's blood-tainted saliva filled my mouth. I swallowed and kissed and swallowed again. His arms pulled me close so our bodies were pressed together as I wrapped my legs around his waist. We continued until he grew hard and spilled me onto my back. Ethan looked down at me, lip still bleeding, kneeling between my legs. He leaned over me, and kissed me again. I reached for his jeans as he reached for mine.

Ethan grabbed my jeans and yanked them off. I had unzipped his pants, then helped him take off his shirt before our lips met again. Cinnamon and apples never tasted so sweet. When I reached into his pants for his dick, he gasped.

He dribbled pre-cum on my hand while our lips were otherwise occupied. I wasn't sure what he was waiting for. "Have you ever had sex with someone who has a vagina?"

He smiled. "I have, but it's been a while. I'm trying to be gentle." His fingers traced the curve of my cheek.

"Don't. This will be pretty one-sided if you're gentle." He was hard, and I gave him a tug and a squeeze to emphasize my point.

"Oh?" His eyes narrowed, and his lust-filled gaze met mine. Did he and Creighton like to play a little rough then? He kissed me to the point of bruising, while his hand used the head of his wayward cock to notch into my opening. There was a lift of his eyebrows as our eyes met. I gave him the slightest nod and closed my eyes. He shoved into me with a grunt that opened my eyes and made me watch his face as he fought with my tight entrance. The slight pain curled my toes as he pulled out a little and slammed into me again, eventually easing as my body responded. His thrusts were more insistent, and I felt his cock harden more with each stroke.

"Mason," he whispered. My hips met his as he panted. I traced his face with my fingertips, which caught his attention. The slap of his hips felt good, but I needed more, and I wasn't sure how far he wanted to go.

"Ask," I prompted. It was the only way to be sure. I wouldn't mind if this was where we ended, but I suspected Ethan wanted a little spice of his own.

"Shit, Mason. Shit." He moaned as I contracted around his length. It only made him thrust harder into me. "Please, Mason. Bite me."

His chest was within striking distance. I leaned up and wet his nipple with my mouth, then slid my fangs into his flesh. He hissed and moaned. His thrusts became erratic as he spilled into me. Once I'd taken enough to sustain myself for another night, I licked the wound and pulled back. Ethan's thrusts slowed as I watched him savor his orgasm. Once the haze cleared, he looked at me. "What about you?"

He dwindled inside me and slowly came to a stop, though didn't pull out. "I drank." This sudden shyness was new. I'd never been that way with Ian or Jason.

Ethan frowned. "You know that's not what I meant."

"I know." I kissed him and traced his face with my hands. "You keep frowning and your face will stick that way." He pulled away, then lay on his back. I propped myself up on an elbow. "It's alright if we're not each other's cup of tea, you know. We were in the moment."

He glanced at me. "You're making me feel selfish."

"It's okay to be selfish sometimes." I shrugged. "I'm sure there are times you've sucked Creighton off after a long and stressful day, and he didn't have enough energy to reciprocate." His gaze landed on me, eyes wide, so I kept poking. "Or maybe he fucks you raw and leaves you hard and wanting. Does he like to edge you? Do you like his lips around your cock? Do you call him the Envoy in bed? Or. . ."

"Enough!" He grabbed my arms, pinned me down, and rolled on top of me. "What the fuck are you doing?"

The grin on my face materialized of its own accord. His eyes narrowed. "I'm not fragile, Ethan. If anything," I moved to wrap my legs around his waist, and rolled him onto his back, "you're the one that could break." I scratched furrows across his chest, and he hissed. "Do you want to be broken?" His renewed hard-on didn't escape my notice. I eased a hand up to his neck and pressed down. He gasped, eyes wide as his hands tightened on my arms.

Without breaking my hold, he let go of my arms and moved his hands to my hips. We adjusted slightly, and then he slammed up into me. "That's it, like that. Maybe if you keep it up, I'll have an orgasm sometime this century." I don't know why I was goading him, but his growl reverberated through my arm about two seconds before he pulled out, knocked my hand away, pushing me off, then grabbed me from behind. His hand went to the back of my neck as he shoved into me, then pressed my face to the floor.

I tried to push up, and he pushed me back down, so I stayed there. The brutal thrusts were winding me up, but without more, I'd still have a proverbial hard-on. "Don't you think I should be punished for my dirty mouth?"

"Yeah, you have a fucking way with words." He moved his hand from my neck, repositioned my hips, then smacked my ass hard. It felt so good I groaned. "So that shut you up, huh?" He slowed down, and put more effort into turning my ass red. "Feeling guilty, Mason?" More hits. "You want to be punished for what you did?" The sounds of his hand hitting my ass reverberated around the sitting room. A place I used to play card games and read with Ian's family. We'd take our midnight tea here.

"For your role in the events that led you here?" Ethan's hand came down, and it was wet, with what I didn't know, but it stung, and I pulled in a breath only to gasp it back out. "Do you want me to drive out your willfulness?" His words rang in my ears as pain seeped through my body. He continued to ask questions while he spanked and fucked me at a steady pace. I was so close I could taste it. "You've taken so much, Mason. You'll just keep taking it." With more hits and I moaned into the cloth still covering the floor.

Ethan yanked me up and pressed my heated backside to his front as he wrapped one hand around my neck and put the other between my legs. He smacked my clit, and I shook from the sheer pain and pleasure. His hand tightened around my neck. "When will you stop running and ask for help? When are you going to stop taking it and ask for what you need?" I sobbed as his questions hit like arrows.

Fuck, we were in deep. How had I lost control of this situation? He was in my head now, not literally, but close enough.

"What do you need?" he whispered.

"Bite me. I need you to bite me. Please. Please. Fuck, Ethan, bite me." As I bounced on his cock and his hand slapped my pussy a few more times. I whined with need until his teeth pressed hard at the nape of my neck on my right side. I shook as it set off fireworks in my body. He rubbed my clit as he continued to bite. I came again and again. The waves never seemed to stop. Even as Ethan let go of my neck, and stopped biting, it didn't stop. His fingers refused to let me come down. He was so hard inside me, I tried to squirm off of him even as I wanted more.

A whimper slipped from my throat as he pushed me back onto my hands and knees. "You're still taking it, aren't you? You just can't help yourself. So greedy, Mason." He put my hand on my clit and wouldn't let go until he felt me rubbing myself. "Don't stop until I say." I whimpered and moaned my agreement, too far gone to even think of doing anything different. He pulled out of me, wiped our collective mess across my asshole, then slowly pushed in. I was so relaxed from my continual orgasm that it didn't take long for my ass to press to his hips. At some point, he must have created some kind of lube, because while it hurt somewhat for him to press into me, it didn't actually hurt when he started fucking me again.

He pulled me back up to press against his chest. His hand pushed mine aside and found my clit again. It set off another wave of pleasure. I shivered as he continued, then he whispered in my ear. "Do you have one more for me? Come with me this time, Mason. I forgive you. You're forgiven. Come with me." He repeated his litany until he throbbed in my ass, then bit down on the other side of my neck while I drenched his hand as we came.

I don't know how long my sexual high lasted, but after a time, Ethan slipped out of me and laid me down like I was fragile glass. I was alone for a bit until he returned with the refilling water bottle and cloth. As I lay there, he wiped me clean. He was so gentle about it; it set off silent sobs. When he was done, he picked me up off the floor and pulled me into his lap. He sat with his legs crossed and his arms wrapped around me, supporting my body as he rocked me gently. He must have put his boxers back on when he retrieved the refilling bottle.

"It's been a rough couple of days for both of us. I'm guessing it normally doesn't take that much to get you off."

I sobbed and chuckled. "I might be a bit broken, Ethan."

He moved my hair and smoothed it back, then kissed my cheek. "You're beautiful, Mason, not broken. And this whole mess is not your fault."

My chest-racking sobs filled the room as Ethan held me and kept repeating, "It's not your fault." I passed out, exhausted from everything. When we woke again, it was midday. While we had cleaned up the sitting room. The catalog of bite marks, bruises, and hickies on both of us was proof of what happened.

We were sitting at the kitchen table sharing a meal, and Ethan's gaze kept returning to the purple bruises on my neck. "Will they be upset?" His face was slightly pinched, and his lips were pressed in a thin line.

I shook my head. "They'll ask for details, but they won't be upset. Knowing Ian and Jason, it will make you more interesting to them."

"How so?"

"I tend to be choosy about whom I sleep with. As you've experienced, I'm not exactly low maintenance in the sexual gratification department."

He smiled. "It was worth it." He took a bite of his sandwich and swallowed while I sipped some broth. "If Lenny and Tabatha had been closer, we could have been a throuple. We were all friends, but it never developed into more than that." I nodded as we continued eating.

The sun felt good through the kitchen windows. I lifted my face and closed my eyes to bask in it. When Ethan spoke again, I almost missed what he said.

"You weren't that far off about Creighton and me. I've acted as his Chief of Staff for a long time. When he's angry or frustrated, I give him something to channel those through. We have our tender moments, but they are more rare than the quick blowjob or fuck between meetings so he can relax and do his job. Though he's never forgotten to return the favor. Better that I'm tense and edged than him making a mistake." He smiled a little.

It was easy to imagine what Ethan was describing. "Plus, we'd sometimes do it as a power move." He smiled a little as he toyed with the rest of his sandwich. "Especially if there were demanding guests with enhanced senses. 'Fucking you is more of a priority than their petty squabbles,' he told me once. It was early in our relationship. And the first time I knew I meant more to him than our jobs or a good lay."

"I hope I'll get to meet Creighton someday."

"I hope so as well."

We finished our lunches and laid down for another nap so we could be ready for whatever the night would bring.

TEARFUL GOODBYE

An unknown vehicle came up the drive around midnight. The first person out was Ian, followed by Dorothea and Jason. Ethan gave me a little push, and I ran to them. Ian caught me in his arms, and Jason came to hug and kiss me as well. Our connection flared between us, and the need to stay physically connected became an obsession.

"Uncle Ethan!" Dorothea squealed as she ran to him. He picked her up like a doting uncle and swung her around as he hugged her close. Jason and Ian flinched, muscles tense, ready to rescue Dorothea from a threat. I shook my head, and they took it down a notch.

"I'm sorry I couldn't tell you about Ethan before you arrived. He's Creighton's Chief of Staff and partner. Let me introduce you, and then I'll tell you what happened." We walked back up to the house together, Ian holding my hand on my left, Jason holding my right. I noticed a few glances at my neck, but they didn't ask, for now.

Once everyone was introduced, things went much easier. Ethan took Dorothea to have a snack and play with the tablet Ian gave her after the long trip. She even had her own suitcase with all the clothes, books, and toys we had bought her. After I explained what happened with Tabatha, how Ethan found me, and my continued struggles with day walking, the guys held me between them and hugged me like they would never let go.

"So if I understand this correctly, you can be awake during the day plus go out into the sunlight. And if you have magical blood in your system, you create a dangerous reaction between your healing ability and direct light." I clearly fascinated Jason.

"I promise to let you experiment with me when we go home." I kissed Jason soundly, and he conveyed his delight for all kinds of reasons.

"When are we going home?" Jason's question made my stomach clench. I'd have preferred we head home now, but I was worried about Dorothea.

"I'd like to say goodbye to Dorothea first. They'll need to leave soon if they are going to meet the plane on time. Though we made sure the basement was lightproof in case it took longer for you to drive out."

Ian nodded. "I don't want to stay in this house. There are too many memories here. I should have torn it down decades ago."

I understood his sadness. "I'm glad you didn't. It was the only place I could think of that we both knew and was likely safe." Ian nodded and placed his hand on my back.

Instead of dwelling on the past, I nudged us toward the future. "Let's go in and say goodbye. If we reach home in time, there's a bathtub with my name written all over it." The guys laughed, and we went inside to find Ethan and Dorothea at the table playing a game.

She jumped up, leaving Ethan high and dry, and wrapped her arms around me. "Mason, I missed you so much. Jason and Ian missed you too. We're glad you're safe." I bent down and gave her a proper hug.

"You've been a very brave little girl. Ian, Jason, and I are so proud of you. We'll miss you, Thea."

"Ethan calls me Thea. So does Daddy." She frowned. "I don't want you to go, Mason."

"Sweetie, Ethan will take care of you, and you'll see your daddy soon."

"What about Mummy?" She must have suspected, or possibly pulled something from my mind. I couldn't be sure, but I didn't want to lie to her, nor tell her the grisly details.

Ethan spoke, saving me. "Thea, sweetheart, we talked about this. Your mother can't take care of you anymore, neither can Marion. Your father and I will. We're going to take a plane ride tomorrow to see him."

"Are you coming with us, Mason?"

I shook my head. "No sweetie. Ethan will take care of you. He took care of me and did great, so I'm sure he'll do just fine." I held her tight. "Maybe someday we can all visit. Would you like that?" Her head nod was enthusiastic. I kissed her forehead and let go.

Jason dropped to her level. "Take care, okay, sweetpea? You study your elements and do well on your maths and before you know it, you'll be a scientist." Dorothea hugged Jason's neck, and he hugged her back.

Ian bent down next and offered a hug. Dorothea latched on. "Be a good girl, alright. Keep practicing your drawing."

We were all having a hard time. It was supposed to be temporary, but we'd all grown close to Dorothea, and this was much harder than any of us thought it would be, though it was the right thing to do. Creighton had lost so much already. I didn't envy him the job he had to do, explaining that Dorothea's mother was never coming home again.

As Ian and Jason stood, they drifted toward Ethan to say goodbye. It's what I would have done too, except I couldn't move. Dorothea quietly picked up her backpack and walked toward the door. I turned to follow as Dorothea's mental control snapped into place with little more than a brush of her hand. I'd forgotten how much power she had, and the lack of personal mental wards was a glaring omission in hindsight.

"Thea, where are you going?" Ethan asked. Thea didn't stop, and neither did I. She shoved a key fob into my hand, and I clicked the button to see which vehicle it belonged to. Ian's ride lit up, and she diverted to the passenger door.

"Mason, what's going on?" Ian shouted. "Dorothea, what are you doing?"

They came closer, and that's when Dorothea turned me on them. My hands came up, a glow started at my fingertips, and all three men bled from their noses, eyes, and ears. Mentally I screamed, but I couldn't say a damn thing.

"You lied to me. Mummy is dead, so is Marion. Gran Papa too." She moved my hands to focus on Ethan, and he dropped to his knees. "Uncle Ethan. You lied."

"Thea," he pleaded. "Your father and I wanted to be together before we told you. You've been through so much already, love. Please. Stop."

Ian and Jason tried to help Ethan, and I tried to stop whatever Dorothea was doing with my magic. Thank the moon that it wasn't daylight. I don't know how much more power Dorothea would have had access to, and it likely would have killed Ethan.

"Dorothea, this is wrong, and you know it. Let Mason go, and we can talk about your fears; your concerns. Like we did at home." Ian held out his hand to her.

"It wasn't my home! You wouldn't have brought me here if it was my home. Why did you bring me here?" she screamed at all of us. Ian dropped his hand as if she had slapped him.

"Your father misses you terribly, Thea. He knows that Jason, Ian, and Mason have kept you safe. Is this the way you thank people for taking care of you?" Ethan's voice trembled as he bled, trying to maintain his composure. My heart hurt to watch myself harm people I cared about. Silent blood tears streamed down my face.

"Fine," Dorothea said. My hands dropped, and I took in a grateful breath. "We'll go see my father."

Ethan moved forward. "Not you, Uncle Ethan. Not you!" My hands came up, and Ethan dropped to his knees.

"You're killing him, Dorothea, stop!" Jason yelled. My hands dropped again.

"Mason will take me to my father. I'll hurt you more if you follow us."

"How do you know where to go?" Ian asked.

"Mason knows." She was right. I did. Which meant she knew a lot about things that were tucked in my head. She moved me to the driver's side, and I slid into the vehicle and tapped the controls. It came to life, and I was in for one hell of a ride. I cried as I turned the vehicle and left the three men standing there, bloody in my rearview imager.

Once we were headed in the right direction, Dorothea released control. "Don't go back, or I'll make you stop, and you won't like it."

"You don't have to do this. Ethan. . ."

"He lied, and so did you. And you did kissy face with him. You made him lie somehow."

Kissy face? A heat crept up my cheeks. I feared what else this child had found rifling through my memories. "We agreed with your father. He wanted to explain things to you. That should be somewhere in my head, too."

"You and Ian told me that hurting people was bad, but you hurt lots of people, including my mum." Tears fell from her eyes, and sympathy caused mine to blur with unshed, blood-tinged tears.

"I know I did. We didn't want that to happen. Your mom was so brave, sweetie. Her family…" I wasn't sure what to say, or how to say that Tabatha's family had betrayed them and left her mom for dead. Her grandfather was part of that family until I killed him, too. "There are a lot of grown-up things with grown-up problems going on. It's hard to explain."

"I hate you," she said. Her voice was full of pure conviction for a child who thought they knew their version of the story was the correct one. "I'll take you to Daddy, and he'll know what to do with you. He's the Envoy. It's his job."

Atlantic Flight

When we reached the airfield, it was about an hour before dawn. The place seemed deserted except for one security guard at the gate. All I had to say was, "the lawyer sent us." The gate opened, and they directed us to a hangar. We were somewhere near Valencia, Spain. I had driven all night while Dorothea slept in the passenger seat. She woke as I pulled to a stop.

Someone came toward the vehicle, and I felt the small minion in the seat next to me take control. I got out of the car and greeted the gentleman in a suit.

"You're not who I expected." His amber eyes glowed, which meant he was magical. Without some other tell, it was impossible to know what species or what kind of magic might be involved.

"There were complications. My consort's Chief of Staff sent us along. He wants us safe as soon as possible." I said, surprised to find that I was pretending to be Tabatha, French accent and all.

Well, that was impressive. Never underestimate a child at any age, especially one with unchecked abilities. Dorothea slipped out of the vehicle, walked up to me, and took my hand, completing the pretty picture. She looked a bit pathetic and sad. The guy in the suit seemed to melt a little.

"Creighton recently oversaw my nephew's case. I wondered what it might cost him, considering the amount of vampire politics that seemed to happen around it." He walked us toward the private plane. Dawn had already arrived, so my heart rate and warmth were already changing. Instead of Dorothea losing control of me, her tendrils seemed to dig deeper.

"We appreciate your generosity under these circumstances." Blessed night did this child have her mother down pat. The guilt I felt doubled.

I shook the lawyer's hand. He didn't react as if anything was remotely off about me. My heart rate was human now. If I had smiled, my fangs would have given me away. Maybe he made the same mistake Ethan did and thought I was a dhampir. "I'm glad I'm able to help in some small way. Please give Creighton my regards."

With that, we boarded the plane and took off about fifteen minutes later. After a decent breakfast for Dorothea and apple juice for me, Dorothea fell asleep. When her control slipped, I begged one of the staff for a phone. They pointed to an in-seat communication device, which I used to call Jason first. I hoped Jason was still awake, Ethan was okay, and they were safe for the day.

"Hello?"

"Ethan?"

"Mason, thank the stars. Where are you?"

"On the plane, headed wherever to meet Creighton. Where are you? What happened to Jason and Ian?"

"We tried to follow at a distance. That was harder than I thought. You really know how to drive." I tried not to grin. "Jason and Ian are fine. They passed out in my vehicle since it has UV blocking properties. I'm going to find a safe place to park them, then work out what to do next."

"She can control me during the day and read my mind, Ethan. I've never been more scared of a kid in my life."

He sighed. "Apparently, you're the only one she can control right now. Ian noticed you didn't have mental wards."

"I dropped them to find Ian." Then didn't put them back in place because having communication with Ian and Jason was more valuable, and Dorothea seemed to respect my bodily autonomy after the first time she controlled me. "I'll need someone's help to put them back in place." The ocean was the only thing I saw as I looked out the window. "I've never been able to block things selectively like Ian can. For me, it's always been all or nothing."

"If I can get a message to Creighton, I'll warn him." Ethan was silent for a bit. I thought I'd lost the connection, then I heard him sigh.

"I'm sorry." I tried to hold back tears, but they came too easily at the images burned into my head of people I cared about being tortured by my own hands.

"Hey, Mason. This isn't your fault. You couldn't have known how she would have reacted, or take advantage of the situation. Hell, it was a surprise to me, and I've known her since she was a baby."

I grabbed a tissue and wiped at my face. They came away clear. "How would you have reacted to finding out someone you trusted killed your mother?"

Another silence passed. "I'll follow as soon as I can, Mason. Tell Creighton if I don't reach him first."

"I will. Be safe."

"You too."

The audio call disconnected, and I slumped back in my chair, exhausted. The co-pilot, who was also the cabin crew, came to check on us. I dared ask a question that I feared wouldn't have an appropriate answer. "Do you happen to have blood onboard?" The co-pilot blinked, then nodded.

"It's synthetic, mostly for emergencies. Are you in distress?" she said.

"Not exactly in need of it for medical reasons. Could you bring me the kit and a Scotch?" Synthetic blood tasted like rotten apples. If it was a choice between going into whatever happened next, depleted of energy, or drinking synthetic, I'd drink the synthetic.

The co-pilot didn't judge when they handed me the kit and returned to the cockpit. The pilot's feminine voice came over the comm system. "We're at cruising altitude now. Our ETA to Chicago is ten hours and twenty-five minutes."

I wanted to ask if that was a layover or where we'd stop, but I didn't really care. I hoped Creighton would retrieve his offspring, let me go home to Ian and Jason, and then I could figure myself out.

PREDICAMENT OF A FATHER

As far as fear goes, I'm not sure who I should have been concerned with more, the eight-year-old that could control me, or her father who could call for my execution based on the death of his partner and six mages related to her family. Or better yet, having sex with his other partner, followed by leaving him injured in the middle of a driveway. Honestly, if I lived beyond stepping off the plane with Dorothea, I'd count myself lucky.

Dorothea's excitement was contagious as she watched the landscapes go by. It was hard to remember that she used me as a living weapon not that long ago. "Mason, is this where you came from? I've never been before."

"It is. But I haven't been here in a while either." How the lawyer managed to not have us flagged by customs or immigration surprised me. Maybe Creighton could do that with his diplomatic status, though that would give away his location. Either way, when the plane shut down, and the door opened, Creighton himself was at the bottom of the steps.

Dorothea skipped down the steps and jumped into his arms. I took two steps and stopped, not of my own accord.

"Hello Daddy!"

"Hello darling. Did you have a nice flight?"

"Yes!" She described several things she saw out of the plane window, and he indulged her while I played mannequin.

When Creighton glanced at me, he frowned. "I wasn't expecting you, Mason." He put his daughter down, and she listed off my crimes as she marched me down the steps to my doom.

She spoke in a clear, bright voice. "Daddy, she killed Mummy, Gran Papa, and Ethan. I brought her here so you can punish her. Because that's your job, to punish bad people." She looked proud of herself. I hadn't expected her to betray me so quickly, but it wasn't like she hadn't spoken the truth, at least in part.

I watched, helpless, as Creighton looked at his child, then me. His eyes looked haunted. What had this man been through?

"Let her go, Thea. Regardless of what she's done, she has a right to defend herself."

"But Gran Papa said she was a killer. That she killed Mummy." That was straight from my mind. I wonder what else she'd dig out to hold against me.

"Thea, I won't say it again. Let her go. I will hold Mason accountable like any other defendant when I see fit. Do you understand?" The girl pouted. I was her new favorite toy, and Creighton was putting his foot down.

"But Daddy, she killed Uncle Ethan."

The lie was so smooth that I saw Creighton flinch, but I couldn't open my mouth to refute it. I didn't want her to know that I had spoken with Ethan already either. Maybe she thought he betrayed her father somehow? It was hard to understand how children interpreted an adult's actions, especially if they didn't have context.

"Are you sure?" Creighton asked with all the indulgence of a father who knew his child was lying but wanted to give her a chance. She confidently nodded. Why wouldn't she try to manipulate the situation? Thankfully, she couldn't kill me with her power, or well, I hoped that was the case.

"Ethan, could you join us?" He stepped out of the vehicle and walked over to Creighton and Dorothea. He had a moment to spare a smile for me. I shed a tear at seeing him safely arrived, though I had no idea how.

Ethan bent down to Dorothea's level. "Thea, I'm happy you are safe, but you need to let Mason go."

The child looked in confusion between the three of us. "It's not fair! She lied to me, and so did Uncle Ethan. They didn't tell me about Mummy or Marion. They lied!"

Creighton gently placed his hands on his daughter's shoulders and dropped to her eye level. "Dorothea, did you ask them why? I told them to wait. I wanted us to be together before I told you."

"Uncle Ethan said you told him, but I couldn't trust him. He and Mason did things to each other. Bad things." The kid was definitely going to need therapy.

Her father sighed. "Dorothea, let's talk about what you've done." He asked her a series of questions that walked her through his job. He explained how she violated the Vampire Accords and how her power, though seemingly limited to one unique vampire, would classify her as a necromancer. Then they talked about other laws regarding privacy and reading another's mind without permission, and then using that information against them. They weren't Creighton's purview, but as an officer of the law, he was sworn to uphold the laws of countries along with the Accords. By the time he was done, I could move again, and Dorothea was a crying mess.

As I approached, Creighton held Dorothea close. Ethan stood and touched my arm. "I'm sorry we had to meet under these circumstances." It was a weak introduction on my part, but I didn't know what else to say.

Creighton continued comforting his child and looked at me. "They wanted to hurt me, and they did. I'm only sorry you've become mixed up in all of this, Mason."

I nodded. "What do you want to do now?"

Creighton didn't say anything as he stood and ushered Dorothea toward the waiting vehicle. Ethan explained as we followed. "We have lodging for the evening. It's better we go there and discuss things." Ethan opened the left rear passenger door for Creighton. He got in with his daughter. Ethan closed the door behind them.

"You can ride up front with me." Ethan nodded to the passenger door as he went to the driver's side. I walked around to it and got in. As long as whatever happened next meant I was going home to Ian and Jason, I was happy with it.

IN TOUCH

We were headed toward Chicago and the famous skyline until Ethan turned due south and kept driving. So, Chicago wasn't our final destination after all. "It's good to see you, Ethan."

"Likewise." He spared me a small smile as he fished something out of the storage compartment. "Here," he said, handing me a small package. I glanced toward the back seat compartment.

The vehicle we were using had an opaque privacy panel between the front and the back seats. People who wanted privacy often used them. Vampires with means used them to travel during the day since a lot of these vehicles came with fully automated options.

"They can't hear us unless the comm unit is activated."

The package contained a phone and two bracelet charms I hadn't seen since the war. They were used to keep vampires safe when there weren't enough mages or other vampires to do mental wards. They felt familiar.

"Ian thought ahead. He made the charms in case I caught up with you. I picked up the phone for you to call them. Ian knows that if you're wearing the charms, it will cut the connection between you and them. The phone is a one-use-only thing. Then we go dark until we can get somewhere safe."

The charms were warm in my hand. Once I got home, I'd have Ian make something more permanent. For now, the quick protection was a comfort. I didn't need the kid in my head ever again. I slipped them on, and the soft buzz that represented Ian and Jason melted away. The silence hurt. Ethan nodded to the phone.

It rang once before Ian picked up. "Mason?"

"It's so good to hear your voice. Is Jason there?"

After a moment of fumbling, Jason spoke. "We're on speaker, baby, are you alright?"

"I'm fine. I got the charms. Thank you both. I'm so glad you're both alright." A sob lodged in my throat. I missed them so much.

"We miss you too, Mason." Ian's voice sounded rough. I could only imagine what not having our connection was doing to him. It brought up too many memories that we hadn't dealt with yet.

"Hopefully, I'll be home before the week is out. Then we can talk about things. I promise. No more heroics after this."

Jason chuckled. "If you can keep that promise for longer than a week, I'll buy you a clinic myself."

"That's a bet." I laughed. God, it was good to laugh a little. "I love you two. Please stay safe, please."

"We will," Ian said. "From what we could tell, and as far as Ethan knows, we aren't being watched or tracked. They've been looking for you and Creighton, though."

"Our advantage is that very few covens have coterie records, and anything else they might have tracked would be nearly impossible, but you should get rid of my bike, just in case." I hated to say it, because I loved that bike, but if they could trace it to me, it could be traced back to Ian and Jason.

"Fuck, seriously? It's a sweet ride. I hate to see it go." Jason's disappointment was mine, too. I loved my Ducati, but if it could be tracked, it needed to be dealt with.

"Me too, Jason. It breaks my heart, but we can replace bikes." Hopefully, that drove home the point.

"We'll take care of it, Mason. Just make sure you come home, alright?" Ian had relaxed a little during the phone call, and so had I. Hearing their voices meant the world to me. Ethan had done that for me. It had been a while since I was surrounded by people who cared whether or not I was safe.

Ethan tapped his watch. "Okay, loves, I'm out of time. I'll try to call again soon, so please stay safe."

"You too, Mason. We love you."

"I love you both." With that, I hung up and covered my face with my hand in a fruitless effort to keep from crying. Ethan tapped my shoulder and made a gimme motion at the phone. Once he had it, he opened his window and tossed it. "Ethan!" I looked at him, astonished. "What if someone picks it up?"

"There won't be anything left. I slagged it. It should dissolve pretty quickly."

"You're full of surprises." I wiped at my face, and Ethan pulled some tissues out from somewhere and handed them to me.

"Targeted acid spell with a delay. Plus biodegradable tech. Works pretty nicely."

It made sense. I was quiet for a bit and then gave up.

"Ethan. . ."

"Are you seriously going to apologize for something you had no control over? Literally zero, Mason. You know that, right?"

"I know, but it's not just that. It's the night before, too. Dorothea knows what we did, and somehow that destroyed her trust in you. It won't be easy to get that back." It destroyed her trust in me too, but there was so much more I'd done besides fucking someone.

"Creighton knows." That surprised me. I wondered if Ethan planned on telling him or not. "He also knows it's part of why

Dorothea doesn't trust us. It's not something we've ever had to explain to her before. The three of us were a family from the day she was born. We had planned to talk with her about things when Tabatha married, but. . ." He shrugged.

"I don't know how much she saw, Ethan. I don't think she understood everything. She called it kissy face."

"Tabatha used to call sex that." Ethan tilted his head as he explained. "She told her if there was a closed door, she needed to knock. When Dorothea asked why, she said that adults might be making kissy faces and it wasn't the kind children should see."

The image came to mind of the prim woman I met when I was first shoved into the oubliette. That changed over time as we continued to suffer. "It sounds like something she would say." My throat tightened. "Tabatha made me promise to take care of Dorothea."

"Hey." Ethan grabbed my hand. "You didn't have a choice. Tabatha knew that as much as you did. You both would have died there if you hadn't done what she asked. It was a shit choice, Mason. You're a doctor. You know that sometimes the shit choices are the only ones we get."

I knew that, but I'd like to think I could do better even when I knew for a fact that it wasn't possible. I squeezed his hand in return, then let go. "However this turns out, I want to stay in touch. Even if it's a small cryptic note from time to time or a holo-postcard from somewhere warm and tropical."

Ethan laughed. "I'll miss you too, Mason."

We arrived at what appeared to be a small condo set into rolling hills. It was one of the older eco-villages that were mostly used for summer homes. Ethan parked in the garage, and Creighton carried his sleeping daughter into the house. I followed Ethan into the kitchen area, where he poured three glasses of wine. It wasn't what I needed, but it would have to do for now. I wouldn't be able to leave to find blood without drawing attention, especially if the covens were looking for me.

He pushed a glass over to me, and I took a large swallow as he watched. "Would you like more?" I nodded, and he filled my glass again. "When was the last time you fed?"

"I had some synthetic on the plane."

Ethan took a sip of wine. "I thought that might be the case." He set down his glass. "Creighton and I discussed it, and until we can return home safely, we can act as donors."

"You can what?" I shook my head and thought maybe I imagined what I heard. "Was your plan to ply me with wine first and then woo me with this brilliant idea?"

"I told you she wouldn't like it." Creighton came into the kitchen area and retrieved his glass.

Ethan shrugged. "It's still her choice, Lenny." Creighton lifted one eyebrow at his partner.

"How's Dorothea?" Her walking in on the current conversation would be one more thing to explain to her, and I didn't have the energy.

"Asleep. She should be out for a while." He turned to Ethan. "I think you've found something, or maybe more accurately, someone, to indulge in." Ethan opened his mouth, then closed it again. "Thank you for that, Mason. We had a rather lively interlude when he found me in Chicago." He pulled back his collar to show off some rather impressive bruises where Ethan had made bite marks.

My face heated. "I'm flattered, but I'll be alright for a few days." I drank and hoped my words were true. It was possible to take blood without sex, but I got the impression that both men would be interested in more. "Besides, shouldn't the two of you be furious with me? Especially you, Creighton. I destroyed your family, for fuck's sake." I put my glass down, picked up the open bottle, and poured out the last of it. Ethan didn't meet my eyes, and Creighton frowned.

"You single-handedly made sure I saw my daughter again." Creighton put down his glass. "Dorothea, her nanny, and Tabatha were all gone by the time I could do anything about it. Ethan found no trace of them. But you and your kindness kept my daughter from forever being lost after someone altered her mind. Ian and Jason watched over her. Educated her. They adored her as if she were theirs. I know you did as well, or Dorothea wouldn't have felt so betrayed when she discovered what you had to do to survive."

I kept wiping at my face until Ethan tossed me a dish towel. "She wasn't wrong. I killed Tabatha. And her grandfather. And I almost killed Ethan too."

"And yet I'm standing here." He smirked.

"I'd love to find out how."

Ethan grinned. "Trade secret."

"Enough flirting," Creighton said playfully. He looked between the two of us with a knowing smile. "It's a rare person who captures Ethan's interests. I happen to know from experience." He came closer and took my hands in his. "Mason. All you're guilty of is protecting a young girl and yourself." He squeezed them gently and let go. "As Envoy, that's the ruling I would make if anyone had requested it from me." He shook his head. "The actual truth is, you and your family are collateral damage due to a coven bent on revenge because I did not rule in their favor."

"But I killed mages!" Was I the only one upset about this?

Creighton nodded. "And that's something you'll have to live with for the rest of your days. However, I would remind you they had you staked and were prepared to kill you if it hadn't been for your unique talents." I glanced between Creighton and Ethan, then back to Creighton.

"You two really tell each other everything?" I heard a soft squeak in my voice. They nodded and gave each other rather proud smiles.

"Communication is important to us. It's why we plan on talking with Dorothea about what she saw in your head and hopefully help her understand, along with explaining that people have boundaries that should not be crossed," said Ethan.

"The child hadn't shown one bit of magical acumen when she was younger. It surprises me she's able to control and read your mind so well with no formal training."

"Or she had those abilities all along and someone took them from her." I set my empty glass down. "Ian said she had layers of compulsions. He suspected someone kept applying a compulsion for various reasons until she ended up in a nearly catatonic state."

"That is a theory." Creighton picked up his glass again and shook his head. "Anyone who would have known is likely dead, so we don't know if they did it to protect her from herself, or keep her from having any abilities at all."

"You have to admit, a child with that much power, however focused, is a little scary." I looked down at my glass and wondered if there was another bottle in the house.

"Yet you're not scared of her, and you're the one she's abused the most," Ethan said in a flat voice, implying that I should be more upset.

While Dorothea's grandfather was a smarmy asshole, her mother was a much better person. Maybe Tabatha was a little self-centered, but she didn't deserve to die. I'll blame myself for the rest of my days that I didn't figure out another way for us to both make it out of that hole.

Silence fell over the kitchen, and I sighed. "I'd like to clean up if I could, and maybe get some rest. It was a long trip." They nodded, and Ethan showed me to a guest room that had its own bathroom. Once he left, I locked the door, stripped out of my clothes and stood in the shower until I was a prune. When I extracted myself from the bathroom, wrapped in a towel, I dropped onto the bed like a sack of potatoes. I should have been tired, but because it was after dark, that wasn't the case.

OUT OF BOUNDS

Once I figured out that I couldn't sleep, I picked up my clothes and sniffed them. They desperately needed a refresh, whether from magical cleansing or an ionic wash, it didn't matter. I re-wrapped myself in a towel, picked up my clothes, and went to see if I could find a sanitation machine. My best bet might be somewhere near or just off the kitchen. It was dark, but I could see perfectly fine. A soft moan caught my attention. My feet froze in place. Maybe if I was lucky, they didn't hear me, and I could worry about clean clothes later.

No matter how many times I tried to tell myself to turn around, my feet, once they were unstuck, followed the soft, earnest noises that I recognized as coming from Ethan. As I glanced around the corner into the living area, I saw Ethan and Creighton on the couch. Ethan straddled Creighton, facing him. They were kissing, and Creighton's arm moved in a rhythmic motion. My body lit up with desire, and the damn towel wasn't helping as the soft fabric rubbed against my nipples. Hunger pangs hit, and I barely kept myself from moaning.

The erotic sounds grew more urgent. I ducked back into the hallway and tried to scoot away from the noise. As my lust-filled thoughts pestered me, I heard two distinct grunts of male completion. It was time to remove myself, or I'd do something extremely forward.

Back in my borrowed room, I dumped my dirty clothes near the door, then dropped onto the bed. I pulled the covers up and the towel off. My fingers immediately went to my clit as I tried to alleviate some of the tension I felt between my legs. I shoved my wrist into my mouth and bit down as my fingers lit upon a particularly sensitive spot. My orgasm quickly washed over me as I licked my wrist and took in one calming breath after another to settle my desires. When my senses noticed two figures in the doorway, I sat up as if something had stung me.

"How long have you both been standing there?" Had I forgotten to shut the door? Fuck, I was so intent on rubbing one out that I didn't even check. I was usually more careful.

They both entered, and Ethan closed the door behind them. "Tell us to go, and we'll leave," Lennix said. Ethan reached around his partner and pulled off his shirt. His hands caressed the lithe body and made my stomach do little flips. Ethan kissed Lennix's shoulder and pulled his own shirt off. My brain went blank.

Lennix Creighton was all dark hair and hazel eyes with a tanned, statuesque body. Contrast that with Ethan's light brown hair, blue-green eyes, and athletic build, and I was practically panting. They waited for me to say something as they kissed and teased each other. Had the act in the living area been on purpose? I buried my fists in the bedding and nearly bit my lip as Ethan's hand opened Lennix's trousers and slipped in to stroke his hardening length.

Why was I finding myself in these situations lately? Was it the fangs? Had to be the fangs. I pulled at the sheet on the bed and wrapped it around myself as I stood. They didn't pause what they were doing, but both men watched as I moved closer. With one hand on the sheet, I reached out to touch the chests and shoulders on display. Scars and blemishes told stories, and these two had plenty, though Ethan certainly had more. With gentle pushes and nudges, I rearranged us so that I was at Lennix's back and Ethan faced us.

"Is this what you're curious about?" I stood on my tiptoes and ran the tips of my fangs and tongue along Lennix's right shoulder. Lennix stilled as Ethan drew a shuttered breath. I let go of the sheet and pressed my breasts to Lennix's back. Both men audibly swallowed. I loved a captivated audience as much as I enjoyed being the audience.

"Ethan, on your knees." He made a graceful drop to the floor as I wrapped my hands around his partner's torso and pushed his trousers down further until they dropped to his ankles. Ethan helped Lennix step out of them as I watched.

My right hand drifted to Lennix's cock and wrapped around his base. With a gentle squeeze, I gave Lennix one firm stroke. He groaned softly and leaned back a little. I wondered if he had fae somewhere in his family tree. Even his cock and balls looked as if someone had lovingly carved them out of marble with a perfect thatch of hair to frame it. The sigh of disappointment when I let go of his cock amused me. I reached out for Ethan and touched his face, then caressed his chin and motioned him forward.

With one hand on Lennix's hip and another that gently caressed his cock, Ethan opened his mouth and slid the length of it inside. It distracted me from my own game for a moment until Lennix's hips moved of their own accord and Ethan's hand reached for my thigh as he moved closer. His head made steady motions that elicited soft groans from Lennix. I kissed along the man's back to tease him until his breathing became more erratic. I nudged Lennix into a wider stance, which dropped him a few inches. Ethan adjusted quickly, and Lennix's desperate groans grew more intense.

I kept my fingernails short because it was good hygiene in the medical profession. It also meant that I didn't have to worry about hurting someone with my nails. I wet my right index finger and slipped it between Lennix's ass cheeks to find and gently tease his tight ring. He flinched, then settled as I played with him, and his left hand shot out to grab Ethan's shoulder.

"Lubricant, Ethan, please." The soft whine in Lennix's voice was like a melody. It must have been part of his vocal powers, though I sensed nothing different. Ethan's questing hand met mine, and his fingers twitched slightly as I heard a soft pop and he uttered some phrase. A substance gushed between Ethan's fingers and mine. His hand disappeared, and I used the lubricant to penetrate Lennix with my finger. His gasp was delicious to my ears. It also explained how easily Ethan had penetrated me the other night. That was a nice party trick. I'd have to learn it before I left.

Lennix didn't move once I found his prostate. I left my finger in position as I asked a crucial question. "Lennix, would you like me to bite you?" Someone could imply they were okay with something all they wanted, but until they asked for it or said it was alright, it was better to know.

"Yes, Mason, please."

I'd think about how wild it was to be in this position later, but with sex in the air and my hunger driving me, I didn't hesitate. I pressed my finger to his prostate and moved to his left to sink my fangs into the crook of the arm he had extended to Ethan's shoulder. Ethan grabbed Lennix's hips as the man came, then licked and swallowed as I sucked. The smell of apples and sex filled the air. I took my finger away from his still-clinching hole, then licked Lennix's arm to stop the flow of blood. Ethan held Lennix up with his muscular arms until the man recovered. I stepped away and sat on the bed while I licked my lips, tasting blood and apples.

The movement drew their attention, and I looked at them to see Lennix tap Ethan's shoulder, which caused the other man to rise gracefully and unbutton his jeans. Ethan slipped them and whatever else he wore to the floor, while his gaze locked with mine. They waited as if they were supplicants and I was someone of great importance. I wondered if the rule about biting dhampirs had something more to it than an admonishment or something taboo.

Lennix caressed Ethan as they watched me. Ethan wasn't significantly larger, but he had more girth. I fidgeted as they played. "Would you like me to watch?"

They looked at each other, then glanced at me as Ethan took a few steps forward and bent down to kiss me and lick the hint of his partner's blood from my lips. In the space of a breath, we moved onto the bed. Ethan lay on his back, and I straddled him while Lennix moved behind me. Hands were everywhere as we shifted with each other and moved, touching and playing with heated flesh. Mine was warmer now because of the blood I had consumed.

Ethan shifted me forward and pushed into me slowly. The feel of him was wonderful, and I suspected the slowness of it was so Lennix could watch. Lennix's hand traced lines down my back. The tips of his fingers briefly brushed my anus, then moved. When Ethan made a noise under me, I suspected where Lennix's fingers had gone.

"Lenny, if you keep doing that and we'll have to switch positions."

I tried to look, but Lennix pressed himself flush to my back and put his head on my shoulder. His cock was hard as it pressed into the small of my back. "Ethan comes rather quickly if you play with his prostate." We moved together in that way that keeps things going but doesn't rush. "But we need him to last for a little while, hmm?" Lennix's hand slipped down my stomach and between my legs. He toyed with my clit for a moment or two before pulling his hand back to my hip. "Would you like more, Mason?" He ground his cock between my asscheeks and I moaned softly. This was either the weirdest revenge plot or the best meal I'd had away from home in a while.

"I can always take more," I said with a sly smile and a challenging tone. Lennix's hand reached under my shoulder and landed on Ethan's chest, making a gimme motion. Ethan made some movements with his hands and said the same words as earlier. Lubricant pooled in Lennix's palm. A moment later, I felt the substance coating my hole. "I really should learn that spell from you, Ethan. It would come in handy." He grinned and nodded. Lennix put a hand on Ethan, which made him stop as Lennix worked himself into me.

"Fuck, you're tight," Lennix hissed as he pressed into me further. I drew a slow breath and tried to relax. The pressure felt good, and I wanted more.

"Lenny?" Ethan's voice asked a question. Lennix nodded, and Ethan's hands went to my hips and urged me to move. The movement worked Lennix in deeper, and I shook with each thrust. Ethan's fingers found my clit, as Lennix's fingers found my nipples. The combination had me on the blurry edge of an orgasm in no time, but I didn't miss it when Ethan urged Lennix on. "Bite her."

With Ethan's bite, it was more pressure and bruising than anything else. When Lennix bit down, I felt his fangs. They were less prominent than mine, but still longer than a human's canines. His bite was sharp enough to draw blood. Small welts, nothing more. The surprise of it and the pain made me shake as my orgasm took me. I couldn't catch a breath to drive back the pinpricks of light around my senses. I came again when Lennix sucked at the wound he made and fucked into me harder. That did something for Ethan because I felt him writhe as he unloaded so much it leaked out of me onto him. Lennix followed, and I felt content and full in my pleasure.

Sometime later, I woke up on the outer edge of our group and extricated myself for a trip to the bathroom. The scene in the bed reminded me of Ian and Jason, who couldn't sense me at all while I had the protective charms on. I didn't feel guilty for anything I'd done with Ethan and Lennix, but I was homesick. Ian and Jason were my home, and this moment with two others crystallized my feelings more than anything else could have.

After another shower, I wrapped myself in a fresh towel and attempted what I had set out to do earlier in the night. Once I found the sanitation machine just off the kitchen area, I busied myself with cleaning my clothes. When I turned to go back to bed, Dorothea surprised me. By the look on her face, she wasn't too happy with me.

ACTIONS AND CONSEQUENCES

"Shit, Thea, you scared me."

She stood there staring at me. "Daddy says you did nothing wrong, but you hurt people. You hurt my mother. I don't understand, Mason." She cried, and that broke my heart. I reached for her, and she came into my arms willingly. She wanted to trust me, but was terrified, and I couldn't blame her. She'd been through a lot in a short amount of time. We all had.

I walked her to the living area, sat down on the couch, and pulled a blanket up for us so we could stay warm. "Your mother and I knew each other for a bit."

"You were in the dark place together the whole time I was with Ian and Jason."

I pushed a few strands of her hair from her face and nodded. "We tried to get out, and she very much wanted to come back to you. She loved you, Dorothea."

"So, why did you hurt her?"

I sighed. "I tried to make her like me, but it didn't work. It was too late. We were both too weak."

"Oh." She wiped at her tiny face while I wiped at mine. I was careful to wipe my blood tears on the towel I wore. "What about the others?"

"They thought I hurt your mother, so they hurt me, too. They wouldn't let me explain and were the same ones that put us in the dark place."

She looked away from me. "That's how I knew you could hurt people. How I learned how to make you hurt people. I can't do that anymore." She touched the charms and pulled her hand away as if she'd been burned.

"I know you're scared, Dorothea, but controlling me isn't the answer. I don't want to hurt people, and I didn't want to hurt the people that hurt me, but I had no choice."

Dorothea sat with that for a while, and something made her face crumple. "Did I hurt you, Mason?" I nodded, and she bawled outright. I hugged her and tried to calm her as she said sorry repeatedly. Lennix appeared, dressed in his trousers and a shirt which looked like Ethan's, but I wasn't one to judge.

"Thea, is everything alright, baby?" She shook her head and let go of me, wiggled out of the blanket, and went to her father. Her adorable pink pajamas with rabbits contrasted the distraught child now in Lennix's arms. "Shhh, tell me what's wrong."

"I hurt Mason, and Ethan, Daddy. Like Gran Papa tried to hurt Mason. I hurt them and did bad things. I'm sorry, I'm sorry!" Ethan appeared behind Lennix and glanced at me, putting his hand on Lennix's back to let him know he was there.

Lennix didn't coddle her, much to my surprise. "You did. But Ethan and Mason love you, and they know you were upset." She nodded, his voice soothing her as she sniffled. "What do we say to people we love that we've hurt?"

"I'm sorry, Ethan." She saw him, and he touched her hand.

"I forgive you, Thea. I know you were scared."

She turned toward me. "I'm sorry, Mason." Her father reassured her while she spoke.

Dorothea's face and eyes were red. I don't know what Ian had unlocked in her, but I wondered if this would be the last time she'd struggle with something of this nature. "I forgive you, Dorothea. It's going to be alright." She nodded, and Lennix gave her a gentle kiss on the cheek.

"Well, there now. All forgiven." He smiled for her, and she tried to smile. "It's supposed to hurt still, but it feels better, doesn't it?" Dorothea nodded. "That's a good girl. Now, are you hungry, love? Shall we see what there is to eat?" She nodded again. Lennix took his daughter into the kitchen while Ethan moved and sat next to me on the couch. He noticed my towel and smirked.

"If you're going to stay with us, we should probably get you a few more clothes."

I smiled. "That would be nice. I'd rather not have to wander around here half naked if I can help it." Which led me to another topic. "How long does Lennix think it will take to clear this mess up?" I wanted to go home. The familiarity and the differences made me ache for the men I was already bonded with. The empty echo that remained because of the charms threatened to break my heart. Maybe it was karmic payback for all the time I'd kept Ian out. If he'd felt like this, it was no wonder that he had become somewhat of a recluse.

"If we can get to some place that isn't connected to Lennix or me, he might have a chance to fix things." Ethan sighed. "But we're out of resources. We have enough to get by, but a lot of our assets were frozen, and now that Tabatha has passed, we've lost our best advocate with the Lafayette family."

I thought about it for a minute. Maybe there was an option to keep everyone safe. I had resources Ian left me, and something else that might work. "Ethan, how do you feel about mountains and snow?"

Over the next week, we slowly made our way to Boulder and my old family home. When Ian and I married, he helped me set up an anonymous trust for my family. After the last of the family moved away, a stasis lock was put on the house. The taxes were always paid, and the lock checked from time to time, but I left the house empty. If someone from my family came back to collect it, they could contact the estate and have it opened. In the last fifty years, no one had. It was an older house made of reclaimed wood and other materials. It would have taken a great deal to bring it up to fire and environmental codes, not to mention that nearly everything but the plumbing would need to be updated.

With the funds Ian had set aside for me so long ago, I'd be able to refurbish it. Maybe even start a practice again, but right now, I wanted to make sure Dorothea, Lennix, and Ethan had the best chance to survive whatever madness the covens were going through. I moved my funds through different accounts, calling in favors and even stashing things in case of an emergency. Ian would know I took the money, which hopefully let him know I was alive.

It was a little before sunset when we arrived at the house. The area it resided in was still used for farming and raising domesticated animals for meat replication. Ethan pulled the vehicle into the drive. We all looked through the windows at the stately old house that needed a lot of work, and the rustic front porch that needed an update. I got out and walked up first.

"Are you sure it's safe, Mason?"

I shrugged. "Safe as any other hundred-year-old house. It needs some work, but that's why we got the materials printer." The printer, a small version, could construct a good deal of replacement items and things we'd need out of what was non-functional in the house. It could also convert garbage, rocks, and dirt if necessary. There was plenty of material around to use.

The protective ward let me pass through easily enough. It recognized me as a family member. I moved to the stasis lock and brought the ward down. The door swung open, and other than the musty smell, everything looked alright, considering how long it was since it was last opened. "Welcome to Worthing House." Dorothea ran inside to explore, and the men followed as we looked around.

We started moving in our things as the sun sank into the tree line. The stars came out, and I took a deep breath of the pine and grass-scented air that I remembered.

"I set up the materials printer to make sleeping gear for us. The fireplace looks alright, but we'll want to test it out before it gets too dark or cold to do anything about the flue," Ethan said as he stood next to me.

"Sounds good." I patted him on the back. "I haven't been back in a long time. It's nice to be home."

"As long as there's hot water, I'll call any place home," Ethan said as he moved inside. As I passed the threshold, it triggered a ward. It was enough to prick Ethan's senses as he turned to see me forcibly thrown from the house. I slammed into our vehicle, and it was lights out for me.

History of Worthing House

Ethan

Mason slumped to the ground, and I couldn't breathe. If she was hurt, or dead, I'm not sure what I'd do. I'm not sure how I'd ever explain it to Ian and Jason, either. They trusted me to keep her safe. I ran out the door toward her and dropped to her side. She wasn't moving, and I wasn't sure if the vampire ward I sensed was a onetime thing or constant. Lenny and Thea ran down the steps toward me when they saw us in the drive.

"What happened?" Lenny knelt down on the other side of Mason.

"I felt a vampire ward trigger. It threw her out of the house and across the drive." Vampires had a pulse, but it was amazingly slow, so it took me a bit to figure out whether Mason was still with us. The lack of desiccation was a good sign.

"Is Mason alright?" Thea asked.

I reached back and touched Thea's shoulder. "I think so. But we'll need to get her inside."

"If the ward only works on full vampires, then we might be able to invite her inside. Assuming this ward works like the tales of old." Lenny looked like he wasn't sure.

"Will that work while she's out?" I didn't want to risk her being hurt more by the house. "Maybe we should wait until she's awake." I turned to Thea. "Could you go back inside and bring some blankets for Mason, sweetie?" Thea nodded and took off. "We can put her in the vehicle for now. I can stay out here with her. . ."

Mason groaned and sat up. "Whoa. What's the trouble?" She looked at Lenny and me, then frowned.

"The house tossed you like a rag doll out onto the drive. It was a vampire ward, from what I sensed."

"Oh? Really? How odd."

Lenny and I looked at each other, then back at Mason. "How do you mean?" Lennix asked.

"My family used wards like that. I wouldn't have thought any of them would still be active." She looked around at everything but us, and I wondered why. "It means someone in my family still comes by and checks on the house."

"It's also likely someone either knows you're still alive, or that an abandoned property looks like prime real estate for a transient vampire." Lenny's suggestion tracked. I looked between Mason and Lennix and saw an understanding pass between them.

"Maybe a bit of both," said Mason as she rolled her head from side to side as if she was checking to make sure it was still attached.

"Could someone please clue me in?" Lenny smiled as I took Mason's offered hand and helped her up. We stood and looked at the house as Thea came back out with a blanket. I glanced at Mason, waiting for an explanation.

"My family used to be vampire hunters. It's the reason we moved. My parents wanted to retire, or so I thought." Could vampire hunters actually retire? I didn't know. "But this is good! It means you'll be safe here."

I shook my head. "What about you?" Mason was in as much danger as Lenny if the covens found her.

She smiled. "This isn't about me. I'm a loose end. And I have a medical degree. I'll figure something out. In the meantime, all of you can stay here. I'll take a sleeping bag and stay in the vehicle. Whoever set the ward will be back."

"What do we do when they find out you're a vampire and you're protecting dhampirs and a fledgling necromancer?" Lennix asked.

Mason looked at the ground. "We find out if they are here to help, or cause trouble, then deal with it accordingly."

We didn't have to wait long. She showed up at dawn. When the front door opened, we assumed it was Mason, but there were two differences. She was blond, and she had a one-handed crossbow.

"Well, well. You realize you are trespassing," the blond stated.

Mason walked up behind her. "They aren't because I let them in. Who are you?" she asked.

Except for the blond hair, it was like looking at Mason's twin. The blond-haired woman turned to face Mason, then turned to keep us all in her sights. Mason walked in as if she owned the place. The ward didn't go off again, and there was color in her cheeks. Magic was so fucking confusing sometimes.

"Look, this is my family's house, and since I'm the only one left, you're trespassing. Simple as that. I'm going to call Public Safety." The blond pulled out her phone as she held the small crossbow on Mason.

"What are you going to tell them?"

"That someone pretending to be me broke into my house with two guys and a kid." Clearly the math didn't add up for her. We certainly didn't look unprepared, and she kept glancing at Mason's face.

Mason stepped closer. "Your toy won't slow a vampire down, so why not drop it and talk?"

"Sure," said the hunter.

The thwack of the bolt hitting Mason's shoulder surprised all of us. Lenny grabbed Thea, and I moved to help Mason as she slumped to the floor.

"What the fuck?" I reached for the bolt in Mason's arm, and her odd doppelgänger stopped me.

"You pull that bolt and I'll put one into you. Answer some questions first."

I held up my hands and tried to protect Mason from any further damage, though the woman seemed pretty indestructible given everything she'd been through.

"How do you know this woman?" The hunter still had her phone in hand.

"We know her because she rescued my daughter," Lenny said, as Thea clung to him. "She brought us here hoping we could use it as a safe house for the time being."

While Lenny distracted the hunter, I checked if Mason was breathing. She moaned a little as I touched her neck. The relief I felt loosened the knot of panic in my throat.

"How did you open the wards?" The blond asked, glancing between us and Mason, trying to figure out the puzzle Mason represented.

"She opened the wards and the house." I pointed at Mason. The woman frowned.

"If that's true, that means she's related to me somehow."

"I think that would be plenty obvious, since you look a lot alike." Lenny pointed out.

I glanced at Lenny and back to the blond. "Look. We've had a hard few weeks and we're tired. We're only trying to find a safe place to stay until we can sort things."

"She's a vampire, though not like any I've seen. You're dhampirs, and the small one... is a mage?" It sounded like a bad joke. If only that were the case. The confusion on the woman's face was comical.

"Now that you've read our auras, could you please let us wake up our benefactor so she may talk with you? I'm certain she'll be able to answer your questions." Lenny, ever the diplomat.

"Fine." The blond tapped my shoulder with her weapon. "Pull the bolt, but if she does anything, I'll put another into her and call for backup." Mason was a force all her own, to be sure. It was odd how she was underestimating the rest of us, assuming Mason was the real threat. Maybe that was the fallacy of being a hunter of vampires.

I pulled the bolt, and blood seeped out of the wound. I pulled off Mason's jacket, and tore off part of my shirt, and wrapped her arm to stop the bleeding. Once she was awake again, I hoped Mason could heal herself.

It took ten minutes before the effects of the bolt wore off. Mason sat up with my help.

"Is everyone okay?" she asked.

"So far. The woman who shot you would like to ask you some questions."

"Sure. How about we start with names? I'm Mason. What's yours?"

"Constance."

"Help me up, Ethan." I pulled Mason up from the floor and let her lean on me until she got her legs under her again. "Constance, you're obviously in the family business, or what used to be the family business. How did you know the ward was tripped and who tripped it?"

"Magical signature. Whoever tripped the ward has to be a vampire, and the ward leaves magical traces I can see."

"Ah, they've updated it then. Usually, it only kept vamps out."

"Interactions with vampires are strictly regulated. Going after the wrong intruder without proof can have consequences. I'd like to stay within the law." She tapped her chest, and that's when I noticed she was wearing a small imager.

"Lucky for us, then." Mason glanced around. "I tripped the ward, but I am also inside the house, and I was yesterday as well. I was able to unlock the place, so you know that means we're related. Yes?"

"But how? Unless..." Constance seemed to add things up in her head. I glanced between the two women and Lenny. Mason straightened, and I reluctantly let her go. "The lost bloodline?"

"Lost?" Mason repeated.

"During the Necromancer War, Madison Worthing disappeared. She told her parents she had enlisted as a medic, but when the war was over, no one could find a record of her."

"Huh, I turned into a family legend. Interesting."

"Madison?" I looked at Mason, curious as to why she changed her name.

She laughed. "I never liked my name. I couldn't be a woman of mystery with a name like Madison. And who wants their parents to track them down while you're having an adventure? They were powerful enough to do it."

"My parents told me the story because they thought I looked like you. If you are actually her." Constance dropped the crossbow to her side. "But you're a vampire."

"Yes, which is another reason I never came home. While my parents moved out here to retire from being hunters, I don't think they would have accepted me."

We all stared at each other, though the tension of the moment leaked away. Thea brought us back to reality.

"Daddy, I have to use the restroom." Lenny let go of her and looked at Mason.

"Down the hall. First door on the right," Mason and Constance said at the same time.

I watched as the two women smiled at each other. "How about you join us for breakfast, and we can fill each other in on the gaps in our history?"

Constance sighed and shut the front door. "Why not? Not every day you meet a family legend."

With that, our strange life became even more interesting. I didn't know what the future held for us, but I hoped Mason would be part of it. If Lenny could figure out a solution to this coven clusterfuck, then all of us could keep Dorothea safe.

HOMECOMING

MASON

A few months later...

I knocked, like I had not so long ago, when I first came back to the Lindquist estate. And exactly like back then, Jason answered the door. I took in his half-dressed form in a pair of pajama pants, a shocked expression on his face.

He didn't take long to reach out, pull me into the house, and close the door. His lips landed on mine, and I kissed him ardently, having missed our discussions and hypotheses. The sexy brain contained within the sexy man was no match for my libido or his apparently until we heard a noise behind us.

"Never should have introduced the two of you," Ian said with a smirk. Jason moved slightly and reached for him. We brought him into our circle, and I kissed him gently, then with more urgency as Jason worked at removing my jacket.

"How are you here?" Jason asked, having realized that things weren't adding up.

I stopped kissing Ian long enough to answer. "I took a plane back, then a train..."

"Mason," Ian growled. Apparently, it was no time for jokes.

I sighed and held my libido at bay. "Lennix resigned. The covens agreed to let him retire in exchange for keeping the political upheaval private. Along with Lennix promising if anything happened to any of us, he'd make sure the world knew the full story."

They both looked at me, stunned. "I don't think that's ever happened in the history of Envoys," Ian said. "It's remarkable."

"It was more about Thea." I glanced at them. "If this continued, she'd never have a chance at a regular life. We'd always be on the run until someone caught up with us."

"I don't think it was only about Thea. Maybe she was the main reason, but this deal let you come home too," Jason said.

I nodded. It was enough of an answer that I didn't have to talk anymore. Their hands drifted over every inch of me they could reach until we were in their bedroom. It smelled like them, and I nearly wept from the familiarity. Clothes disappeared, and we all lay down together, pressing as much skin to each other as possible. Ian reached out and removed the charm bracelets last.

The bonds the three of us had flared to life. The only living thing between three undead people. Mentally, we reached for each other and renewed our connections. Emotions and images were there. Overwhelming need and satisfaction. The promise of things to come and a life together for as long as we could manage it.

Jason spoke first as he nuzzled into my neck. "You can't leave again. Not without us. Everything was off without you. Ian and I . . ."

I reached for Jason and then looked at Ian. They had been lovers before I had showed up, but we had started something and bonded. Both men keenly felt my absence.

"We're not the same without you, Mason. We never will be." Ian kissed me softly on the temple.

Images of dark days where neither of them left this bed. Some arguments that they never had before as a couple were about me. The pain they caused each other over my absence. Ian was right—I'd hurt them. I'd had others act as a balm in their absence, but they only had each other.

"I promise, whatever I do next, wherever I go, you'll come with me. We'll stay together. The two of you are my home. You always will be." It was the truth, and I wanted nothing more than to keep the promise I'd just made.

"What about the others?" Ian asked. He was always too good at pilfering information from my brain.

"I care about them. They helped me and I helped them, plus they are Dorothea's family." I took a breath. "But you're who I love and who I want to be with, both of you."

"Good," Jason said.

Ian kissed me again as Jason caressed me. When Ian was done, I turned my head to kiss Jason. We spent the night reconnecting, sharing ourselves, and relearning each other. After sleeping through the day, we did it all over again.

Eventually, we slowly opened the house to other family members who lived nearby. I was able to greet them during the day and explain a few things about the family. Some took it well, others wanted nothing to do with us. We had parties and holidays with those who wanted to be involved. Ian opened up more, and Jason continued to chase the mystery that was me.

Our hopes of having children of our own were dashed somewhat by my changing state of being. Jason had ideas for that too, but needed a daytime assistant to help him with experiments he couldn't perform. We discovered that one of Ian's distant cousins was a nurse. The perky twenty-two-year-old named Helen arrived at the estate one evening and offered her services.

Since then, Helen and I have had a close friendship and have worked together not only in Jason's lab but also in my clinic that Jason helped me set up nearby.

A year after I'd left Dorothea, Ethan, Lennix, and Constance, a package arrived. When I pried open the box, the large item swaddled within revealed itself to be a scrying mirror.

That evening, after everyone was awake, I followed the instructions and activated it. When the image resolved on the other side, Dorothea was waving at us as Lennix came into view. Constance and Ethan entered the picture, and they all smiled at us.

Ian choked up as Jason rubbed his back.

"Hi Mason! Hi Ian! Hi Jason!" Dorothea waved.

"Hello darling, it's lovely to see you," I said.

IMPORTANT EVENTS IN HISTORY

MAGICAL SPECIES PACT OF 1452

As trade and expansion became more prevalent, territorial wars and colonization became more commonplace. While harvesting parts of magical beings had always been unseemly, the trade and expansion of different empires pushed it into high gear. It was at this point that the Council of Elders, the wisest and oldest magical beings in Europe, came together to create the Magical Species Pact to protect magical beings or anyone who used magic. The pact made magical beings inert or non-magical upon death. If any part of the being was magical, it would render any magic that part or person carried inert. It effectively enforced tolerance between species that shared the same continent.

What they did not understand at the time was how this would affect beings with regenerative powers, such as phoenixes. Magical species that go through a cycle of renewal, such as phoenixes, have a duality of power, as their death generates magic that causes a rebirth, allowing the individual to keep their magical abilities, whatever those were. There's been some side effects attributed to the pact, as phoenixes have reported issues with memory loss since its enactment.

Nor was death magic taken into account. Of the number of elders that were represented by the council, very few had any dominion over the dead or undead. This was the loophole that allowed Joseph Florentine to thrive.

NECROMANTIC WAR: 1873 TO 1878 (THE NECRO WAR)

The major theater of war was in Europe and the Prussian Empire, though it spilled over into parts of the Russian Empire as well. Joseph Florentine had been an exceptional necromancer who rose to power in the mid-1800s. His platform centered on allowing magic users the rights and freedoms to use magic as they pleased. He and his followers wanted to abolish the Magical Species Pact created by the Council of Elders to protect magic users. Florentine considered it the height of hubris that one of the most powerful groups of magical beings in Europe had forced magic users on that continent into the pact.

It took many magical species, including necromancers, vampires, and non-magical species (mostly humans) to fight off Florentine's forces.

AUTHOR'S NOTE

Of all the myths and legends, the one that's captivated me as much as dragons are vampires. I played a lot of LARP through my college years. Eventually, I ran LARP games and had people willing to make a character and come along for whatever plot I had cooked up for the night. This story is, in a lot of ways, an homage to those times, stories, and especially the people that participated. Many of who became lifelong friends. Some of who have passed too soon.

Some of the hand-waving I've done around the world building for the Mythical Desires Universe was solidified because of this book. The Vampire Accords being one of them. Some of the original world setting and background were, at best, misinformed whitewashing of historical events. Thankfully, Tori, my editor, marked several things she thought required a sensitivity read and I follow up on that.

I'd like to thank Dr. Joe Stahlman from the Seneca Iroquois National Museum for keeping me from making a rather large world building appropriation mistake, on top of that, teaching me basic indigenous history of North and South America. The very little time he spent with me on the topic made me realize how vast and rich a history indigenous people have. Having grown up with a euro-centric, evangelical background, I couldn't hope to do it any justice whatsoever. I won't go into the details here. (It might be in a blog post later.) Anything taught about history, anthropology, and archeology should be questioned and evaluated by the viewpoint presenting the information. Especially if that viewpoint is euro-centric. It very much annoys me that I didn't question these things in college and I took them for face value more often than I would like to admit.

To my beta readers, Shawn D., Sherri S., Josh H., and several folks on the Tapas platform—thank you! Your attention to detail, and help with tuning the story, and even some of the plot for the next book in this series, was greatly appreciated. To the eternal support of the Inclusive Romance Project Crit group. They read and critiqued the first draft of the first chapter, which put me on a path to publishing this book.

One final note, if you like the vampire myths and genre as much as I do, you'll want to look up "Blood Libel: The Anti-Semitic Roots of Vampirism" by Heather McCallum. It's an eye-opener. I credit this article with reminding me that I needed to be careful with this myth. Hopefully, I managed it.

To my friends and family, thank you for being supportive of this venture. I've appreciated every encouragement and commiseration during this wild process. Here's to hoping I have some things figured out by the next time around.

Sincerely,
M.L. Eaden

About the Author

M.L. (Mel) Eaden works by day in the tech industry, but at night, she reads books, writes stories, and is an avid board gamer. Originally from the sunflower state, she migrated to one with a lone star for work and sunshine. She has indie-published several books and short stories from the same queer-centric universe. She's also published several contemporary short stories in anthologies.

There are more great things to find at mleaden.com—blogs, reviews, and her latest newsletter.
Sign up today at mleaden.com and receive a free downloadable short story!

ALSO BY M.L. EADEN

You can find more books from the
Mythical Desires Universe at:
mleaden.com/books

Or sign up for the newsletter:
mleaden.substack.com